Life without Daddy

To Betsy

It's such a joy to see
you again. May this book
be a blessing to you.
Let's keep in touch.

Your friend,

Cameron Grady

a story of fatherlessness in society today

Life without
Daddy

Janessa Grady

Includes Resources & Suggestions for Helping Fatherless Children

Contact the author in care of:
Foundation House Publishing, PO Box 2526, Wheaton, MD 20915
Phone: 301-681-9137 • E-mail: Jlgrady218@aol.com

Hardback ISBN: 0-9749899-0-8
Paperback ISBN: 0-9749899-1-6
LCCN 2004102294

Cover and Interior Book Design by Pneuma Books, LLC
For more info, visit www.pneumabooks.com

Cover photograph by Jason Latshaw
Printed in the United States of America by Thomson Shore, Dexter Michigan
09 08 07 06 05 04   6 5 4 3 2 1

Publisher's Cataloging-in-Publication Data
(Prepared by The Donohue Group, Inc.)

Grady, Janessa.
   Life without daddy : a story of fatherlessness in society today /
Janessa Grady.

   p. ; cm.
   Includes bibliographical references.
   ISBN: 0-9749899-0-8 (hardcover)
   ISBN: 0-9749899-1-6 (pbk.)

1. Fatherless families--United States--Fiction. 2. Paternal deprivation--United States--Fiction. 3. Children of single parents--United States--Fiction. 4. Father and child--United States--Fiction.
I. Title.

PS3557.R14 L54 2004
813.54   2004102294

To my son, Vincent — the apple of my eye.
To my recently departed grandfather, John Grady, Sr.
and my recently departed grandmother, "Mommy Rose" —
I thank you for depositing in me your amazing strength, unshakable
faith, and fierce determination — I will see you again!

Acknowledgments

To my loving and supportive parents, Paul and Carrie Grady —
your confidence in me and unwavering love have brought me this
far. Thanks, dad, for giving me a "life with daddy." Thanks,
mom, for your "perfect" response after reading a freshly written
page 1. Because of it, page 2 was born. I must acknowledge my
dynamic brothers — Kevin, Paul and Jendayo. Thanks for always
being there for Vincent, and for me. Thanks to Kellie and LaShe-
da, my two loving and generous sisters (in-law, really?), for your
constant support. Cheerie, you were there when this project was
conceived, and your encouraging words have helped me to hold
on whenever the going gets rough.

Muchas gracias to Pastor Lionel and Michelle Pointer for spiritual guidance, "familyship," as well as the constant reminder that,
"It can be done!" Round Oak, we are family! Many thanks to Tom
and YoAnne Barnett and the entire Barnett family for your help
and for just being you (please don't move to Las Vegas)! Chris-
tine, thanks for your comment, "you have something here!" after
you read the 1st draft — it convinced me to forge ahead. Annette,
I'm so grateful for your fine "proof" job and your friendship.

Kellie, Jendayo, Genea and William, Mary, Nan, and Martha
— thank you for reading and for your helpful comments on early
manuscripts. Thank you, Pneuma, for your fine edit job, the
amazing cover, and everything else you've done and continue to
do! Vince, thank you for your honesty, understanding, and
compassion. I love you. Last, but by no means least — I thank
God for leading me to write this book and for providing every
single thing that I needed from start to finish. I love you, Lord!

Table of Contents

Foreword

Life Without Daddy is is a sobering and challenging book that captures the "voice," or essence, of the experience of fatherless families. It is not a definitive scientific treatise but a clear portrait of what often gets lost in the minutia of long-running demographic and statistical analyses. Written in the time-honored tradition of storytelling, Janessa Grady has captured the unspoken voice of families that for a host of reasons find themselves fatherless. The voices reveal the trauma of impending separation or divorce, the falsely perceived tug of war about which parent to love, the pain of visitation disagreements and holiday disappointments, and resentment. This book carries the reader through the fully lived experiences of fatherless families. Captured, in part, in the dialogue of fatherless children now grown, Grady explores the depth, feeling, and impact of fatherlessness and the sense of abandonment and disconnection.

The story is not a victim analysis or a "let's blame those Dead-beat-Dads" assault. This book shows us that none of the packaged theories of family dysfunctioning — victim analyses, poverty-acculturation, pathological systems of social organization, and so forth — are useful for understanding the critical life issues of management and maintenance surrounding the absence of fathers.

Life Without Daddy doesn't just let us know what's going on in fatherless families, it allows us to feel the emotional texture of the everyday life events that become extraordinary and often-times difficult. The result is that Ms. Grady reveals the physical, psychological, and spiritual importance of the presence of fathers in the family.

Equally embedded in this book is the importance of culture in understanding human dynamics. *Culture* is the vast structure of behaviors, ideas, attitudes, values, habits, beliefs, customs, language, rituals ceremonies, and practices peculiar to a particular group of people that *provides them with a general design for living and patterns for interpreting reality.* This is not culture as song and dance or heroines and holidays, but culture as the medium in which life develops. This story of fatherless families is one picture of a particular medium in which life develops with its own special set of issues, attitudes, beliefs, customs, holidays, values, and so forth.

Life Without Daddy openly knocks on the cultural door at its conclusion when a South African mother notes that where she comes from her husband's brothers would take her sons in and in effect become their fathers. Not so in America. Or is that so? What *are* our cultural traditions and which of these traditions can be retrieved in the service of African American family management and maintenance?

While modernity and acculturation are rapidly eroding the traditions and indigenous value systems of Black people in

America, this book should provoke an examination of our positive and valuable cultural traditions. The traditional Black family features of child-centeredness, elasticity, role flexibility and parenting or eldership based on unconditional love, reciprocity, restraint, responsibility, adaptability, inclusivity, and respect must all be reconsidered and reclaimed. Clearly, African American family life reflects, even when we don't realize it, a combination of African retentions/residuals and American inventions/adoptions. In America the notion of family co-terminates with the notion of household. However, in our tradition a "house is not a home" (that is, a family). If properly examined, our African heritage would teach us that a particular *household* may be fatherless but families can never be fatherless.

In its well-constructed guidelines for restoring relationships and assisting fatherless children and their families, *Life Without Daddy* clearly invites the reader to adopt a plan of family support and, I believe, to re-examine our family traditions. Every aspect of our living that impacts family life should be subject to adoption or rejection in order to guarantee the development of African American children who have an authentic sense of family, an affirmed sense of purpose, and an assured sense of power.

Janessa Grady has captured the voice of fatherless families in our society while simultaneously stimulating and perhaps unintentionally calling for us to find solutions within our cultural selves. *Life Without Daddy* is a must read for absent fathers and more importantly for everyone concerned with the healthy development of human beings and the management and maintenance of the affairs of family. I invite the reader to read, to ponder, to embrace, and to do better.

—Wade W. Nobles, Ph.D.,
Executive Director, The Institute for the
Advanced Study of Black Family Life & Culture

Preface

This book began as a book about single mother-
hood. Within the book, I planned to capture the
cries of children to their fathers in a chapter entitled, "Seen but Not Heard." But those cries would not remain
confined to just one chapter. I came to realize that the book I was
writing was not about me. My voice wasn't quite as important
as the voice of the fatherless.

So three years ago I set out to explore the thoughts, feelings,
joys, frustrations, and hopes of scores of people, young and old,
regarding their fathers. I set out to explore what life is like
growing up without a father. I asked point blank: "What would
you want your father to know if you had the opportunity to
speak to him right now?" The varied answers are revealed in the
words and actions of the characters within this book. Some sons
and daughters remarked that their fathers were dead and that it
was too late. I challenged them to tell me anyway. As many

poured out their hearts to me, I have thus poured their hearts into the young men and women that live on these pages and in the world of the Springridge Community Center.

I must confess that I was not raised fatherless, but I am the single mother of a teenage boy. I've seen the pain, the hopes, the anticipation, the good times, and the failed visits. I've witnessed his longing to be with his father. I've seen his anticipation for a visit, as well as the joy and increased confidence that comes after time spent with him. But I've also seen my son's insecurity and disappointment when he was the only team member whose father wasn't at the game. I've seen his eyes wander to a place, a world I know nothing of. So I've asked questions. "Where are you? What's on your mind?" I've concluded that sometimes he just inhabits a different world — a world known only to the fatherless.

We all know the statistics and I certainly have poured over scores of reports and studies to get the big picture. Everyone is familiar with Judith Wallerstein's *The Unexpected Legacy of Divorce*. We've heard from the pundits and the experts. We've seen the charts, the graphs, the Health and Human Services studies, and the census report, yet few have heard the voices. Sometimes we can't even hear the voices of our *own* fatherless children. But stories can take us to places that graphs and charts never can. I want my readers to know the experiences, see the faces, and hear the voices behind the statistics.

I developed the characters in this book after conducting more than 150 interviews with people of all ages, ethnic and racial backgrounds, and socioeconomic classes over a period of two years. Throughout the writing process, their voices haunted me, demanding representation, even in the very title of this book. One thirteen-year-old daughter of divorced parents suggested that I name the book, "Daddy, Did You Mean to Make Me Cry?" Indeed,

Hagar cried out to the Lord when she and Ishmael were no longer in the house of Abraham, and God answered, "I have heard the voice of the lad." It is that voice that needs to be heard.

Introduction

This book is not a study of the current statistics on fatherlessness. It is not a prescription to alleviate its effects, nor does it contain empty promises. Instead, this book is a vehicle for understanding. It provides an inside look at the everyday existence of fatherless children — their life without daddy. Told in story form, it is an opportunity to sneak a glimpse at the real world behind the statistics — the world of fatherless children.

Statistics tell us that the presence or absence of fathers is *the* factor that will determine the overall success of our society. Consider this:

- Children who do not live with their biological father are twice as likely to drop out of school as their counterparts from intact families.[1]

- Children reared in fatherless homes are twice as likely to become male adolescent delinquents or teen mothers.[2]

- In a study of juveniles in treatment for sex offenses, 72 percent did not live with both biological parents.[3]

- A study of juveniles in state reform institutions found that 70 percent grew up in single-parent homes.[4]

- The probability of poverty for mother/child families doubles from 18.5 percent to 37.6 percent during the first four months following a divorce.[5]

- Children who do not live with their biological fathers have higher mortality rates, perform more poorly academically, are more likely to commit violent crimes, and suffer significantly more childhood illnesses, abuse, and injuries.[6] Also frightening is the increased likelihood of child abuse and neglect for children in single-parent homes. Health care is also a problem. Even when single mothers have the same degree of health insurance as married mothers, single mothers are less likely to obtain the physical care needed to treat their children's illnesses. Consequently, the children receive less medical care.[7] As a single parent, I can only surmise the reason for this is that missing work when a child is sick might jeopardize her job.

There's more. According to one study, the number of single-parent households in a community is proportionate to its rate of violent crime and burglary, but the community's poverty level is not. Specifically, the study compared African-American boys in the same low-income neighborhood and found that the children who did not have a biological father in the home were twice as likely to be incarcerated as the children whose fathers were still in the home.[8] Clearly, the overriding factor was the physical presence of a father.

Much of society's focus on the effects of fatherlessness is focused on boys and their resulting criminal activity, gang participation, and poor academic performance. But girls suffer in many different ways. While criminal activity and academic performance are also indicators of trouble in fatherless girls, promiscuity is probably the most pronounced effect. A girl who has never lived with her father is three times more likely to lose her virginity before her sixteenth birthday than a girl who has lived with both biological parents.[9] Indeed, teenage girls who grow up without their biological fathers tend to have sex at an earlier age (two years earlier on average) and more often than the girls who grow up with both biological parents.[10]

The statistics sound daunting, but the story is so much more complex. That is the reason for this book. This book reveals the sometimes surprising perspectives of fatherless children – the way they look at everyday events as well as celebrations, such as Christmas or Father's Day. Throughout their lives, the presence or absence of their fathers shapes birthdays, graduations, Christmases, back-to-school nights, and proms. That presence or absence also influences the company they keep and the vices that grip their lives. It frames their experiences and emotions, their worldview, and how they approach every aspect of life. To a great extent, our children's sense of who they are and what they have to offer this world *is* wrapped up in their fathers. After all, the father is an earthly representation of the Heavenly Father. Through that position, fathers bring protection, honor, self-worth, and a sense of identity to their children. No wonder the statistics about fatherlessness are so startling. Surely they should prompt us to focus our efforts on preserving families, reducing divorce rates, and discouraging births outside of the institution of marriage.

Conservatives and liberals have long debated whether it is society's moral breakdown or more external factors — such as racism, failing schools, and poverty — that have had the greater role in the decline of America's youth, particularly African-American youth. Unfortunately, too little emphasis has been placed on divorce and non-marital births as a root cause of societal ills or as a conduit by which other factors (e.g., racism, failing schools, etc.) have a greater effect. It follows, therefore, that too little emphasis is placed on restoring and facilitating father/child relationships, preserving families, and encouraging marriage. William Galston, domestic policy advisor to former President Bill Clinton, observed that "the disintegrating American family is at the root of America's declining educational achievement … An overwhelming body of data suggests that the 'hidden curriculum of the home,' … is directly related to children's later success in school." [11]

THE CHARACTERS IN this book are composites drawn from my interviews with more than 100 fatherless children, teens, and adults. The setting for much of their interaction is the fictional Springridge Community Center. This book takes you there, allowing you to listen to intimate discussions about fathers and fatherlessness from the mouths of fatherless children; then it takes you to their homes and schools and sporting events.

In America, we're always looking for the perfect how-to book. I will tell you now — this is not a how-to-fix fatherlessness book. Instead it is intended to be a lamp that illuminates the issues of fatherlessness. This lamp will shine its light for single fathers and mothers, fatherless children, clergy, educators, and anyone searching for greater understanding. Fathers may understand their importance and be encouraged to pursue their children. Mothers may view themselves more realistically and understand their role in facilitating a relationship between father and child. Children may grasp that all hope is not lost – that it's never lost when God is around. And all of us may see that we have a role to play in restoring these broken relationships and serving fatherless children. This book provides strategies on how to do our part and, equally important, why it's important to make the effort and what's at stake if we don't. These strategies come in the guidelines found in appendix A. I have also provided a resource list of organizations that provide resource materials, research information, tools, videos, counseling options, and strategies for reconciliation.

Whether contact with the father has been consistent or sporadic, whether the absent father has proven faithful or patently unreliable, no transgression is unpardonable. This story doesn't seek to cast blame on fathers or mothers, but it is designed to open the eyes of our understanding, move us to action, and be the catalyst that sparks our desire to take another glimpse at fathers as key to the survival and success of our children. Proverbs 17:6 says, "...the glory of children are their fathers." I challenge you to look closely at fathers everywhere and see the enormous value they bring to society. Know that the American family's emotional, psychological, and even financial well-being is, truly, *in the hands of the father.*

Prologue

Derek was jolted awake by the sound of his mother's shouting. His mother, Kim, was hurling insults at his father. His dad, Damon, was returning the favor. Derek grabbed his pillow and squeezed it tightly as his parents ripped into each other. He lay there under his pro-basketball comforter as his eyes began to well up and his heart began to race. Derek stared at the door with a look of confusion, unsure of why they were fighting this time. Was Mom spending too much money? Was Dad mean to Mom? Did Dad come home too late? Did she catch him with another woman? Were the bills paid late? Or not at all? Eight-year-old Derek had heard it all before.

Kim told him he wasn't a man. He called her the *b* word, and Derek started crying. He sat up, but he was afraid to get out of bed. Derek covered both ears with his hands and started rocking back and forth, moaning. He actually sounded as if he was in physical pain. Derek's parents always fought. They would scream and holler, and one parent would run into a room and slam the door. Or his father would jump in the car and drive off for hours at a time. But he always came home, and they would always calm down. Sometimes his mother would grab Derek and his sister, and they would stay at Nana's house for a few days after a big fight. But this morning, Derek knew there was something unusual about the fight. Suddenly, there was a loud thump. It sounded as if someone had fallen against the wall. Derek flinched as he heard his mother scream.

"Get away from me, or I'll call the police!" she hissed.

"You are crazy! I didn't touch you!"

Derek heard footsteps moving quickly across the hardwood floor of the upstairs hallway. Then he heard his father's raging command. "Give me that phone! You ain't calling anybody! I didn't touch you!"

"Help!" his mom screamed.

Derek flew to his bedroom door. Flinging it open, he yelled, "Stop it! Daddy, stop it! Leave Mommy alone!" Then he charged his father who was gripping his mother's left arm. His mother was terrified and crying hysterically. Derek could hear his sister's sobs through her closed bedroom door.

"Go back to your room now!"

"No, Daddy!" he retorted as he wrapped himself around the bottom of his father's pajama-clad leg. At that moment, his mother broke free and darted toward the stairs. But in her haste, she slipped on the first step and began to fall down the hardwood stairs. She reached desperately for the oak banister but couldn't get a grip. She shrieked as she tumbled.

"Mommy!" cried Derek.

"Kim!" exclaimed Damon.

Derek's mother lay whimpering at the bottom of the stairs.

Derek tugged on her left shoulder as he wept. His father rushed down the stairs, and stepping over Derek and his wife, he turned about-face to help her up. But when he reached to touch her, Kim screamed, "Don't touch me! Don't you ever touch me again!"

"Get away! God help me!" she screamed. Her head was drooping low and shaking, as if in disbelief that things had come to this. Derek, still in superhero pajamas, sitting next to his mom on the floor, gently patted her head.

"It's okay, Mommy. Everything's going to be okay. Mommy, like you say, God's gonna make it better. Just believe, Mommy," he whimpered.

Damon stood up and turned around, his arms crossed tightly across his chest. Derek looked at his father, who was equally stunned, and realized he was also crying.

"Let me call an ambulance," his father pleaded.

"No! Just leave me alone," she shrugged away from his touch.

"Kim, you should get checked out," said Damon.

"Just leave me alone!" Her trembling voice was growing louder and sharper. Her right hand covered her forehead.

"Derek, you need to get ready for school. Help me up," she whimpered, reaching for the wooden banister.

"Mommy!" he shrieked. "I want to stay with you today. Please let me take care of you. I'll protect you."

"No baby, you have to get to school. Mommy's okay. Come on, get dressed. Hurry, hurry."

Derek wiped his tears and fiddled through his chest of drawers looking for clothes. He couldn't concentrate and ended up with his black sweatshirt on backward. No one even noticed. His mother grabbed both Derek and his younger sister and led them to the car. Sorrowfully, Derek turned and glanced back at the house where his father stood in the doorway, a look of helplessness etched on his face.

At 8:45 A.M. Derek's mom pulled up in front of Ridgepoint Elementary School, put the Toyota in park, and lowered her head onto the steering wheel. She let out a long sigh. After a momentary silence, she looked past Derek, who sat next to her, and watched Lisa, who had already jumped out of the car. Derek's eyes were transfixed on the swaying weeping willows along the street ahead of him.

"Go on, Derek. Get out of the car and go into school," urged his mother.

Derek just sat there — stern, still, and stoic. He was breathing more heavily than normal.

"Derek, go on, now!" she demanded.

Derek unlocked the door and thrust it open. He slammed it with all his might and bolted for the school.

At home Kim cried herself to sleep. The phone jolted her awake.

"Mrs. Miller?"

"Yes, this is she."

"This is Mrs. Anderson, Ridgepoint's school nurse. Derek is not feeling well. In fact, he couldn't keep his lunch down, and he can't seem to catch his breath. He's running a fever of 103. He's laying down right now, but you need to come pick him up."

"I'm on my way."

When Kim arrived at the school nurse's office, she found her son lying on the sick bed with a white blanket covering him. "Let's go, honey," Kim said, as she helped her listless child off the table.

Derek climbed into the backseat and lay down. He placed his hands together under his face, closed his eyes, and resumed his crying. Before Derek knew it, he was sitting in triage. He noticed the "mediciny" odor of the place as he looked around the room. Moments later, Derek was nursing the thermometer nestled under his tongue. Meanwhile, Kim used the hospital phone to call her friend Brenda to ask for help.

"Brenda, it's Kim. Hi. Well, it's a long story, but I'm in the emergency room with Derek. He's okay. I'll explain later. Can you pick Lisa up from school and keep her until we get home? She and Mayra play so well together ... Thanks, Brenda. It's been a rough day." Then she whispered, "I don't know if we're going to make it," and she hung up the phone. Brenda, divorced from Mayra's father since Mayra was a toddler, knew the pain of a family tearing apart and she felt for her friend.

The nurse gave Derek something for the fever and began to discuss his condition with Kim. "He has a fever of 102 and he's trembling. He seems to be wheezing a little. Does he have asthma?" asked the nurse.

"Not that I know of."

"Well, the doctor may need to test for asthma. In the meantime, is he complaining of any kind of pain? I notice his eyes are rather red and puffy. It looks like he's been crying."

Nervous, Kim answered, "I don't know, maybe."

Turning to Derek, the nurse asked, "Son, is it sometimes hard to breathe?"

Derek looked as if he wanted to say something. He paused, looked at his mom, dropped his head, and whispered, "Yes."

"Do you have any other pain?"

"No, ma'am," he said, still looking at the floor.

"Well, are any other kids sick?"

"I don't know," he said.

The nurse continued with her inquiries. "Have you noticed any shortness of breath or wheezing?"

"No, not that I can recall," answered Kim.

"Well, asthma can be exacerbated by stress. Anything going on in his life?"

Kim was not going to pour her personal business into the hospital walls, so she sternly answered, "No, nothing apart from the normal stresses of everyday life, thank you."

"Alright, you two can wait in the waiting area, and we'll call you momentarily."

Kim walked her child to the chairs and sat down next to him, placing her hand first on his clammy forehead and then on top of his head, running her fingers through his tightly curled black hair. She pulled him close to her side as she looked around the waiting room to see who else was there. She immediately noticed another woman, presumably a mother, waiting with a child about Derek's age. Kim wondered if that child went to Derek's school. Noticing that the woman wasn't wearing a wedding ring, Kim began to wonder if this woman was divorced or perhaps never married to the child's father. She then looked off into the distance as if looking down the road and wondered whether Derek's father would ever take Derek to the doctor again.

"Did you call my daddy?" Derek asked.

Kim looked around to see who had heard her son's question and, more to the point, who would hear her response. "No."

"Mommy, if I die, promise me you won't leave Daddy. I think I might die today and be in heaven tonight. So you have to promise me you won't leave him. He loves you; he really does. And he's trying. Give him another chance, please."

Her eyes instantly filled with tears. "Die? No one's going to die, Pumpkin! You're not going to die." Then she covered her face with her hands.

"Mommy, are you going to die? Or is Daddy going to die?"

"Baby, you're not going to die. I'm not dying, and your father isn't going to die. Where is this coming from? You just have a fever. You'll be okay. Mommy isn't going to let anything happen to you." She grabbed him and held him tightly.

LATER, KIM FOUND HER six-year-old daughter Lisa fast asleep next to five-year-old Mayra. Kim stood over Mayra and Lisa in the dark. She didn't want Lisa to wake up and remember the day's events. At that moment, Kim vowed things would be different. She would make it work, or at least she would make sure her kids still had their father. Or perhaps she'd find another father.

Two weeks later, Derek came home from school after a Christmas party to find his father gone. Damon had moved out of the house.

"Derek, I need to talk with you and your sister," his mom said.

"Where's my dad?"

"He's not coming back. We've decided to spend some time apart."

Derek and Lisa both began to cry.

"I want to call him and tell him to come home, Mommy. I'll make him come back; just call him for me," said Derek, pulling on her sleeve.

"Derek, it's not that simple. I asked him to leave."

"Why, Mommy?!" he screamed. "He's not your daddy! You can't tell him to leave us!" With that, Derek turned his face to the pillow on the sofa and cried.

DEREK ALWAYS BELIEVED his father knew that he chose his mother during the custody trial. Toward the end of the week-long divorce and custody trial, the judge's clerk escorted Derek and Lisa to his chambers one after the other and explained to each child that in order to determine what was in their best interests, he needed to factor their wishes into the equation. The judge assured Derek that neither parent would ever know what he told the judge.

Derek had planned to choose his father until the day before

the meeting with the judge. His mother came home from trial and accused Derek of telling his father that she had left him and Lisa home alone one day. His father had brought the issue up in court. She screamed, "Don't you know they'll take you and Lisa away from me if they think I leave you kids home alone? They'll give you to your father, and he doesn't know the first thing about taking care of you kids. If the judge asks you who you want to live with, remember this — you might think you want to live with your father, but after a while, things change. When he's not around, you'll be calling for me. You'll be calling for me when his girlfriends are mean to you and treat you badly. I can't tell you who to choose, but you know I love you and have given you kids everything I have. I would die for you. You know it would break my heart if your father took you away from me. You're all I have. I wouldn't be able to take it."

The next day in the judge's chambers, Derek chose his mother. So did Lisa. Several months later when the frequency of their visits with their father diminished, Lisa confided in Derek. "I think he knows we chose Mom and he's punishing us by not calling."

"No, he's not. He's just busy and works hard."

"You know I'm right," she insisted. Derek looked at her but didn't respond.

A COUPLE OF YEARS LATER, Derek's mom married John, a real estate agent with his own rapidly expanding company. He encouraged Kim to leave her position as a manager of compensation at a large government agency and brought her into the business with him. Despite the addition of a stepfather to their family, Derek spent most of his youth hanging out in the streets. He rarely saw his mother or stepfather. They were too busy trying to build their real estate business. They were successful, but the odd hours were hard on Derek and Lisa. Kim and her new husband showed homes mainly at night and on the weekends, so they were rarely home. For the most part, Derek raised himself. He rarely saw his natural father.

One day when Derek was ten, a classmate asked where his father was.

Derek simply said, "I don't know. I think he's around."

The friend replied, "What if he's dead? Maybe he died."

"My father's not dead!"

"How do you know? Have you checked the obits?"

"Obits? What's that?" Derek said, agitated and fearful.

"It's the part of the newspaper that tells when people die. It lists the names of everyone in the whole city and state who died. Maybe you didn't hear from him because he died. If he died, it'll be in the paper," said the boy.

From that moment on, even through his teen years, Derek checked the "obits" every day for his father's name. Derek always had the same thoughts when he read the obituaries. *Would my name be listed in here like other sons and daughters listed in the paper? Would someone even call us to let us know? Would my mother know about it? Would she tell me? Would I be allowed to go to the funeral? Would I want to go? What if I died first, would he come? Would he care? Would she tell him? What if I did something really, really bad — would he come then? What if I was sick and going to die, would he come see me in the hospital?*

In the evenings when he returned home from school, or the street, or a game, Derek would find *The Washington Post*. The B section contained the obituaries. As he would check them, he'd think, *He's dead. That must be why he doesn't call. She just hasn't told us. If he's dead, then at least I won't have to wonder anymore. Not knowing is the worst of all.*

On the rare occasions Derek and Lisa did visit their father, they usually sat in their rooms watching TV. Their dad would take them to the McDonalds drive through. He never seemed to have the time to go in, sit down, and eat with them. He would occasionally take Derek for a haircut and give him the generic speech about school, obeying his mother, and staying out of trouble.

Throughout his school years, Derek earned "needs improvement" in all areas pertaining to behavior, listening, and attention skills. By eighth grade, Derek had amassed a string of suspensions and was bordering on expulsion. His mother was called to the school every month. During ninth grade, school officials, acting on a tip, found a small bag of marijuana in Derek's locker during a locker search, and Derek faced expulsion. He was charged with possession and completed two weekends in a juvenile detention center — the first of many. It was only after his mother and step-father's attorney threatened to sue the school board that the principal downgraded the expulsion to a ten-day suspension. Despite these difficulties, Derek possessed an unusually high aptitude and always performed well on standardized tests. He routinely scored higher than his grade level average, although his grades rarely reflected his true ability. Derek just barely managed to advance to the next grade.

DEREK IS SIXTEEN. It had been nearly a year since he had last seen his father. On a warm Friday morning in May, Derek's mother flicked on the light in his bedroom. "Get up. You're late!" she snapped.

Derek was still drowsy and inebriated. He had been drinking and drugging for three nights in a row behind his high school. Clothing, dirty socks, and empty soda bottles were strewn about. A few empty beer bottles were hidden under the bed. Against his mother's wishes, posters of rap groups hung on his walls. Since Derek was filled with anger, these groups were his idols.

"It stinks in here and it's a filthy mess! Get up *now* and when you get home today you need to clean up this mess. You can't even see the floor! This is embarrassing," scolded his mother. Derek hadn't budged an inch when he heard the front door close behind his mother. Moments later, Derek slowly crawled out of bed. From downstairs, his sister Lisa yelled, "You're gonna miss the bus again, Stupid!" as she closed the front door behind her.

He didn't care. Derek staggered to the bathroom and then back to his room to find his cigarettes. Derek searched his pants, then the jacket he had worn the night before. He frantically dug into the left pocket, then the right, where he finally found them. He sighed and walked downstairs to the kitchen as he lit his cigarette. Derek took one long drag, held it, closed his eyes, and dropped his head back to gaze at the ceiling, savoring his first joy of the day. Seated at the kitchen table, Derek used his foot to drag another chair close enough to rest his feet on as he smoked. He reached for the Metro section of the paper and opened to the obituaries.

Derek looked around the well-decorated kitchen and noticed the yellow lace curtains and matching tablecloth, which had been selected to complement the imported countertop that Derek's mother was particularly proud of. He glanced toward the mirror in the dining room and saw his baggy red eyes. He held his face and compared the mirror image to the clean-shaven, innocent young man in an earlier picture fastened to the refrigerator by a magnet. His mother always believed that one day he'd look at that picture and see who he was and who he could be again. Derek's eyes began to water. He fell back into his chair and began to cry.

Derek pulled the last possible drag from his cigarette, took his basketball team picture from his wallet, and shook his head in disbelief. He remembered how neither his natural father, who lived only twenty minutes away, nor his mother and stepfather had attended any of his games. Until last year Derek was on the high school basketball team. As point guard, Derek was second in the county in assists and fourth in scoring. Derek assumed his parents didn't come because of their work schedule or because they just didn't care. They told him the reason was that they believed sports interfered with his schoolwork, and they didn't want to encourage that neglectful behavior. At that moment, the hurt converted to anger again. Derek sniffled a few times, then defiantly wiped his tears.

Suddenly, the phone rang, startling Derek.

"Who could that be?" he wondered aloud, looking at his dog. *Is it the school? But class hasn't even started yet, so probably not. Is it Mom? Is it Lisa? Like she cares. She's got enough troubles of her own. It must be Mom,* he thought to himself after the fifth ring.

"Nah, it couldn't be her." Derek reasoned. "She doesn't care." *Well, maybe she cares a little, but even if she spared a few moments to think about me, her mind would quickly wander to the newest house she has to sell.* "At least I know you care," he said, patting the black lab on the head.

But she did care. Derek's mother knew that morning when she left that her son had no intention of going to school. She knew before she even opened his bedroom door that he hadn't gone to school all week.

She loved him with all her heart. He was the driving force, she believed, behind everything she did, and it was her tough love, Kim reasoned during an earlier family counseling session, that had preserved her wayward child thus far. She wasn't perfect and was tired all the time, but she did try. She had explained to the counselor that she hoped getting married again would provide her children with the father-figure they lost when she divorced Damon.

Yet despite all her efforts, the back talking continued. Derek was on restriction every weekend. No phone. No TV. But that didn't stop the drinking. She even let him spend the night in juvenile detention for smoking pot. She did not rescue him until two days later. Kim thought this would teach him just how outrageous his behavior had been.

Derek's stepfather finally told him that there were rules in this house and that if he couldn't obey those rules, he would have to leave. So he left. Two days later, he was in jail.

The hospital visit that preceded the divorce was the first of many. Derek's entire fifth and sixth grade years were spent in and out of the emergency room, the pediatrician's office, and the vice-principal's office. Because of the stress of it all, Kim found distractions. She couldn't bear the thought of failing her son, so she withdrew from him and his problems. She never knew from one day to the next in what condition she would find her son, her daughter, or even her home.

So she needed an escape. Real estate was her refuge from the chaos at home. When she opened the lockbox to the house she was to show that day, Kim knew she would enter her fantasy world. She could walk into this empty house and picture herself, the kids, and her husband starting over. She imagined unpacking the moving boxes and decorating the den, painting the kitchen and then eating together as a family. She pictured her family gathered together around the fireplace, finally fulfilled. She saw all the things she would do differently. This real estate business was her salvation, of a sort, for there she could see the possibilities. Through it she found some hope, though not much, but more than that, she found an escape.

Therefore, having suffered these trials and having tried all that she knew to do — counseling, church, grandparents — she came to the end of her rope.

"It's time to bring Derek's father to the table. It's time for *him* to share in this responsibility, to share in this trial and this heartache," she said to her husband while nursing a cup of French roast coffee as they sat together in the kitchen one evening after showing a house. "Why should *I* bear this pain and difficulty alone? Why should he get off so easily? He's been getting off too easily. That's been the problem all along now that I think about it. I need a break. I can't deal with this anymore. I'm just too tired of all of this," she said.

So Kim called Damon the next morning when she got to work. She knew Derek would probably skip school as he had done all week. She was desperate. She'd tried everything.

"Damon, it's Kim. Listen, I'm at work, so I'll get right to the point … "

"And good morning and how are you," he interrupted. "I know you're busy, but we can at least say good morning to each other – can't we?"

"Fine, good morning, Damon. Look, Derek needs help. I'm sure he's still at home, cutting school, which he has done all week. He thinks I don't know … "

"He probably doesn't care," said Damon, "and from the way I hear it, you're obviously more concerned with your next home sale than you are with the company your son keeps and the trouble he's getting into."

"What! You have nerve! I KNOW you didn't just tell me his problems are all MY fault when you haven't seen or even so much as picked up the phone to call your son in, what … four months? Six months? A year? Please! I do my part. I'm there. And who have you been hearing things from, huh? Lisa? Derek? Get your facts straight."

"Look, why did you call? You get your money, don't you?"

"Well, I think he's at that age where he needs his father — because he won't do a thing I tell him to do. He's not stupid, but he's so rebellious and so angry. I think he's really angry at you … "

"Angry at *me*? Oh give me a break!"

"Let's not get into the blame game … "

"You started it! As you always do. You cut me down and then say, let's not get into the blame game after you fire the first shot!" He didn't even notice that his Newport cigarette was already burning through the filter.

"Look, Damon, I'm not going to argue … "

"So you call ME and want me to clean up YOUR mess."

"MY mess?!!!"

"Okay, I see this is going nowhere. Call me when you're ready to take some responsibility for all this."

"Jesus, Damon, it's so hard to talk to you. Are we going to try and help our son or not?"

"Look, I'm going to be late for work. Say what's on your mind!"

"Fine, can you call him this morning? Can you at least try to talk to him and see where he is? I really don't know what to do next. I know he's angry at me, at John, at you, at his teachers, at God. Basically, he's mad at the whole world. He won't talk to us. You know he's still doing the stuff and he's drinking. I thought the detention center would help, but it didn't. Now I think he hates me for leaving him there for two days. I'm sure of it. John has even threatened to put him out. In fact, John put the chain on the door one night and wouldn't let me open the door for my own son. Derek was so high that night, it was awful. We watched him from the window. I just cried … Maybe you could spend a little time with him. Do you think you can take him this weekend? Just to see if you can talk to him, convince him to go to church with us?"

"You still go? Last time Derek was here, he said you guys hadn't gone in a while."

"We still go, but yeah, it's been a while. I mean we go when we can, but, you know, Sunday is the best time to show houses. I need Sunday morning to get ready and to prepare the houses. So it's been a while," she said honestly. "You have to talk to him. We have to get him off that stuff. I'm really nervous about his mixing all that stuff with his asthma. It's just not good."

"Sure, I'll try. He can come this weekend. I don't know if it'll help, but it can't hurt to try. Now, you know what he's going to ask me, and it's just not possible right now," said Damon squeamishly.

"Yes, I know, Damon!" she snapped. "And that's fine. He doesn't have to live with you for you to help him, you know."

"I'm just not prepared for that. I mean, he can visit more often, that's no problem. But with my job and all, I just can't deal with the responsibility like you guys can. My job is too unpredictable. I have late hours sometimes and he needs someone at home."

"I'm not asking for that, Damon," she said, her voice growing louder.

"Okay, I'll get him over to my place this weekend and I'll call you on Monday."

"Thanks," she said and hung up.

Thirty minutes later, Damon called his son.

Derek answered the phone, "Yeah."

"Derek?" asked the caller.

"Dad?"

"Derek, I thought the machine would answer. What are you doing home? Don't you have school?"

"Uh, I'm running late because I was sick this morning. Mom knows." Before Damon could squeeze out any more stern inquiries,

Derek blurted, "What ya doin' this weekend? Can I come over?" He didn't want to deal with his anxious mother and detached stepfather after a week of not going to school. For the moment, there was no fear of rejection. This unexpected request to visit his dad was easy because the superficial motive was to get away from his mother.

"Uh, well … " his dad mumbled.

"Oh, come on, I just need to get away. We don't need to do anything or go anywhere. I just need to chill. I can get a ride. You can even hide the key somewhere for me. It's no big deal. I'll eat before I come."

"All right, it's okay," said Damon. "Oh, and don't forget your inhaler."

"I won't."

Derek hung up the phone, flashed a wide grin, and exclaimed, "Yes!" Since the answer was yes, he was free to admit he wanted to see his dad and that he needed his dad. Derek then leaped to his feet, looked over at the pile of dirty dishes, and began to clean up the kitchen. Just maybe, this visit with his father would be different from all the others. Just maybe something would happen this time. Just maybe something would be said that would change everything. On the other hand, he might feel rejected by something said, or even something not said. Maybe his dad would disappear — just like old times. But, just like old times, Derek was willing to risk it.

A few hours later, Derek climbed off the bus and walked about six blocks to his father's house in northeast D.C. As expected, the key was under the black spare tire on the end of the porch. Derek smiled as a warm feeling rushed through his body. His dad thought about him, looked out for him, anticipated his arrival, and welcomed him by leaving that key. Though Derek would eventually have to return the key, he stood there for just a few moments, staring at it in his hand. He eventually went in, stood in the middle of the foyer, and took in the stale aroma of his father's cigarette smoke.

"Oh yeah, the Newports," he said. Mixed in with the smoke scent was a faint fishy smell. Derek wandered around the small rowhouse and into the kitchen. The counter was piled high with food-encrusted dishes. On the stove there was a frying pan coated with gritty cooking oil and nearly burned cornmeal granules surrounding leftover catfish scraps and bones. There were a few morsels left in the pan and on a nearby plate. Derek dropped his duffel bag and picked over what was left of the fish. He looked around and found some broken heels of white bread and sopped up the oil and gritty leftover cornmeal to eat with the fish. It was 3:30 P.M., and he hadn't eaten all day. Then Derek finished washing the dishes out of gratitude for the key his dad had left.

With the kitchen cleaned up, Derek plopped onto the soft brown sofa in the den. An eight-by-ten framed photo of Derek rested on the mantle. He was dressed in his red and black basketball jersey and shorts. Derek froze. He remembered sending the picture to his dad the year before. He sat up and moved to the edge of his seat. As he stared at the propped-up photo, Derek wondered. *How could he hang this photo as if he were proud of my basketball playing?*

Basketball was the one thing Derek was proud of. It was the one area of his life where he was certain he could succeed. But no one ever seemed to notice, including his father. Derek glared angrily at the photo, but the sour feelings were soon neutralized by the sweetness of knowing his father at least took the time to frame the photo and place it on the mantle. He knew that's where people feature the things they value.

My dad remembers me and has to think about me whenever he's in the den because he has to see the photo. He put it in a place where he can see it. I know he's in here everyday watching TV. So he has to see me. My dad remembers me.

Derek wandered the house, searching for more clues to knowing the elusive man he'd missed so terribly. He also searched for more evidence of his father's connection to him. Derek found himself in his dad's bedroom. "Whew!" he said, flashing the widest grin of the day. Adorning the nightstand were homemade aluminum foil ashtrays filled to the rim. Derek grabbed and shook a Newport box, hoping to satisfy his own craving for a square. It was empty, so he crushed the box in his right hand and put it back on the nightstand next to another crushed box. There were ashes everywhere — on the bathroom vanity, the rug, and the dresser. Clothes, sports magazines, and old newspapers littered the floor.

"Wow," he said, smiling. "I'm just like my dad. Now I see why I have a messy room. That's cool." The distinctive musky scent of his father's cologne filled the air. *A real man — not like John.* His stepfather, who was heavier and wore glasses, preferred a more subtle upscale cologne. Although his stepfather occasionally tried to reach out to Derek, he usually deferred to Derek's mom for fear of crossing boundaries. Derek resented his stepfather because he didn't fight his wife's control and her decision not to support Derek in his pursuits. When his stepdad wanted to come out to the driveway to play basketball with Derek, Kim admonished him not to encourage Derek in "that basketball thing" but to follow up on Derek's homework instead. Derek believed his stepfather and his mother were only interested in their usual pursuit — money and more money.

His real dad, thought Derek, kept it real. After all, he was a sports fan. He wore dingy jerseys, smoked cigarettes, worked on his car, and had girlfriends. He wasn't perfect, and he didn't even try to be. Most importantly, he didn't completely shut Derek out of his world.

Derek decided to check out his father's closet. "Here we go!" he said. He sifted through shirts, sweatshirts, slacks, and ties to examine his father's fashion leanings. His eyes widened at the sight of a multi-hued Hawaiian shirt. "I KNOW you didn't go to Hawaii and not tell nobody!" he said as if he was scolding his dad. "I bet I could fit into this." He pulled the shirt off the hanger and before long, Derek had tried on nearly everything in the closet.

Dusk was moving in. A slight breeze from the open window grazed Derek's arms, and Derek suddenly heard his father's Oldsmobile. Derek heard the engine stop, the door open and close, and then the sound of footsteps. Joy, pride, and anticipation rushed over Derek. Derek darted out of the room and down the stairs. Derek was on the first step when the door opened.

"Hey, hey!' exclaimed his dad.

"What's up, Pop!" said Derek jubilantly as he reached to do the cool manly hug. Derek realized as he pulled away that he needed a real hug, not the cool manly hug. He wanted to rest in his dad's embrace for a few moments just like he had as a little boy. He wanted his dad to say, "I love you," and he wanted to reply without hesitation or fear, "I love you too, Dad."

Moments later, Damon collapsed in his slightly torn leather lounge chair in the den, exhausted from a long day of lifting heavy furniture. He flung his feet up on the footrest and pulled out a pack of cigarettes. As Damon prepared to light the cigarette, Derek said, "Oh, let me have one of those."

"Boy, are you crazy?"

"Dad, come on, we've smoked together before. I had my own cigarettes the last time I was here. You had run out of yours, remember? I gave you one of mine," he said, almost righteously indignant. "I'm sixteen years old. Give me a break."

"I didn't forget, and I don't know what I was thinking of to smoke with you. I don't know why I didn't take those smokes away from you!" On the one hand, Damon felt fatherly — he knew smoking was not good and that smoking with Derek wouldn't go over too well with Kim either. On the other hand, Damon didn't want to ostracize his son. He knew something Derek didn't know — this time together was a setup.

"Does your mother know we've smoked together? I hope you don't go around telling your friends that you smoke with your father!"

"No, Dad, are you kidding? I wouldn't do that."

But Derek had done just that. He had told his friends about how he and his dad smoke together — to prove that he did have a dad and that his dad was cool. To Derek, this was their thing. This was their father-son moment. Derek didn't regard smoking with his father as a sign of bad parenting. Derek needed a friend, someone who could relate to him right where he was. Derek obviously couldn't articulate this to his father.

Derek needed to know that someone actually loved him with all his faults and failures — the drug use, booze, DUIs, juvenile record, truancy, suspensions, attorneys fees, misdemeanor theft, bad grades, lies, profanity, violent rap music, filthy bedroom, ash-stained and cigarette-burned carpet, all-nighters. Derek needed to know that someone could regard him as a person — someone worthy of relating to — rather than just a mess in need of condemnation, correction, threats, and punishment. He wanted to know that there was something in him that was worthy of love. Derek knew that punishment was a part of growing up and that it was probably good for him, but it had been a long time since he had received praise, affection, kind words, or even a loving glance from his mother. He'd forgotten what those expressions of love felt like.

By now, Damon had learned that the most certain way to sever communication with his son and ruin any hope he had of reaching Derek would be to jump down his throat. Damon realized by his son's vulnerable expression that this moment was pivotal for Derek. His father knew he would have to try an alternative to the domineering authority figure condemning the juvenile delinquent approach. This time, Damon finally realized, things would be different. They had to be.

"Okay, here — need a light?"

Derek was thrilled and astonished. Wow, this has got to be one of the greatest moments of my life. Derek reveled in the moment as he leaned forward to connect his cigarette to the flame of his dad's lighter. They hadn't seen each other in almost a year — the last time his father tried to "talk" to him. Derek remembered how he had blasted his dad on their last visit, flatly stating that his father had forfeited any right to tell him what to do because he hadn't been there. He looked into his father's eyes and remembered how he had told him, "No, no, unh, uh. You can't just come in here after all this time and decide you want to be a father. Uh, no! It doesn't work like that."

But this time, Derek felt he was being treated as an equal, like a man. He inhaled, but not too hard — after all, he *was* with a grown up and Derek wasn't entirely sure if this was some sort of trap. So he leaned back and relaxed into the sofa after exhaling the first drag.

"So, how was work, Dad? You still with that moving company? I know you make good money. Aren't you the boss?" asked Derek.

"Yeah, I'm the manager of new accounts, but I still have to help out with moving when we're short-staffed, and that's after fifteen years in the same job AND I'm only the first line manager. There are three more over me. I'm a figurehead with no real power. Since I didn't go to college, it's much harder for me to get ahead, and I take a whole lot of crap on the job. I'm really sorry now that I didn't work harder in school," said his dad, hoping to open the door to discuss the issue.

"Oh God, is this gonna be the school lecture again?"

"No, no, no. I'm not saying a word about school. If you want to talk about it, that's cool, but you asked about my job and I was telling you how things really are and why. Hey, what you do is up to you. I sure can't make you do anything you don't want to do. I'm just trying to tell you about my life and the choices I made. As a matter of fact, let's make a deal — no talk about school this weekend, or your mother, or that house, or any of the stuff I bet your mother thinks I'm going to talk to you about. Deal?"

Derek's eyes grew wide. He hadn't anticipated his father's angle and was not programmed to respond to it. As a result, truth instinctively surfaced and began to pour out of him. He only realized it after it happened.

"No, it's not that I don't want to talk about school, but no one ever listens to me, to my side, to what I have to say and what's going on with me. I'm just having it kind of rough right now, and Mom is tripping," he said, looking toward the floor.

"Oh, I know all about that," said Damon, smirking. "But go on."

Sharing in that father-son chuckle at his mother's expense, Derek was lured into sharing more and more. His dad empathized at every turn.

"Dad, can I ask you a question?"

"Yeah, what's up?"

"I don't see why I can't just live here."

"Hey, hey, hold on a bit. You just got here. Let's just chill for a while and enjoy the day. We'll get to those matters later. Let's just kick back and maybe grab a bite. You hungry?"

"Yeah, I'm starved. I see you framed the picture I sent you last fall. It looks good," Derek commented, looking up at the mantle.

"I know you play."

"Dad, you ought to come see me play. The summer league is starting next month. I'm pretty good," Derek said, suppressing what he really wanted to say. *Why haven't you come to any of my games?*

"I'll try next time. It's tough with my schedule. You need to call me more and tell me about what's going on in your life. I'll come if you let me know about things every once in a while."

"Dad, you're kidding, right? I mean, you're joking when you say that. You know I've called you a lot."

"Son, don't make things up now."

"DAD! I used to call you all the time. Remember? Remember when I was around nine or ten years old. I called for you to come pick me up. I called and asked you to come for my birthday, though you missed most of them! I called for you to come to my Boys and Girls Club basketball games, and I always had to leave a message — that's if I even had your phone number."

Derek stopped suddenly, as if he realized he had violated the unspoken cardinal rule for children of divorce — never accuse your father of not coming to visit you. At stake were future visits. Derek always feared that if he ever confronted his dad, his dad would withdraw — perhaps from guilt, perhaps from anger. He knew deep down that forcing his dad to face bad parenting might backfire, but Derek also figured that he really had nothing to lose. It had been a year since he had seen his dad. He had confronted him during the last visit, and Derek felt as if his dad had been punishing him for that confrontation by keeping his distance for so long.

"Can you hear me out, or do you want me to go because you don't want to hear this? The last time I tried to talk to you, it seemed like you punished me by not calling for so long. But that's cool. No sweat. I'm just going to say what I gotta say and then I'll leave."

"Sit down, son. Nobody said you have to leave."

"Yeah, nobody said I have to leave. I didn't say you *said* it. I said you were *thinking* it — so, Dad, are you thinking it? Come on, be honest."

Derek discovered something about himself at that moment. All this time, he had thought that just being around his dad was all he ever needed — despite the fact that he was afraid to tell his dad how he really felt — that he was always the one to reach out and that he never felt free to express his hurt or disappointment. He'd figured that as long as his dad didn't turn him away, he'd be alright. Derek now realized that this consolation-prize relationship came at a great price — truth, open communication, and the expectation of a real father-son relationship. Derek now realized that the D+ relationship wasn't good enough anymore.

"Derek, you know you can call me anytime," said Damon, now looking at the floor.

"But why should I always be the one to take the first step? It's not all my responsibility! When I call you, I open myself up to get hurt. I know you're not going to call me back. Why should I bother, man? Why should I risk more rejection? That's why my defenses stay high. You never come to my games. You won't believe this, but I saw you at a game once. You had gone to the basketball game of one of your girlfriend's sons. I saw you. You couldn't come to MY games, but you could go to some stranger's game."

Damon reached for the TV remote.

"See, there you go. As soon as the truth comes out, you close down," said Derek, finally able to look directly at his father.

"Are you just going to keep bringing up all these things from the past? Is hurting me so important to you? Is that why you came

— to hurt me? Well, you've succeeded. Is that what you want to hear? That I messed up and that I'm a terrible father. That's why I called YOU and invited YOU over because I'm such a terrible father ... " he said as he flipped furiously through the channels.

Standing up with his back to his father, Derek responded, "Dad, I have never felt like I could just tell you how I feel. Don't you realize how important that is? You're a grown-up, and I figured you'd understand that."

Silence hung heavy on the room. Derek knew he had struck below the belt, but he knew his dad was erecting the self-defense force field and he had to do something quick. Damon leaned back in the recliner, defensively crossed his arms, put his feet back up, threw the remote on the coffee table, and said, "Okay, Son, give me your best shot — what's on your mind?"

The two finally made eye contact. Derek knew this was it. This was his moment of truth and he had to let it all out, because he might never have the opportunity again. He drew a deep breath and slowly began to speak. "When I saw you there that day, I just figured you would have to be as excited as I was to see you. I mean, you're my dad! I hadn't seen you in so long. You were it, man. But when you couldn't make time for me, but somehow you found it for some other boy who isn't even your son, you dissed me. It was like telling me I was nothing, I was dirt and unimportant. So that's how I felt — like I was nothing. I've felt that way ever since. Before you get bent out of shape, I'm not saying I blame all my problems on you, but, Dad, you're a part of all of it. You had a part to play. I think that's why God gave us parents, both parents, to raise us, to teach us, and to help us become good people in this world, to help us not do all the bad things that I know I've done." Derek stood up and began to pace the floor. With his back to his father, he continued, "So that's why I stay high. When I'm down, I don't laugh. I want to cry and I want to break everything I see. So, I just stay high," Derek paused, waiting to be lambasted by his father.

"Go on," said Damon quietly, visibly moved.

"I'm trying to say that I stayed high to forget you, Dad. Did you know I read the obituaries every day, looking for your name? I figured that must be the reason you didn't call me or come for us. Death was the only thing that could justify your actions. I stopped calling you because I didn't want to open up just to be rejected again, and I know I told you that you have nothing I want. And yes, I remember telling you that you're not my father and that you're nothing to me. But the truth is, you're the world to me. I still have everything you ever gave me. I'll never forget the football jersey you gave me. I actually thought you played. I wanted to be just like you. I wanted to look like you, act like you, walk like you — be you. I was always so proud and happy when my mom and other people said I looked like you. 'Spit him right out,' they would say and I would love it! Even when she called me a troublemaker, she'd say I was acting just like you — and I loved it."

Damon smiled at his son.

"Well, the truth is that I'm pissed off and I'm scared. Yeah, I said it, ok? On the one hand, I'm so angry, but on the other hand, I need you dad. But you haven't been there. I can't believe you haven't been to any of my games! Not one game! There's no excuse for that, and don't try to pretend that I never told you about them. Wanna know something else?"

Damon nodded his head.

"Every time you say I can't live with you, it hurts even more. I'm not trying to mooch off of you or cause you problems. I know it might not work out, but you've never even given me a chance. You have no faith in me or in the possibility of a real relationship with your own son. Again, what I hear you telling me is that you don't want me. How do you think it feels when someone tells you they don't want you? Do you have any idea how that feels?"

"Yes, I do. Your mother told me that when she divorced me. I do know how it feels."

"Then you should know how much it hurts. You should know."

Damon was speechless. After dealing with his own anger and feelings of rejection and guilt, Damon wanted to hear it all. He wanted to hear what he had run from for so long. He hungered to know more of his son's needs and hurts. It no longer mattered what it exposed about him as a parent. "Come give your old man a hug," said Damon, standing up to extend both arms toward his son.

"Dad, I'm not finished!" cried Derek, backing away. "How do I explain this — I'm almost paralyzed, like I can't move or something. Dad, the drugs make it easier. Otherwise I would explode with all kinds of feelings. It's like I want to hurt someone. I guess it's me I'm actually hurting. So, yeah, I know I'm hurting myself, but it also keeps me busy — so busy that I don't have to think about feeling like a nothing. In fact, that's just it. I feel nothing while I'm high. It's the only time I don't have to feel thrown away. I just don't care about anything. You think I don't know all I've done? Do you think I don't know that drugs and drinking and even smoking can kill you? You think I don't know how much I've hurt my mother? How I've embarrassed my family and myself? Y'all must think I'm stupid. I'm not stupid, just hurt, man. You just don't know," he closed his eyes and shook his head. "And I know that I've basically ruined my future. I know there's no chance for me to do anything good with my life."

"Stop right there!" interrupted Damon, rising to his feet. "You've made mistakes. We all have. But it's not too late for you. You are somebody special, and you can do great things. You *can*

put all this behind you, and you will because I see great poten-
tial in you. Son, one day you will make a difference in this world.
I feel it deep down in my soul." Damon grabbed his son by the
shoulders and looked him straight in the eye. "Do you understand
me?" Derek dropped his head. "Look at me, Son. You are destined
for great things. Agreed?"

"Yes Dad. Agreed," said Derek, still unsure.

"C'mon give your old man a hug. You may not think you
need it but I sure do need a hug from you right now. Since your
mother married John, I always wondered if he replaced me in
your heart." Damon reached over and grabbed his son by the
sleeve, pulling him close and clinging to him. Damon closed his
eyes and silently thanked God for the confrontation he had
avoided for so long. Yes, it was painful, but not nearly as painful
as he thought it would be.

"Go on, Son, go on."

"Dad," said Derek, as he turned away to hide the tears pouring from his eyes, "there's no point in starting up again if you're
going to drop me again. That's worse than never trying at all. I'm
glad you called, but if it's going to be another six or eight months
before I hear from you again or see you again, then just forget it.
Just forget it. I'm tired of hoping and looking for you. I'm tired
of wondering if you're going to come around and teach me how
to be a man. My question is — can you keep it up?"

"Look, I'm not all the man you think I am. I'm not perfect,
Son. Far from it. I've made lots of mistakes. Let's face it, I've
screwed up with you and your sister. How I've treated you guys
is a prime example. But I want to do better. I really do. I even
went to church last week — I know you don't believe it …"

"You're right, I don't," answered Derek jokingly.

"Nah, it's true! It was Easter. You know, I'm the Easter, Mother's Day, lose my job, and Christmas churchgoer. But maybe we

can do better together. I'll work on seeing you more, and you can work on school and letting the drugs go. What do you say?"

"It's a deal," they shook hands and hugged again.

"I'll do better, but, remember, it's a two-way street. You have a part to play."

"Dad, you don't have to say anything. I just needed to talk. I needed to let it out without fear. Let me just say one more thing. What I don't need are promises of what you can't deliver. I've had those, and they don't work. Let's start over. But not so much by planning events and outings. Can we just keep in touch? You can even email me. Something, though — anything. Let's start out that way. I know I can call you, but it's always been harder for me to reach you than the other way around. Maybe that's why I'm so hard to find now, because I wanted to out-disappear you. Ever since that time you hit Mom … "

Damon leaped to his feet. "WAIT A MINUTE! I didn't hit your mother."

"Dad, you don't have to be defensive. We all make mistakes, but you have to face them."

"Look, now — I never hit your mother in my life, not once. Is that the lie she's telling you? And you actually believe it?" he asked furiously.

"Dad! I was there that morning. I remember everything. You pushed her down the stairs. Why are you going to start lying now?" said Derek, stunned.

"Listen, if that's what you think of your father, then you're right, we can just end this conversation now. I NEVER, EVER hit your mother. I took her arm, she broke free, ran to the stairs and tripped, ON HER OWN. I tried to help her, but she wouldn't let me. I loved your mother and still do. Don't you ever form your lips to tell that lie again, do you understand me?" he said, almost towering over a seated Derek.

"Yeah, alright Dad. This has been a waste," he said, squeezing past his father. All the tension was back.

"Derek, get back here!" his father hollered.

"Some man you are! Can't even admit when you're wrong. I was there, remember?" said Derek, storming upstairs.

"Get back here or get out!" threatened his father. "I'm talking to you!" he screamed louder and louder. "I'm talking to you!"

"I'M TALKING TO YOU! I'm talking to you!" is all Andrew Derek Miller heard before waking to the sound of his alarm clock. He lunged forward from his pillow, sweat beads pouring down his face. He looked behind him and saw that his pillow was wet. This was the fifth such nightmare in as many days, each culminating in the same clash with his father.

"God!" he sighed. He looked at his hands. They were trembling. "When is it going to stop?" he asked himself with a cracked voice. Thirty minutes later after a shower and shave, Drew took his usual glance at the only picture on his lamp stand — that of him and his father when he was eight years old, taken two months before the split. Then he grabbed his blazer and headed toward the front door. He stole a quick glance in the mirror hanging in the foyer, pulling on the bags that sagged under his eyes.

"Man, what is with these dreams? Jeez, it's been seven years! Will I *ever* get some sleep?"

Andrew Miller, who had discarded his childhood name of Derek in favor of "Drew," was twenty-three and heading out the door to his first real job. Drew left the house and drove his sleek Honda Civic to the Springridge Boys and Girls Center in Rockville, Maryland. He was the new executive director. Drew believed in his heart of hearts that it was providence that sent him to this job. He wanted to save the world, and he had decided to begin with "troubled kids." What better job could there be than at a community center where most of the neighborhood kids passed their time and what better case study than a group of juveniles from families no longer intact?

The research he was conducting for his master's thesis told him these kids were likely to drop out, get pregnant, earn less money, and be more depressed than their "intact" counterparts. He was familiar with current research and the most recent news from the census on the breakdown of the family, but Drew was still surprised to learn during his interview about a center where all but ten of its thirty-five regular attendees no longer had a father living in the home. All but ten. Some of their parents were professionals, teachers, managers, and secretaries. Yet their status and their education seemed to have no effect on the peculiar situation in which the children were now living.

Drew pulled up to the community center at 7:30 A.M. His hours would be noon to 9 P.M., allowing for his two morning classes as well as permitting him to direct evening activities at the center. Today he had to be there early. Bruce Conrad, President of the Springridge board of directors, was waiting inside the front door to meet him.

"Drew! We're glad you made it, and we're truly excited to have you on board," he said, reaching to shake Drew's hand. "Come on in." Bruce pulled Drew inside.

"Thanks Mr. Conrad," said Drew, slightly nervous.

"Oh, call me Bruce. We're going to be working closely together this year, and I'm hoping we're going to accomplish some great things for this center. These kids need someone new, young, and with fresh ideas. With the challenges you faced and overcame in your early years, I think you have something unique to bring to the Springridge experience. You have a 'been there, done that, and overcame' story and methodology that you've got to share with these kids." Bruce led Drew upstairs toward Drew's new office. "We were so impressed with your interview and delighted to be a part of your research."

Drew followed him into the office, and although he saw the chair behind the desk, he moved toward the chair in front of the desk.

"No, sir, that's your chair. Go on, you're the new boss around here. In fact, I'm going to introduce you to the staff and get out of your way. But first, let me leave you with some important numbers and pointers. First, always keep in mind that we have to answer to the parents. If they don't like what we're doing, we need to make adjustments. Also, read and reread the grants and the operating requirements that are attached to those grants. We want to keep our donors happy because when we do so, they keep funding us. And that's what it's all about. No funding, no center. Got that?" he asked, as he scribbled on his pad.

Drew, trying to peer onto the pad, answered, "Of course."

"Good. So if you ever have any trouble or concerns, or if you want to try new things, check with me first. We'll be meeting every two months, but the various committees will meet a little more frequently. They'll probably want to invite you in to stay on top of what's going on. Also, while I certainly agree with the rest of the board members about your ideas for the weekly talk sessions with kids, just try not to go too deep, if you know what I mean. I know we agreed to help you with your thesis, but just remember you can't save the world in one day. Keep it light. After all, we don't want to drive the parents away. If that happens, there'll be no one here for you to save, right?"

"Of course."

"Good. Well, let's go meet the staff."

Bruce's instructions had somewhat squelched Drew's exuberance. Apprehension began to set in.

Journal

I truly wish I could rewrite my past instead of just reliving it. Dr. Valentine Jackson, my group counseling professor, insists that capturing these dreams in writing will help me come to terms with my past. I hope so. Dad, you were right — I did turn things around. Now I have a chance to arrest the downward spiral of someone else's life — just like you did for me. I miss you so much. — A.D.M.

CHAPTER ONE

The Heart of the Matter

The flyers and phone calls to existing members had evidently done the trick because the all-purpose room where Drew planned to conduct the Friday evening "Keep It Real" sessions was nearly filled to capacity. By 8:15 P.M., most of the kids had gravitated from the gym next to the all-purpose room. The usual four-on-four pickup games left most of the boys and the few girls who played exhausted. The other girls had practiced cheerleading routines, played ping pong, and talked about the usual — boys. But all were ready for food and more fun. The kids straggled into the all-purpose room and collapsed into seats, some sitting on the back of chairs, others leaping onto the long rectangular tables near the kitchen. Those who actually sat *in* the chairs made sure to slouch.

"Nothing leaves this room, deal?" asked Drew, who was calmly leaning against a tan rectangular table with his arms folded across his chest. "If we can all agree not to let what we say leave this room, then maybe we can rap." Drew was casually dressed in faded jeans, a number twenty-eight Redskins jersey, and visibly worn Air Jordans. He studied the faces of about twenty kids whose ages ranged from eight to seventeen. Some were there because their mothers preferred the structure of the club to after school day care. Some were there because of the year-round basketball league. Whatever the reason, Drew planned to keep the doors open and host a game night each Friday for anyone who wanted to come. Part of the night would feature "Keep It Real," the new name Drew had assigned to the rap session formerly called "Let's Rap."

"Everyone turn your chair into a circle so we can face each other," said Drew as he walked toward Jason. "Jason, help me pull these chairs over. In fact, everyone grab a chair. Hey, why don't we order a pizza?"

"That's what I'm talking about! What kind should we get?" said Jason, allowing himself to be lured into cooperation. "Come on y'all, let's get these chairs in line so we can have some pizza." Predictably, the other kids all did as their unofficial leader directed.

Meanwhile, in the kitchen filling cups with ice was Mayra, Drew's closest friend from childhood. Twenty-year-old Mayra knew the nature of the subject matter for this evening's rap session and wanted no part of it. Drew insisted she come anyway. A junior at nearby Howard University, Mayra was excited to see her friend land this job and hit the ground running. She was proud of him, although she had no intentions of joining in the conversation tonight.

"Drew," she whispered from the kitchen, "you want me to order the pizza?"

"No, I got it," he pulled his cell phone from his back pocket and placed the pizza order. He turned his chair around to hear better as the group grew rowdy.

"Okay, I just want you guys to shake loose what's on your mind. Tell me what you want to talk about. Ask me things you've always wanted to know. If I have answers, I'll give them. And if I don't have the answers, I'll find someone who does," said Drew, confidently.

"I have a question," said Dion, standing with a serious demeanor. "Can anyone tell me why when Kalia stepped on the scale, it said, 'to infinity and beyond'?"

Laughter roared throughout the room.

"Oh, you are so unbelievably stupid!" retorted Kalia. "If you study really hard, your I.Q. might reach zero."

"You guys stink," added Jason. "Didn't anybody teach you losers how to *jone*?" he chided. Popular with the girls at his high school, Jason considered himself a good basketball player and a force to be reckoned with on the court. He was six-foot-two and known for his skyhooks and finger rolls. He really was as good as he thought. Jason lived with his mom in a tiny two-bedroom townhouse in Aspen Hill, just outside Rockville.

"Yeah, well, your daddy's so stupid that he stared for one hour at the orange juice carton because it said 'concentrate,'" Dion said in Kalia's general direction.

"Oooh, that's a good one. Whoa, that's deep," said Jason, as he dropped his head to silently chuckle.

"Yeah, well, that one doesn't hurt because if my dad was buying OJ, he wouldn't be buying it for me anyway, so you can talk about him all you want," said Kalia out of nowhere, betraying her inner feelings in her bluster. "But you better not say anything about my momma!" she added.

"Cool it! Why do you guys always think you need to jone on each other?"

"Like you didn't jone, Drew," said Jason.

"Yeah, but then I finally grew up and realized that it always leads to hurt. I lost a lot of friends joking around like this. I see some things never change."

"Like what?" asked Jason.

"Oh, like you can't talk about nobody's momma — that is if you don't want to get hurt. But anyway, I know we can find something better to discuss tonight than jonin'. I happened to notice in that little exchange that it's okay to talk about anybody but the mom. Am I right that you can even talk about someone's daddy?" he said, looking in Kalia's direction. Some of the kids giggled.

"Come on, at least I'd like to know who you guys are and what you're all about. Who'll start us off, huh?" asked Drew.

No one spoke.

"Hey guys, let's take some time to get to know each other. Many of you know each other but some don't. I'm new here, so I'd like to put faces to names. Go around and tell us your name, age, a little about yourself and your family, what sports you play, and what you want to do with your life. We'll start with the oldest. Who's the oldest in here? Any takers?" Drew was gazing directly into Jason's eyes. Drew noticed his intensity on the court and the deference the younger boys showed him. Drew had also noticed that Jason caught the attention of at least one young lady, fourteen-year-old Kalia.

"Alright, I'll start. I'm Jason Phillips and I'm sixteen. I shoot hoops and go to Rockview High. I live with my mom."

"And you promise to keep … "

"I know, I know, it's confidential. I won't blab," said Jason. He looked around the room at friends Dion and Kalia and smirked. "It's cool; this'll be fun. So let's talk." He leaned his chair onto its two back legs and began to rock.

"Okay," said Dion, always eager to please adults. "I'm Dion and I'm twelve. This is my brother Ray," he said leaning to his right side in the direction of his thirteen-year-old brother. "We live with our mom and go to Red Oak Middle. I'm a ballplayer, and I plan to play football."

"Ray?" motioned Drew.

"Dion said it," he answered, nodding his head toward Kalia as if it were now her turn to speak.

"Ray, what do you like to do?"

After a pause, Ray placed his right hand on his chin like Rodin's *Thinker*, looked up toward the ceiling, and spoke. "Umh … Umh, I play football and played here last year. I like playstation and, uh, movies."

"Well, what's your favorite movie?" asked Drew.

"He likes *Big Daddy*," blurted Dion. "I like that one too."

"Let's let Ray answer for himself," Drew said gently.

"That one's okay," said Ray.

Drew saw this as his chance to move into the subject he really wanted to broach. "So, why do you like that movie?"

"It's funny," said Ray timidly.

Drew waited for more, but more didn't come. "Okay, who's next? Kalia. Tell us about yourself."

Kalia's cute face was overshadowed by some extra pounds. She suffered her share of fat jokes, most centering around her love of eating. But buffalo wings weren't the only things she loved — Jason was next on the list. Kalia's mother had once overheard her leave a voicemail message for Jason and scolded the child, telling her, "Stop looking for your daddy in all those older boys. Stop it now!" After that, Kalia was careful when she dialed his number.

"Okay, I'm fourteen and I like school most of the time. I live with my mom and my sister. My dad and mom divorced, and sometimes I see him and it's totally cool, and sometimes it stinks because he forgets important things and days. I know he loves me, but ooh, I get so mad sometimes."

"Hey, Kalia," shouted Jared from across the room. "Don't forget to tell everybody how much you like Jason and ... " laughing uncontrollably, he added, "and food!"

"Whoa!" said Tony, snickering with nearly everyone else except Jason.

"Man, you need help," said Jason.

"Whatever!" said Kalia. "You are so sick," she said as she looked to see if Giselle was looking at Jason.

Giselle was a tall honey-colored high school senior whose parents divorced when she was eleven. She loved hanging out at the youth center where she could play basketball, use the computers to do her schoolwork, write for the school newspaper, and be near all the cute boys — including Jason. "Grow up, Jared," she said, rolling her hazel eyes.

"If we're going to do this, let's be kind to each other. If nothing else, can we agree on that?" asked Drew.

They all nodded, including Danny, who continued with his giggling.

"Tony, what about you? If your best friend were to answer the question, *who is Tony*, what would he say?" asked Drew.

Tony glanced around the room to see who was looking at him. He was a curly-topped cutie with eyes like marble. Tony peeked through his glasses at Dion as if expecting Dion to crack on him and said, "I'm eleven and I live with my mom. I don't have any brothers or sisters. I like my game boy, and, um, I play baseball. I like basketball too." Tony didn't mention Boy Scouts because some kids had called him a nerd and said he was uncool for being a scout.

"Thanks, Tony. We look forward to getting to know you and everyone else better. So tell me, what's on your heart, what's on your mind? Where do you want to go this year?"

"When's the trip to Six Flags?" asked Dion.

"Next week. So is the family picnic. Did your parents get the flyers in the mail? We're having the annual kids versus grownups basketball tournament. Who's bringing their dad or mom?"

"I am," said RJ.

"My dad's coming," said Marcus. Drew looked around the room, waiting for responses but no other hands were raised.

"Any other dads coming?" asked Drew.

Again no one answered. The kids looked around at each other. Some snickered.

"Moms can play too, you know. So what else is going on?" asked Drew.

"It's kind of scary these days because of 9/11," said Kalia.

"Yeah, yeah!" said Dion. "It's weird now. They keep talking about more attacks. That day was so scary. My dad called me and told me he was thinking about me and that there was nothing to worry about."

"What was the first thing you thought about when you heard what happened?" asked Drew.

"I was in school, and I kept thinking about my mom," said Kalia. "And my dad."

"Oh yeah? What was going on inside?"

"Well, my mom works in D.C., and I was so scared. My dad lives in D.C. and my mom said he was doing some work near the Pentagon. I just broke down crying at school," said Kalia.

"Did you talk to your father after that?" asked Drew.

"No, I called my grandmother to try to speak to him but he wasn't there. My grandma said he was fine. I don't know if he ever got my message," she said, folding her arms.

"Well, when was the last time you talked to him?" probed Drew.

"Like around June. He came to bring my mother some money."

"I have a question," said Dion, looking around the room as if building up to fire off a live one. "Do you know why God would let this happen to us?" asked Dion. All eyes followed Dion's eyes directly to Drew.

"Whoa!" said Drew. "I guess from your perspective it might look like God has abandoned us. But I think truth is all in how you look at things. From my vantage point, I saw God all up in the middle of it all, protecting us."

"What? Are you talking about the same 9/11 we're talking about?" asked Jason.

"Absolutely. Think of it this way — 95 percent of the people in the twin towers escaped alive. I saw the hand of God holding those structures up until most of those people escaped. I saw the hand of God move that plane away from the Capitol and into the nearly vacant side of the Pentagon, killing far fewer people than could have been killed. I also saw the hand of God raise up some modern commandos to take that plane out in Pennsylvania. Do you know what anarchy is?"

"No," replied Tony.

"It's when you have no government. Everyone and everything goes buck wild. Can you imagine your school with no teachers or adults?" he asked. The question stilled the room. The youngsters all smiled. "But that didn't happen. Just because you didn't see him clearly didn't mean he wasn't there," said Drew.

"Anyone else? What's been going on?" Drew stood up to move around the circle.

"It's just been really sad. I really wish my dad was here," said Kalia.

"How many of you thought about your fathers after 9/11?" he asked. Every soul raised a hand.

"We were afraid we'd have to leave Washington if they attacked us again, and I just kept wondering whether my dad would come help us or take us or whether he would just leave without us," said Kalia.

"Listen, who here lives with both parents?" Counting around

the room, Drew said, "I see six hands out of twenty of you." He noticed the silence. "I know this is touchy. If this is too uncomfortable for you, we can change the subject," he said sincerely.

The room remained silent as most eyes descended upon Jason, who paused a few moments, then commented, "It's cool. We can talk about fathers."

"Um, I don't think so," said Kalia.

"It's up to you guys," said Drew, leaning back in his chair and clasping his hands behind his head. "It's up to you."

"Okay, we can talk about dads," said Dion, eagerly sitting up in his chair. Most of the kids looked in Jason's direction as he spoke.

"Sure, let's do it. But like the man said, nobody blabs," said Jason. "Kalia?" he asked.

"Okay," she agreed.

"Can you talk about your dad or mom if you live with both of them?" asked RJ.

"Absolutely!" reassured Drew. "We need input from everyone. So, someone tell me something about fathers. It doesn't have to be your father. Just fathers in general. What do you think of? What feelings come to heart?"

His words were greeted with utter silence. He prompted further, "Everyone knows that many kids these days don't live with their fathers."

Still no takers.

"How about this … you don't have to talk about yourselves. You can just talk about things that someone you know has experienced. Maybe your best friend or a cousin. You don't have to use their name. But let's find out what the deal is." Drew could see he had their attention.

As Drew looked her way, Kalia dropped her head to avoid being singled out. But then she decided to speak. "My dad's okay. It's just that he's never there. But hey, he's cool," she said laughing.

Jason spoke up. "It's kind of hard to just open up and start talking about a dad who's not there. I mean, what do you say?" He looked around as if to see if anyone else would agree with his comment. His glances were met with silence. "Okay, my dad's not around. He never shows up when it's important, and I'm pissed. Is that what you're looking for? If so, I know a lot of people in that boat. Just about everyone I know can tell you that story."

"Listen, everyone. I can tell you all a story about someone whose father was not around," said Drew. But first we need to get some things straight. I'm going to give you a peek into someone's life, and I'm only going to ask a few things from you guys. First, I just want to make sure you want to be here. I presume that you *want* to be part of Keep It Real since you're not still in the gym or game room, right?"

Nods followed.

"Yeah!" said Jason emphatically.

Drew glanced toward Jason with a puzzled expression, wondering if Jason was being sincere or sarcastic.

"Second, I need some confidentiality. Do you know what that means? I know you guys like to jone on each other but you can't do that with the things you share or learn in here. Plain and simple, I won't allow it. If any of us hears that something said here was repeated outside these walls, the squealer is not welcome back to Keep It Real. Are we agreed? Do you think that's a fair enforcement tool for breaking a confidence?" he asked sternly. "I need everyone to agree. If you agree, raise your hand, and if not, these sessions are simply not for you. And that's okay too. We can still be friends. You can go back to the game room or the gym. It's cool."

Drew looked around the room again, and he was pleasantly surprised as he noticed all the raised hands. He sighed, leaned back in his chair, and was about to speak when Jason chimed in. "What difference does it make? My dad hasn't been there lately, so I just got over it. Y'all need to just get over it like I did."

"Oh, you got over it?" said Drew, smiling as he acknowledged the first challenge to his mission.

"Yeah, I'm not pressed anymore. I don't think about him and my life goes on. I'm cool."

"Well, you may be just fine, but I sure know beaucoup kids who went through big time changes when their parents split."

"Whatever you say," mumbled Jason. Drew ignored him and looked around the group for more participants …

PERCHED IN THE KITCHEN doorway, twenty-year-old Mayra was intent on remaining inconspicuous, but she was hanging on Drew's every word.

"I knew they would have nothing to say," she mumbled to herself, shaking her head.

But as Mayra peered around the corner into those timid faces, she remembered her own defining fatherless moment when she first heard her mother tell her, "He's not coming." Mayra had been sure her mother was wrong. She had to be. Suspended somewhere between faith and fear, Mayra refused to yield to her mother's prediction that her daddy was not coming to take her out for her birthday. Mayra was eight at the time and she lived with her mother and her aunt. Her parents had split up while she was a baby and Mayra had no memory of her father's presence in the home. She vaguely remembered a tall handsome man named "daddy" who would occasionally stop by with a doll or some other toy and leave shortly thereafter. Her father, Rick, was a successful local photographer and artist, and shortly after his breakup with Brenda, became involved with a woman named Barbara. She gave birth to Mayra's half-sister Gwen one year after Mayra was born. By the time Mayra was four years old her parents were divorced, and she had a father and a sister she barely knew. Rick and Barbara married years later.

By the age of seven Mayra knew from other children what a father was, what a father did, where a father lived, and, most importantly, that her father did none of these things. Mayra knew that most of her friends had something she didn't have. Mayra imagined those daddies were like the ones Mayra watched on television, and, in her imagination, Cliff Huxtable became her daddy.

Every Thursday evening, Mayra found her *Cosby Show* father looking after her brother and sisters. Mayra was Rudy and Cliff was daddy because for the most part, there was no one else. Yet every Thursday evening at 8:00 P.M., she found daddy on television. Mayra learned that there are good and reliable daddies in the world and that hers was not that kind.

WHEN MAYRA TUNED back in she heard Drew telling his unofficial clients that it was okay that no one had anything to add to the father discussion and that there'd be plenty of opportunities in the coming weeks.

"*If* anyone comes back after tonight," Mayra said to herself as she turned to eat the last slice of pizza. "I told you."

As the group wrapped up and cleaned up, Drew walked over to Jason who was waiting for his mother to pick him up.

"I heard you in the session. I heard you loud and clear," said Drew. "You got a few minutes? I want to share something with you."

"Yeah, my mom won't be here for a few more minutes. She has to take dinner to my gramma who lives in a nursing home. Mom usually just stops at home to make dinner and then heads back out until around 8:30 or 9:00. So, yeah, I've got a few minutes."

"Well, what do you usually do until your mother gets home?"

"Oh, I just hang out at the courts shooting hoops."

"Well, you can start coming here every day to help out with the younger kids, but right now there's something I want to talk to you about," said Drew, leading Jason toward his office.

As they walked, Tony and his mother Linda passed by on their way to the door. Tony turned to his mother and said, "That's him, Mom. And he said he's coming to some of my games."

"Okay, that'll be nice," she said, urging him toward the door.

"Drew, I'll bring my baseball schedule next week, okay?" asked Tony, who paused despite his mother's nudges.

"I got you, man. I'll make some of those games for sure. See you later."

Jason followed Drew into the office and sat down in a chair by the doorway.

Drew said, "Listen, I want to tell you about this boy named Derek. His parents split when he was eight years old. It was unbelievably hard on him. His relationship with his father began to unravel because they never saw each other. They just couldn't get it together. Trust me when I say Derek had a hole the size of Montana in his heart. He felt rejected. He felt as if something was wrong with him because his father didn't want to be with him. He felt like he was defective and unwanted."

Jason cradled his head in his hands, resting his elbows on his legs.

"So, when your father doesn't want you, what's the point? Who do you live for? Derek thought he had no strength to face life — no strength to fight, to succeed, to push. So he fell into the wrong crowd. That meant drugs, drinking, staying out — early on now, early on. But if you asked him, he'd say his father's absence didn't affect him. He got over it."

Jason glanced up briefly before folding his arms tightly across his chest. He didn't say a word.

"But it did affect him. It hurt, man, it hurt. One day it all came crashing down on him. His father called and wanted to see him. Derek's dad said, 'I want to see you, son.' Derek could have melted. So he made it to his dad's house. He was there. He was whole. He was happy. That was the beginning of his healing."

"And where are they now?" asked Jason. "Does he live with his father? Did things work out? Was he a part of Derek's life after that? Did Derek get off drugs? What happened?"

Before Drew could answer, they both heard Vicky calling for Jason. "We'll finish this later, but all I can say now is don't give up. You need him and it does affect you. And that's okay. It's an okay thing that you're struggling with how you feel. It is a struggle."

Vicky walked in the office. "Oh, there you are. Someone named Mayra said I'd find you guys in here. Jason, let's head home. Nice to see you again, Drew."

"Nice to see you too, Mrs. Phillips," said Drew, hurrying behind them to escort Jason and his mother to the door. "See you next week, Jason."

"We'll see what his schedule looks like," said Vicky as they disappeared into the night.

Journal

I suppose you could say these kids represent the glaring census truths fleshed out. But somehow, studying statistics and reading psychology books pale in comparison to what I see and hear these half-winged angels say as they air their secret wounds and desires. Some I'm sure I can help. Others, I'm not so sure. Either way, Dr. Jackson has admonished me to keep the parents involved every step of the way. I hope I can do that. — A.D.M.

CHAPTER TWO

Separation Anxiety

The following Friday, only three stayed for Keep It Real — Jason, Giselle, and RJ. "Basketball season starts in a few weeks and, man, I hope my dad can come to my games this year. He hardly made any last year because of his job," said Jason.

Drew was surprised since Jason had said nothing the previous week. Drew figured the empty room helped. "Well, you need to invite him. Call him before every game. Does he have directions? You need to make it easy for him." Drew rattled off directions as if he'd been there.

"It's not that easy," said Mayra, emerging from the kitchen.

"Well, well, well. Seems like everyone's got something to say tonight. Mayra Taylor, come on down!" quipped Drew sarcastically.

"That's all I'm going to say. Drew, it's just not always that easy. Let's leave it at that," she said, shaking her head as she returned to the kitchen. Giselle leaped from her seat and darted toward the kitchen, muttering, "I'll be back." Mayra saw her coming and turned her back toward Giselle, twisting on the faucet to wash her hands.

"Hi," said Giselle softly. "Is there anything else to drink?" She decided not to advance further into the kitchen until feeling welcome to do so.

"Oh, uh, sure."

"Are you Drew's girlfriend?" asked Giselle.

"No! But we're like best friends when he isn't too busy thinking he knows everything."

"Talking about fathers is hard. Shoot, talking about mothers is hard, and I live with my mother," said Giselle, hoping to draw Mayra out.

"My mom's pretty cool most of the time. You'll feel that way when you get older. You're, what, in the eleventh grade?" asked Mayra.

"No twelfth."

"Oh, twelfth. Yeah, as soon as you get to college, you'll see. My mom has been there for me like nobody else. I realize that now," said Mayra.

"Well, my dad's not there and my mom has it hard, although she hasn't made it easy for him either. And, well, sometimes she just does things to really tick me off. Like before he moved away, he missed a lot of things in my life, but, guess what — so did she. All she ever talked about was what he didn't do, but she didn't do a lot of things either. She always said it was because she was too busy trying to do all the things he was supposed to do. But that gets old after a while." She looked at Mayra and waited for a response — some direction, empathy, correction, opposing view — anything.

Mayra finally asked, "Do you see your father much now?"

"Um, not really. He remarried and moved away. Get this, I now have a baby brother."

"Really?"

My sister Kiarra and I go every now and then. It's okay," she said, looking toward the floor.

"I know what you mean," said Mayra as she turned to open the refrigerator door. "Here, have some more punch before I pour it all back in the jug."

"You know what it's like?" asked Giselle.

"What do you mean?" asked Mayra. Her face was still buried in the refrigerator as if she were studying x-ray photos.

"You said, I know what you mean."

"Oh, that. Well, I mean, you know, I know what you mean," Mayra said, trying to avoid discussing her own life. She had told Drew she believed that bringing their personal lives into the work at the club was unprofessional. That was her stated basis for not participating in the group sessions.

"Soooo, are your parents still married?" Giselle asked reluctantly.

"Huh?" said Mayra, glaring harshly at Giselle to suggest that she had just asked an improper question. "Okay, no. So, I do know what you mean. Is there anything else you'd like to know?"

"Well, I see you turned out okay, so I guess I'll be alright. Right? I mean, it probably wasn't so bad for you. Your dad probably came to see you and kept you in his life, didn't he?"

Mayra looked upward, drew a deep breath, exhaled, and smiled at Giselle. Then she finally began to talk. "Come sit down. Trust me when I say that life without daddy is no picnic, and I still have issues."

"*You* have issues?"

"Yes, I have issues. My dad is a famous photographer. He's actually pretty good, and scores of people know him and his work. So growing up, sometimes I would go to a friend's house

… in fact, it's still the same today … but I'd go to a friend's house and see one of my dad's photographs. This one time, I was at my friend Denise's house … "

"How old were you?"

"Twelve, and I walked into the living room and saw one of my dad's famous photos above the mantle. I still remember," she said, looking past Giselle to the blank wall.

"The picture was of my cousins on the playground. It was my favorite. It still is. But beneath the photo and on the mantle was one of my father's brochures.

"You're joking, right?"

"No, trust me when I say I know what it is to be left out. Anyway, when I saw the picture, I just screamed, 'That's my daddy's picture!' Then, Denise's dad, who had just walked in behind us, said, 'No, no.' I hadn't even heard him come in. He said, 'I know Rick Taylor and he only has one child and her name is Gwen. I met her. I know him well. Young lady, you shouldn't go around calling people your daddy.' Then he picked up the brochure and showed it to me. I wasn't in it."

"You okay?" asked Giselle, trying to make eye contact with Mayra.

"Oh, girl, I'm fine. I'm over all that, and anyway, I didn't care what that man said. I said, 'He IS my dad.' I couldn't really move, though. I just stood there, almost frozen. Then I wondered — is he my daddy? Am I wrong? I knew he was my daddy, but this grown up was so sure of himself, and I *was* left off the brochure. I still can't believe I let that foolish man make me doubt myself."

"Well, what did you do?"

"I just walked out and whispered, 'My name *IS* Mayra Taylor and my daddy *IS* Rick Taylor.' I thought, how dare you?!"

"What did HE say?"

"Nothing."

"Why didn't you try and prove it to him? You could've called your mother and she would've set him straight," said Giselle defiantly.

"Yeah, but, well, I don't know. Would you believe that when I told my mother, she told me not to go around telling everybody, that it wasn't important? I never understood that. He wouldn't accept me as Rick's daughter. That hurt. You know, I really wanted Denise's dad to know. I wanted my dad's friends to know. I wanted his customers to know. After that, I wanted everybody to know all about me," she said, rising to dig through the cabinet for tea bags.

"Wow, you should tell your story to the group," said Giselle. "I think you should join us next time. Have you noticed? It's quiet in there. Since no one really opened up, I think they went back to the gym. But you should open up to the group. It could help us, really."

"I saw him later that summer, after the brochure incident. I went to the mall with my cousin and I saw my dad. I walked into the City Place Mall and there's a frame shop on the right when you walk in and there he was. I wasn't expecting that. My heart skipped a few beats! I was lightheaded. So, there he was, displaying his photos in the frame shop," Mayra said, dramatizing the scene. "So I said, 'Hi Daddy.' I was so nervous."

"What did he say?!" screamed Giselle.

"He said, 'Hi, baby girl.' And that was it. That's all he said. I stood in that shop, waiting and hoping for my father to be fatherly, hoping that man would say something to let me know he cared, but all he said was, 'Hi, baby girl.' I just waited. Then my cousin Celeste said, 'let's go into the mall.' So I said, 'bye, Daddy.' And he said, 'bye, baby girl. I'll be talking to you soon.'

"So we wandered in the mall, and I have to admit I hoped my

dad would come looking for me. I expected to see him following, trying to catch up with me, but he didn't. So when we left
about an hour later, I couldn't help but look in the frame shop
one last time, but he was gone. When I got home, I bugged out
I was so angry. I mean, I wanted to scream at him, ask him, 'Is that
all you could think of to say to me? It's been months since you've
seen your own flesh and blood, your daughter, your first born.
Isn't there anything else you want to say?' I thought he'd want to
know about what was going on in my life, how I was doing in
school, what I needed, you know."

"Shoot, I just want to know if my dad even thinks about me,
even if we don't talk," said Giselle. Then she stood up, finished
her drink, and walked out, hoping to find Jason in the gym.

AN HOUR LATER GISELLE WAS looking at the mailbox to the right
of the door.

"It's okay, I got the mail," said her mother, aware of her
daughter's apprehensions in light of the anthrax scare. "My, my,
you are growing taller by the minute. You obviously get your
height from your father's side of the family. You look like his two
sisters." At seventeen Giselle towered over her mother. "Oh, I
wish you had kept up with the dancing. You are so graceful.
You're my gazelle. Yes, you are," she said affectionately.

"Mom!" said Giselle, embarrassed. Then she added, "Well, it's
been years since I've seen them, so I wouldn't know." Giselle sat
down at the kitchen table. "You're not afraid to touch the mail
with everything going on?"

"Child, no! When it's your time, it's your time. I can't afford
not to open these bills. Do you actually think those companies
wouldn't add all those late charges just because I said I was afraid
of anthrax?"

"I guess not. Well, did any of my college applications come in the mail today?"

"Uh, let me see. Oh, here's Spelman College, BU, and University of Maryland. Good, you're applying to Maryland. You need a fallback," said her mother as she began to open the Spelman college application.

"Mom! Let me open them!" cried Giselle as she stood to reach for her mail. Her mother playfully stood up and turned her back to Giselle.

"Girl, I need to see what this tuition is going to be. And, speaking of tuition ... " she said, walking down the hall, prompting her daughter to pursue her. "You need to call your father. There's simply no way I'm going to be able to afford the tuition at the schools you're applying to. And I shouldn't have to."

Giselle slowed her hot pursuit and sat down on the sofa in the living room. "I'll apply for loans and grants. I have good grades, so I'll probably qualify for at least a partial scholarship," she said, folding her arms.

Giselle's mother joined her on the sofa, cradled her daughter's face in her hands, and looked directly into her eyes.

"The point, my dear, is that he needs to do his part. You need to involve him, make him contribute his share. You are his daughter. He is your father and owes you at least part of this. I'm going to do my part. So will you. So must he," she paused before continuing. Giselle didn't respond.

"And, you need to call him sooner rather than later, because I can assure you that his little wife will definitely throw a monkey wrench into the mix, especially if you wait too long."

"Mom, leave her out of this. Dad said he would help me and I believe he will," said Giselle, defiantly.

"Child of mine, how naïve are you? This is all I'm going to say on this. I know how you are — you're a procrastinator. You let things drag on and you think things will just somehow fall into place. Well, they won't this time. This is one call you're going to have to make or you may come up short."

Giselle dropped her head into her hands and sighed.

SEVERAL NIGHTS LATER, the all-purpose room was packed. The gang was gathered for their customary pickup game and rap session.

"Drew, so what happened after Derek got to his dad's house?" asked Jason as he twirled the basketball on his right forefinger.

"Are you sure you want to know about him? You didn't seem all that interested when I was talking the other week," said Drew from the free throw line. "Pass it," he said, motioning for Jason to pass him the ball. Drew took a free throw shot.

"Brick!" yelled Dion.

"Yeah, well, you can't win 'em all," said Drew turning to exit the gym. Drew noticed the usual suspects slowly finding their way to "The War Room" – what the group called the all-purpose room. Jason pulled his chair close to Drew's and insisted that Drew continue his story about Derek.

"Let me just ask you, was two weeks ago too heavy for you guys? I mean, we talked about a lot of things but we also talked about fathers and mothers. Should we pick up where we left off, or should we talk about something lighter? If you can't handle this now, I'll understand."

"I like talking about my dad." interrupted Dion. "We can talk about fathers. If no one else wants to talk, I'll talk."

"It's all good," said Jason, surprising everyone. Drew immediately looked around the room and noticed even more heads slowly nodding up and down to signal a willingness to open up.

"Okay, Dion — tell us what you'd like to share," said Drew, leaning back in his familiar chair.

He felt a bit timid this time around, but he was ready to describe the defining father moment that was forever embedded in his memory. "The only time I felt really close to my dad and older brother was when I was five. I remember it like it was yesterday, and I go back to that place whenever I feel like I'm not a part of my dad's family. We had gone to my grandmother's Baptist church in Virginia. I still remember the small white wooden church that sat a ways off from the main road. The paint was peeling, and it smelled damp, like it was leaking water in the basement or something. And it was so hot in there, especially when the organ played and everyone got up to sing. But when it was finally over, I remember we all got together in the church backyard. I think it was a church picnic, or something. There was music, food, and a lot of people. My dad and older brother were there. I remember hearing jazz playing from somewhere. There was a playground and I remember climbing on the swing. My dad walked over to stand behind me and he began pushing me to the jazzy beat. He was pushing me and humming to the beat. Then, my brother came and stood in front of me and began to push me back toward my dad. Me and my brother started humming with him to the beat. Man, it was so tight! There I was, rocking and swinging back and forth with my dad pushing me higher and higher right to my brother who would catch me and push me right back to my daddy — all in this perfect rhythm, this perfect beat. I dropped my head back and felt the wind on my face. There I was, free like an eagle with nothing and no one to stop me, nothing to hold me back. I was flying. I was the prince. There was no place on earth I would rather have been then — or even now. Now I just wish he'd call every now and then. I mean I do talk to him many times, but I know he's just so busy."

Ray looked at him in disbelief.

"Ray, is there something you want to add?" probed Drew.

"Well, it's just that Dion doesn't always remember exactly as things are," said Ray, cutting his eyes toward his brother. "You know Dad doesn't call as much as you say he does."

"Alright, Ray — do you call your dad often since he's not calling you?" challenged Drew.

"I used to, but I don't do it much anymore," he said, folding his arms.

"I wish my dad would call and ask me about school or boyfriends, you know, let me know he cares about those things. I always watch on TV where the dad wants to know who the daughter is going with and the dads like to scare the boyfriends into acting right," said Kalia.

"Kalia, you can scare them all by yourself!" said Dion.

"You need to shut up before I hurt you, boy!"

"Now, now. Kalia, go on, please," said Drew, trying to keep the discussion moving.

"Well, I wish I knew if he cared if my life was in danger or not, like on 9/11, that he cared whether I lived or died. Sometimes, I think that he'd rather that I die so he wouldn't have to pay child support."

The room was silent.

"Oh, like I'm the only one who feels that way," she said, glaring at everyone.

"She is soooo right!" added Tony. "Whenever my mom goes back to court about child support, it's a whole year before I hear from my dad again. It's like he's punishing me because of her."

"Or like whenever he has a new girlfriend, my mother starts trippin'," said Jason. "I can never see my dad if he has a new girlfriend, unless my mom wants the scoop on her. Then I have to go and be grilled by her when I get back. That scene is so wild. It's deep. It's so deep," he said, sighing and shaking his low-hanging head.

"Do you really believe all that?" asked Drew.

"I don't know."

"I'm not a father, but I know it can be hard for them — to be torn or, yes, even walk away from someone they love and only see them every now and then. It's almost easier to just let the person go. I once read that many parents actually reduce their visits to terminally ill children because they need a break from the pain and need to begin to let go. I'm not saying that's what's going on. One day, I'll ask the moms and dads to come in for a session and let them talk it out themselves."

"Yeah! Invite our fathers and mothers to come and talk about us and why they won't come see us!" said Dion.

"Or why they, our moms that is, won't let us see our dads," said Jason, leaning forward in his chair.

"We can ask my dad," said R.J. "I have an older brother from my dad's first marriage and he comes to stay with us all the time. But I do hear my dad arguing with his mother sometimes because she won't let him take trips with us. She wouldn't even let him come to my grandmother's funeral. She said he had a band concert for school. Like his own grandmother's funeral isn't more important than a band concert. He's fifteen years old. It's crazy sometimes. He says she even talks bad about us, but he doesn't listen to it. My brother Devon is cool to me all the time, despite how his mother acts."

"Drew, you're in psychology — why does it seem like they never have time for us? It's like we're in the way of their lives," said Giselle.

"Gang, I don't have all the answers, but I know who does. Your father has many of the answers to the questions you're posing."

"Oh, like I'm going to call my dad and say, 'Hey Dad, and why is it you haven't called or come by in a year? Huh? Huh?'" said Kalia sarcastically.

"I'm always nervous when my father comes or when I go see him," added Dion. "It's weird. I'm just nervous."

"I try to see my dad, but sometimes my mom changes our plans and says we have to go to my grandmother's house or to see some other relatives. It's wacked, that's all I can say," said Jason, looking down at the floor and slouching further into his chair.

Drew looked over at Tony, expecting him to join in. Instead, Tony seemed captivated by the openness of the older kids but had nothing more to add. "I got a question for you guys," said Drew. "Whose fault is it when two people break up? Or when the parent doesn't come to visit like they're supposed to?"

The room was silent.

"Well, you know, there are three sides to every story," said Drew to close out. He stood up and folded his chair.

"No, two sides," said Jason.

"Actually, there are three. Try and figure it out. But let me just add this: It's not easy after two people with children break up or divorce. Trust me on this one. It's hard keeping the father-kid relationship together and it's hard on the mother. Hey, it's hard on both parents. You need to try and understand what they're going through too and try to figure out a way to be part of the solution. You guys are intelligent and resourceful. I know. I see some of you on the court every day. You know how to find the open man for the impossible play. Let's learn how to take that persistence and creativity into the relationships with your mothers and fathers," said Drew. "Let me close with this question: Can you lose something that you don't have?" He was confident there would be no smart comeback. There wasn't.

"So, let's clean up our mess here and go home. It's getting late. Whose mother is *not* on her way?" he asked.

No one raised a hand.

"Okay, then. See you guys later."

A few mothers began filing in.

"Hey, Drew, can you come to my baseball game tomorrow morning?" Tony asked, as he was leaving. "I'll be playing short-stop."

"Oh yeah? Sure, I'll come. Where's the game?"

"It's off Bonifant by the Old Trolley Museum," answered Tony's mom, Linda. "The game begins at 10:30 and lasts, oh, about an hour and a half."

"Cool. I know where that is. I've been meaning to come, and I've been telling him I'll come. I'll be there. I wouldn't miss this for anything. Tony's my boy. This way I can say I knew him when, before he wins the MVP award. Hold up, just let me get my keys and jacket and I'll walk you guys out." Drew darted into his office to turn off the lights and grab his keys and jacket. As they walked out, Tony and Linda regaled Drew with baseball tales of third base steals, near homeruns, and sensational diving catches.

KALIA'S MOM, JOANNE, WAS POSITIONED at the front door wait-ing for her daughter to be dropped off. She was waiting to ask Kalia about a phone call she'd made. Kalia had called her grand-mother Lois to try to get a message to her father.

"Oh God, what have I done now?" asked Kalia as she walked in.

"Just get inside first. Besides, you know what you did. How many times have I told you not to call that woman, especially not to ask for any money? The last thing I need is for them to start talking about how we want something from them. I can't believe you did that!"

"Mom, I didn't ask her for any money. I just left a message on her machine to give to Dad if she saw him. I just said that I needed some money for a movie and I didn't want to ask you, that's all. But I didn't ask *her*."

"It's the same thing."

"I asked you for money for the movie and food, and you told me you just didn't have the money. You said they were about to cut off the gas and the phone, and that money to see a movie was the last thing on the money list. I understood all that. I just wanted to go to the movie, to have a good time for once, just once."

"Have you ever stopped to think about how this makes me look? If your father paid child support, maybe I could send you to the movies. Did you tell her that — that if he paid like he was supposed to, we wouldn't be worried about whether the gas would be cut off tomorrow or whether I'd have enough to feed you girls? Maybe I wouldn't have to work two damn jobs!"

"Aaaaaaaaaaaaaaah!" screamed Kalia. "Mom! I'm sick of hearing about the rent, the gas bill, the light bill, the food bill, and everything else. I just wanted to go to the movies and have some money for food," said Kalia, sighing. She shook her head as she dropped it into her hands.

The phone rang. She ran to the phone in her mother's bedroom, hoping it was her father.

"Oh, hi, Mrs. Westley," said Kalia. "I don't think I'm going to be able to go to the movies because I have too much homework to do."

"Nonsense. Tomorrow is Saturday and no one has that much homework. Since we already have the tickets, what would we do with yours if you don't go?"

"Okay, Mrs. Westley. I'll go; what time should I be ready?"

"We'll be there at noon. We want plenty of time to get in the popcorn line and buy all those goodies."

"Okay, I'll be ready. Thank you, Mrs. Westley. I'll tell my mom everything you said." *Well, I'm sure Mom can scrape up a few dollars for popcorn. I might have some change,* thought Kalia. She could already smell the buttery popcorn. The salty crunch was already in her mouth. Kalia went to bed somewhat hopeful.

MAYRA HADN'T EATEN AT SPRINGRIDGE and she was famished. *A Night to Remember*, an old black and white flick, was playing on the thirty-six-inch TV, and a few of the girls were braiding each other's hair, and others were eating pepperoni pizza.

Kellie immediately noticed Mayra's sunken mood. "Mayra, you okay?"

"I'm fine, but I just left a community center rap session and all these kids were talking about their no-good fathers, and well, needless to say, that's all I needed to hear after my dad just missed my birthday again!"

"I know how you feel," said Kellie. She sat down next to Mayra and they began to talk. The evening-hour discussions in the all-girls dorm consisted mainly of boy talk. Who was cute, who was not. Who went with whom, and who was on the side. But as the night wore on, layers peeled away and souls were bared and the girls usually began to share the real issues of life — family, pain, and fathers. By 1:00 A.M., two more girls had joined the discussion, and by the wee hours the numbers had swelled as girls returned from partying. Those who endured and stayed awake till the pre-dawn hours would hear the heartfelt confessions and the broken-hearted laments.

"I have friends who are daddy's girls. While most of them didn't experience living without their father, a few did — a very few," Mayra said. "Unlike my dad, those dads were there every step of the way. They called regularly. They took their daughters to dinner once in a while. They sent them a card or even flowers. Really now, how hard is it to pick up the phone, call FTD, and place an order? But my dad never could seem to muster up whatever it took to place that call."

The girls compared no-shows and letdowns. They hugged each other and fetched tissues for each other. They also compared themselves with those who had fathers involved in their lives.

"There's just a difference," said Mayra.

"We're more insecure — if we're honest about it," said Kellie.

"I think I'm more depressed," added Robin.

"Yeah, we obviously feel the need to sit around all night and obsess over not having the love of our fathers," said Tanya.

The daddy's girls are asleep," concluded Mayra. The room erupted with laughter but then grew strangely silent.

"Yeah, you notice how Lisa and Michelle went to bed an hour ago. Why is it just us always left behind?" asked Tanya softly.

"Nah, it just seems that way," said Kellie.

Through her tears, Mayra confessed, "Basically I don't trust men and am pretty sure that sooner or later they're going to leave me. When guys ask me out, I'm desperately afraid that eventually they'll stand me up, leave me hanging and waiting by the door. It's like the minute after they ask me out, my anxiety level begins to rise, because the one who should have reassured me that I am worthy of affection was the one who showed me that I'm *not* worthy ... "

The girls were all nodding; some had tears streaming down their faces.

"I've been thinking about this a lot lately – this fear of being stood up. And it finally dawned on me where it comes from. I mean, I know it comes from my messed up relationship with my father. But I have this vivid memory of the time he didn't show up for my eighth birthday. I'll never forget it. He promised me he would come, and that was all I cared about. Really. I didn't care about presents, cake, or anything else that year. So I waited all day out on the porch. I spent the whole day watching for him. Every time I heard a car coming, my heart beat faster. I remember that in the middle of the afternoon my mom tried to talk me into getting some friends to come over for cake and ice cream. She said she'd take us to the movies. But I wouldn't give up. I insisted he was coming, and we argued. Looking back on it now, I know she tried to let me down gently – telling me his car probably broke down or something. Eventually I fell asleep out on the porch. When I woke up, my mom and my aunt brought me my presents and a cake and sang Happy Birthday. I'll never forget that feeling. I blew out the candles, but I refused to make a wish. He never even called."

"Oh, Mayra, that's a horrible memory," said Tanya. "My father did show for my birthdays, but those were just about the only times I saw him."

"Uh huh, my dad did me the same way. He was a trip. But I don't really even think about it anymore," said Monique.

The other girls looked at her in disbelief.

"Mayra, didn't you just want to give up? I just gave up on my dad," Monique insisted.

"Yeah, but after those visits, I held on to the feelings, the words, the expressions of love — even the gifts he gave to me. I held on to those gifts like they were a lifeline to him. He had touched them. They represented him and it was all I had until the next time. All I ever wanted to hear and believe was that 'daddy's here to make it all better.' It's so amazing. Here I am grown up and it's four in the morning and I'm still tripping over my father," Mayra said, cradling her head on her pillow. She finally curled up, closed her eyes, and quietly drifted to sleep.

Journal
I feel like I scratched the surface. But I'm afraid that I may unearth feelings, deep hurts and rage, that I'm not prepared to handle. Jason is the angriest one of them all. But if I can get his father out to the center, I'm sure I can help him reach out to his son. I'm curious about what role their

mothers play in the struggle to work out their father issues. I pray that Mayra is touched and becomes willing to give of herself and share her past to help these girls handle their future. — A.D.M.

CHAPTER THREE

The Hail Mary

Early Saturday morning Drew was jolted from his sleep by the telephone. He had forgotten to turn the ringer off like he usually did before bed on Friday night. He rolled over and answered it.

"Yeah."

"Hey, it's me," said Mayra.

"Oh, hey. What's up?"

"You don't even know who you're talking to, do you?"

"Of course, I do," he said, grinning.

"No, you don't."

"Okay, wait a minute. Talk a little more."

"Drew!" she screamed.

"Oh, yes, Mayra. I recognized the shrill."

"Okay, I'll remember that."

"Along with everything else, I suppose. Anyway, what time is it?" He grabbed his watch. "Good grief, girl! Have you lost your mind? It's eight-thirty in the morning."

"Oh, it's not that early."

"I was up late."

"And I don't want to know why. Anyway, I just called you because I wanted to tell you to be careful with those kids. I know you. You promise the world and then have trouble following through."

"Yeah okay, alright."

"Yeah okay, back at you because I know what I'm talking about. How do I say this without getting you all riled up? You're not their father and you can't save them. You can do your part, we all can do our part ... "

"Oh and uh, what part have you played, Miss 'I don't want to participate' Taylor?"

"See, I knew you'd get upset."

"I'm not upset, just sleepy and frustrated. Don't judge me if you don't have any better ideas and you don't want to really help by getting into the thick of things. It's easy to stay out of the game like the armchair coach and second guess the plays, but try getting into the game and then you can criticize me. But not until then, because frankly, I don't want to hear it. If there's one thing I know, it's how to manage. I took three summer school classes to finish high school after everything that happened, worked, and took the SAT, then juggled college and two jobs, one of which was running a group home — the night shift, that is. Get in the game, baby, then talk," he snipped. "And you woke me up for this? Huh? I don't see you jumping at the gate. I don't recall hearing you chime in with input from your vast experience with loser dads."

Silence followed his acidic remark.

"Oh, now I *know* you're in too deep. I was just trying to help, but I see that you're the man. You're the self-appointed father to the fatherless, although you could barely save yourself from all the no-daddy drama, but hey, that's another story. But no, you've got it all under control so I'll check you later, cowboy."

"Wait, Mayra, don't hang up. I'm sorry, that loser daddy crack was wrong. Hello? Are you still there?"

"Yeah, I'm still here, and, yeah, you were wrong. Do me a favor, leave my dad out of this, okay? That whole situation is still, fluid, if I may borrow the word *du jour*."

"I'm really sorry. Anyway, can we talk about this later? I have to get up in a few to go to Tony's baseball game."

"Okay, so call me after the game. I'd like to hear how it went."

"Okay … Wait a minute. I have another call. Hold on, don't hang up!" he said.

Moments later Drew returned to Mayra's call.

"Aah man! Mayra! I'm in a serious jam!"

"What is it?"

"That was Ray's mom with directions to their house where I'm supposed to pick up Ray and Dion to take them to Ray's football game. Man, I totally forgot that I promised two weeks ago to take them because she had to work. But last night I promised Tony I'd come to his baseball game." Drew was now furiously pacing the parquet floor of his apartment. During Mayra's very audible silence, Drew returned to the bed, sat down, and tried to compose himself. "Go ahead and say it."

"No. Actually I have nothing to say that I haven't already said. I'm just going to pray that you get it all together."

"Wait, you can help me out!"

"Oh no! Leave me out of this. I'm not going to enable you. That's what's wrong with men today, too many women enabling them. No way, Jose. You're on your own."

"Oh, here we go with your no-good black man soapbox."

"I didn't say *black*. Enabling knows no color, deary."

"Oh man! Just don't go there. If you can't help, then just say so. I don't need a lecture. All I was going to ask was if you could stop by Tony's game for a few minutes in my place, but it's cool. I got it, bye."

By nine-thirty, Drew was showered, dressed, and on his way to pick up Ray and Dion. And, he was armed with a plan.

Moments before the first inning of the baseball game, Tony watched Ken's dad, also the assistant coach, help Ken with his swing. He also watched the parking lot, snapping his neck to look every time a car rolled up. But when he saw the driver wasn't his father or Drew, he returned his attention to Ken's dad, who smiled every time Ken swung correctly. Tony couldn't help but notice after three weeks of preseason practice that these coach's helpers weren't just men off the streets or men from the community center that organized the league play. They were his teammates' fathers. And amazingly, all of the dads were available most of the time to help — all except for his dad. All their dads were there during those practices. They lingered behind the backstop, cheering and coaching. One worked with Ben and his batting. Daniel and Mike practiced pitching to Ray-Ray's dad. Finally, Coach Hawley called the team together to give his season-opening speech —

"I want to talk to you about this season. I think we're going to have a lot of fun, and you'll see that every kid is going to have a chance to play equally, meaning the exact number of innings. Everyone is going to play every position because I believe that's the only way we'll know what you're good at. You kids are all different ages and levels of experience. Some are better than others, but you already know that. But don't worry about that, because to me, you're all the same. I want you to learn. And I want you to do your best and work together as a team. We will win as a team and we will lose as a team. We'll win some and we'll lose some. If we lose, it's nobody's fault. We lost as a team.

"I'm never going to pull you from the game just because you're struggling. You can strike out ten at bats in a row. I'm not going to embarrass you. You'll have family and friends here, friends from your school, and I know that.

"The umpires are there to manage the game and they do a pretty good job of it, but they're going to miss some calls. Get over it. Don't let it steal your game day.

"Everyone has strengths and weaknesses and we're here to help you. Whatever you need — hitting — we'll help. Wherever you are now, I promise, you'll be better by season's end. Also, trust me when I say, it hurts when you get hit by the ball. So crying is okay. I expect it, so go ahead and cry, then shake it off. If you get hurt, we'll take care of you.

"When you're up to bat, I want you to go after the ball. I don't want you walking. Go after it! Swing at the ball. Don't worry about strikes. This is important. My kids don't go down standing. My kids don't go down looking at the ball. You'll never hit the ball if you don't swing. I'd rather you strike out than just stand there. If you gotta go down, go down swinging.

"Let me leave you with this. You're a team and you must play like it. Over time, you'll get to know each other. You'll learn to trust each other. You'll learn to rely on each other — you'll have to. That's how we succeed. But remember, we're all here to have fun. It's my job to make sure you learn baseball and have a whole lot of fun playing the game and I promise to do my best to make it happen. Okay, team, let's go get 'em!"

Tony had never experienced a father-son baseball moment. As he sat on the splintery team bench, he searched his memory for any recollection of his father ever playing baseball with him. When Tony and his dad got together, the time was usually spent watching sports on television or going, going, going. "We've got big plans for this weekend, he would say. First we're going to my mom's house so you can see your grandmother, then to your Uncle Eddie's, then to a church picnic. After that we'll go … "

DREW HAD MAPPED the route from Ray's community center game held at Blair High School to Tony's game at the field near the Old Trolley. It would be tricky but he figured he'd get to Blair, stay for the first quarter, cut out, and head to the baseball game. Then he could catch two innings and swing back to see the fourth quarter of the football game. How hard could that be?

Fifteen minutes shy of kickoff, they pulled up to Blair's rapidly filling parking lot.

"This must really be the game of the season. Look at all these people!" said Dion.

"Look at these cars. At least we found a good parking spot," said Drew as he turned into the lone spot in a sea of cars. "Alright, let's hit it."

Ray scrambled to meet up with his team as Drew and Dion made their way to the bleachers. Drew took in the crisp, cool air as he watched metal bleachers fill up. He stretched back and noticed fathers giving their boys last minute strategy. Other boys stood close by to listen in. Drew kept his eye on the clock.

With six minutes to go in the first quarter, Drew was about to make his move.

"Hey, Dion, I need to make a quick run. I figured I'd catch an inning or two of your boy Tony's baseball game. It's only over at Bonifant field by the Old Trolley Museum. Wanna come?" he asked.

"Um, yeah, but Ray would kill me if I missed some big play. You go. It'll be cool."

"Okaaaay. You sure?" said Drew, standing to dig for his car keys.

"Yeah, I'm sure."

"Okay, I'll be back by the fourth quarter."

Drew then skipped down the bleachers and squeezed past the wall of people plastered against the fence. He made it to the parking lot and walked briskly toward his car. "Whew," said Drew, noticing several double-parked cars. He rushed toward his row and was greeted by the unthinkable. Drew's black 2000 Honda Civic was blocked by a double-parked car. There was no chance of squeezing out. "Damn!" He pounded on his hood before hustling back to the officials surrounding the refreshment table.

"Excuse me. My car's blocked in and I have to get out. Where are announcements made?" he asked, cutting in line to demand help.

"I guess the P.A. announcer's table on the field, but I don't know if security is going to let you on the field. I guess you can try," said the lady collecting the hot dog money.

Drew looked up and saw a crowd as thick as oatmeal. But he forged his way through anyhow. Moments later, he saw a security guard standing watch over the door to the gate. "Sir, I need to get onto the field. My car is blocked in and I need an announcement made." Drew tried to squeeze past the guard as he spoke.

"Is this a medical emergency?"

"No, but I have a commitment, okay? It's urgent," huffed Drew. The guard placed his hands at his sides and adopted a defensive stance. "Then you'll have to wait until halftime," said the guard, sounding official.

"That'll be too late!" said Drew through clenched teeth.

"Well, they're not going to make the announcement until halftime anyway, so I'll have to ask you to step back and return to the bleachers," said the guard. Drew left the guard with a loud sigh and slowly returned to his seat next to Dion.

"Whew, that was quick. What happened? You're not going now?" asked Dion.

"No. It looks like I'm going to stick around after all. Besides, I don't want to miss Ray's TD," said Drew. He shoved his hands into his pockets, slouched as far back as he could, and watched the rest of the game. The TD came late in the fourth quarter. When the pre-play huddle broke, Ray lined up at the forty-five-yard line. Smiling, he briefly glanced into the stands in Drew and Dion's direction. Dion sat up quickly.

"Uh oh, that's his signal that the play is to him," said Dion. The center snapped the ball. The quarterback faked a handoff and dropped back to pass. The pigskin ball spiraled high in the air right down mid-field. Defenders followed the course of the ball to stave off the easy score, but the ball sank right into Ray's arms. Clutching the ball, he accelerated past the approaching cornerbacks and sailed into the end zone.

"Oh, no way! It's the Hail Mary!" shouted Dion, jumping to his feet.

"Touchdown!" declared the referee. The stands erupted and Ray's exuberant teammates ran to him and tackled him. When he rose to trot off the field, Ray looked into the stands but not in the direction of Drew and Dion. It was as if he was looking at someone else.

TONY WAS NEXT AT BAT, but he hadn't moved from the bench. Linda waited as long as she could before speaking up from her beach chair. "Tony, why don't you get up and take some practice swings."

"Mom, I'm okay," he snapped.

"Tony, come here."

"Mom, stop it, okay? I got it. Is anyone coming to my game?"

"Who did you invite?" she asked.

"Drew's coming. Did you tell Granddad? What about Uncle Brian or Uncle Jedediah?"

"Well, I haven't heard from Drew. I know he said he'd be here but you do know how things come up, right? So don't get all worked up. Just focus on your game. I'm here. Your coach is here."

"Mom, I'm not getting worked up and my coach has to be here because he has to be here," said Tony, visibly annoyed.

Suddenly, the coach called out for Tony.

"Tony, you're in the hole."

Tony leaped to his feet and dug into the bat bag. He settled on the long silver bat with the red tape at the head.

"Okay, now take some practice swings," said Linda, looming near his space.

"Mom! Stop it!" He stormed ten feet further away and cut his eyes at his mother.

"I'm just trying to help. The best hitters on your team all practice swinging when they step into the hole."

Tony ignored her. Linda returned to her seat and slipped her dark glasses across her eyes and sighed. Moments later, Tony stepped up to the plate. Distracted, Tony turned his head and blew steam from puffy cheeks when he heard his mother say, "Step back off the plate. You're too close, and choke up on the bat. Get that elbow up."

"Okaaaay!"

Linda turned to another mother. "Why is it they won't listen to mothers? Oh, I suppose moms don't know anything. Well, I'm not saying another word."

"Two balls, two strikes," said the umpire.

Tony raised his elbow.

"Strike threeeeee! Batter's out."

Tony stomped out of the batter's box and dropped his bat, but not without smarting at his mother. "There, I did what you said and I struck out!"

About thirty minutes later, Tony was back in the hole. This time, Linda decided to take a stroll around the adjoining field. The first pitch came. Tony swung.

"Strike."

"Good cut, Tony," reassured the coach. Tony's right elbow suddenly began to move up and back. The pitcher looked left, then right. He wound his arm and let loose a high-flying ball.

Tony wacked a fly out into left field, right in the hole. From across the field Linda screamed, "Run, Tony, run!" Tony sent two runners home and landed at third.

BY SATURDAY AT 11:00, Kalia had cleaned her sister's bedroom, as well as her own. She even washed the dishes while trying to build up the nerve to ask her mother for five dollars for popcorn. She approached her mother in the kitchen.

"Mom, do you have five bucks for popcorn? I don't need money for the movie. I only need a little for popcorn. Hey Mom, did you notice, we cooked this morning. I mean the gas is still on and the lights are still on. God did that, didn't he, Mom?"

Her mom couldn't even smile. "Sweetie, I don't have any money at all. I don't have five dollars. I added up all my change and even rolled pennies and took them to the bank yesterday for the money that I used on gas and to buy beans and bread and milk. That should last this weekend and I'm expecting some money on Monday, but I won't have a dime until then."

"Mom, not even three dollars?"

"No honey, not even three dollars."

When Mrs. Westley pulled up, Kalia walked out the door as her mom stood there waving to Mrs. Westley. Kalia turned around and asked, "Mom, do you have maybe just one dollar?" as her voice began to buckle. Kalia didn't want it to sink in that at fourteen years old she was a poor little black girl living with no daddy. They hadn't had that much more when her parents were together, but somehow they always seemed to make it. Her family had never really gone without, or if they did, she hadn't noticed. But now that her dad was gone, she felt for the first time what it was like to be poor, to struggle, to have the lights cut off, to have the phone disconnected, and to see her mom move the car around the block so the "snatchman" wouldn't take it. She knew how it felt to lose her dad and not see her mom, who had taken a second job, until ten-thirty at night.

So Kalia turned away from her mom and headed toward Mrs. Westley's van. Her mom slowly shook her head from side to side to tell her daughter one last time, once and for all, she didn't even have a dollar. Kalia climbed into the van, covered her face, and cried. Mrs. Westley kept driving but at a light, she reached in the glove compartment and pulled out some tissues for Kalia. She didn't say a single word until she pulled up at the theater and parked the car. Then she turned to Kalia and said, "Sweetie, whatever it is, God's going to make it alright in no time at all. I mean no time at all."

Kalia stopped crying and wiped all the tears from her face. She turned to look out the window and saw all the other girls standing out front. As she stepped out of the van, one of the girls shouted, "Kalia, come on in. Deborah's in line and she's buyng popcorn and soda for all of us! Come on, hurry!"

As DAYLIGHT SAVINGS TIME ENDED, the available evening daylight was reduced by an hour. The days also grew colder. Thanksgiving approached, as did the talk of war in Afghanistan. Drew did his best to draw the young in for fun, answers, and hope. At 9:00 P.M. that Friday night, the group was still busy in the gym while waiting for parents to arrive.

"Giselle, pass the ball!" urged Dion, trying to slip past Tony for the layup.

Drew, Tony, and Ray were up fourteen points to Dion, Giselle, and Jason's ten in one of their usual four-on-four pickup games at the center.

"Here!" cried Giselle as she slipped a bounce pass to Dion who quickly threw it up for the layup only to have the shot blocked by Drew.

"Bam! In your face!" screamed Tony.

"Oh yeah, oh yeah!" said Drew who quickly caught a pass from Tony. Always mindful of his mission and slightly out of breath, he stopped and dribbled in place, turning his attention to Tony. "Hey, Tony, I thought you weren't coming tonight. Don't get me wrong, I'm glad to see you, but weren't you going to work on your boat for some upcoming Cub Scout race?"

"Well, my mom said she had to go to church but that she'd buy the paint and decals this weekend and we'd finish then."

"Sounds good. Guys, game point and I'm ready to put you out of your misery. So this next jumper will end it, right?"

"Jason, cover him tight!" yelled Dion. Drew faked to his left and released the three-point jumper. It swooshed into the basket.

"Game!" bragged Drew.

"Okay, okay, you got us this time. Let's run it back, I'm just warming up," said Jason, hoping to play again.

"I know you don't want more of this!" said Drew, sinking another three pointer.

"Nice shot!" cheered Jason.

"Well, we'll see!" said Dion, trying to steal the ball from Drew.

"Son, it's going to take more than that!" said Drew as he dribbled around Dion and made his way to the basket for a layup. "You youngsters really need some practice."

"So, Tony, when is this race again?" said Drew, preparing to close up.

"It's Monday night."

"You need any help?" asked Drew.

"No, I'm cool. My mom's going to help me."

"Okay," said Drew.

LAST YEAR TONY HAD WON the sportsmanship award for how well he handled himself during the race. He'd been ready to race again ever since. When the regatta boat kits were handed out about a month before the annual race, Tony couldn't wait to get started.

"I want my boat to be red and yellow and be called *Jaguar!*" he had told his mother. "I'm gonna win this time and I'm gonna have the coolest boat." Unfortunately Tony was never fully prepared for the workshops when the boys worked on their boats, using first the sanding machine, then paint and decals. Some fathers helped their sons at home. On the night of the race, Tony's boat wasn't even decorated yet.

At around 6:30 p.m. on a brisk November Monday night, the adrenaline-pumped scouts entered the social hall of the Presbyterian church with their carefully crafted boats. The water-filled raingutters were impressively decorated. By 6:40 p.m., boys were gearing up to blow the boats down the raingutters with their breath. The room was filled with energy. In one corner, parents prepared to judge the race and evaluate the quality of the workmanship. At 6:45 p.m., Tony was still at day care. At 6:50 p.m., Linda sped through the parking lot, parked, and hurried into the day care where Tony waited with his coat and backpack in hand. He turned his pouting lips and seething glare toward his mother.

"You're soooooooo late! Did you buy the paint and decals?"

"We'll talk about it when we get home," she said, looking back at Mrs. Campbell, the day care director, hoping to find sympathy.

"You said you'd get off early and buy the things to finish my boat! You promised! Come on, let's get out of here!"

"Tony, calm down, you're too upset right now."

"We have to hurry!" his voice trembled as the tears began to flow.

Moments later, they crossed the threshold of their townhouse located two blocks from the school.

"We have to hurry!" urged Tony.

"Tony, let me get in the door for God's sake," she huffed. "How about hi Mom, how was your day?" Linda wanted to fall right into her bed. Cub Scouts was the last thing on her mind. She barely had what it took to cook dinner.

"Hi Mom, how was your day? Are you tired again? I can eat dinner after we get back. I'm not even hungry. Please Mom. Come on, let's go. I did my homework already and I got an A on my spelling test..." he followed her into the kitchen.

"Tony! Just wait. I want to take you, I really do, but Mommy is so tired, honey," she said sorrowfully. "I just can't." She felt her forehead and realized she was running a low-grade fever.

Tony grimaced and exploded in protest. "Mom, you promised! I missed most of the workshops because of you. You lied! First you said you'd take me this weekend, then last night, but you were tired then too. You promised it would be today! I have NO ONE to ever take me anywhere and I've already missed a lot of activities! I missed both campouts and I didn't get to go to the summer camp because of your job. It's not fair! You don't care about me! Why won't you try, just try. You don't have to do anything once we get there. Please, Mom."

Linda closed her eyes and lowered her head onto her folded arms as they rested on the table. She didn't respond. Tony sat down next to her, leaned over as if to peak into the world under the lowered head, and asked, "Can we call someone? They have extra boats there, loaners. Maybe Drew can take me. All we have to do is paint it and put the decals on because it's already sanded. Maybe we have leftover paint or can get some at the drug store. Pleeaaaaase, Mom, pleeeeaaaase! Can't we call Drew? He told me he would help me."

"Oh, have we forgotten that Drew already missed your base-ball game? Can't you see it's just us? It's you and me. There's no one else! When will you figure that out!" she fired back. Linda looked off into the distance and tried to figure it out. *Maybe we could work this out. Maybe we can find some quick paint and do with-out the decals and, yes, maybe I can dry the boat with my blowdryer, and we could get there at 7:30.* She noticed the clock; it was 7:05 P.M. Then she looked back at Tony, slowly shook her head, and said, "We're not going to make it. Even if we tried, we'd be too late, and … we didn't finish your boat. I'm sorry. The answer has to be no this time. I'll make it up to you, I promise," she reached to pat his head. Tony reflexively withdrew from her touch and lunged to his feet.

"You're lying and you always make promises and then break them. I miss my daddy," he yelled, as he stormed out of the door-way of the kitchen and to his room. He slammed his door, opened it, and slammed it again furiously.

"Tony!!" she screamed, leaping from the table to quash what she considered disrespect, but then she froze. Moments later, Linda quietly walked past his room and could hear the gameboy's electronic music. About thirty minutes later she returned to his door to hear the same sound. Though she had hoped to steal a few minutes to try and explain once more, she didn't want to spoil his period of calm, so she returned to her room. An hour later Linda heard the soft sound of rippling water emanating from the bathroom. She followed the sound to the door and found Tony playing with his boat. He had put the sail on it and was now sailing his sand-colored, unpainted, undecaled, unremarkable, and unjudged boat around the bathtub.

Journal

Was Mayra right? Mentoring this group is a bit more complicated than I first thought. I think I helped Dion and Ray, but I know I let Tony down. But if I listen to Mayra, I should do nothing — that way no one gets hurt. Of course, no one is helped. Well, I'm going to proceed full steam ahead and plan to have fathers and mothers in this place by the time our annual Christmas party rolls around. Thank God Dr. Jackson accepted my paper late. — A.D.M.

CHAPTER FOUR

Christmas: Some Assembly Required

Jason went to the center immediately after school to help the staff decorate for the holiday party.

Weeks earlier, Drew had reminded the kids to invite both parents to the holiday party.

Despite his father's no-show, Jason couldn't wait to show Drew his grocery bag stuffed with cans of peas, corn, and yams — items purchased with the money he had earned raking leaves. He also wanted to hang out with Drew.

Drew, single and in between relationships, had begun to informally mentor Jason, taking an interest in his performance at school, his father issues, and his game, and he chose to remain at the center for many of the evening activities, though he wasn't required to do so. At first, his reason was to develop case studies for his research. By now, his heart was in it all the way.

Mayra had just completed her last final exam for the semester, and Drew had succeeded in getting her to help out with the party. He was still trying to draw her into a deeper level of involvement with the kids.

"Where should I hang the streamers?" she asked, tearing open the plastic bag of black, purple, and gray streamers.

Jason looked over and laughed. "Streamers? Are you kidding? I hope you don't have party hats too!"

"No! I happen to like streamers and they're not for babies."

"Oh yeah? Let's ask Drew. Hey Drew, what's up with these streamers?"

Drew turned from his Christmas tree decorating to look at the streamers. "My concern is what's up with the black and gray? Is there a funeral tonight that someone just forgot to tell me about?" He paused and then commented, "Oh yeah, I remember your thing with Christmas. I'll leave that one alone."

"Fine," said Mayra, grinning as she put the streamers back in the package.

Jason watched Mayra return to the kitchen and quietly moved toward Drew. "Look, people are coming in," he said.

"Hello, R.J. Hello, Randy," Drew said as R.J. and his dad crossed the threshold. As they arrived, the children and their parents congregated in the party room to drop off their food donations, get to know each other, and help wrap presents for the patients at the local children's hospital. The younger ones played billiards, video games, and held a Ping-Pong tournament.

Everyone devoured overloaded plates of sliced turkey and dressing, jellied cranberry sauce, mashed potatoes, green beans, and apple pie with ice cream. Christmas music, hip-hop style, played most of the night.

Toward the end of the evening, Drew rolled out a huge red wagon filled with at least two dozen individually wrapped gifts. The kids had worked feverishly throughout the fall selling wrapping paper and collecting donations of food and toys for the needy and for sick children, so this Christmas party was especially meaningful for them. The twenty-three young fundraisers had raised $2,436.50, enabling the center to purchase toys and food for many needy families. The kids had broken the club record.

When Drew emerged with the wagon overflowing with gifts, the young people were confused. They were surprised when he said, "Well, what are you waiting for? Come get *your* gifts!"

The youngsters froze.

"But we thought … " began Jason.

"Guess what?" interrupted Drew. "Tomorrow we're going to take the other gifts to the children, and those of you who want to go are free to come along. But we always, *always* save money to treat and bless the kids who come to this club. It's a club rule! So look for the gift with your name on it. There's something for everyone.

"Jason, we've got something else besides what's in the wagon for you. Listen up everybody. Every year we award a special gift to the youth who raises the most money, or who has contributed the most to the club's mission overall. This year that person was Jason Phillips. Give it up for Jason!"

Everyone cheered.

"As an assistant coach, Jason gave of his time to teach elementary students how to shoot hoops, and he served as a tutor in the more important task of helping them with their school work. So, come here Jason. We have two tickets to … wait, drum roll, please … we have two tickets to the Wizards-Hawks game in February!"

"Oh, wow! Thanks man!" he said, trying to read the tickets.

"You earned it," said Drew.

Jason grabbed Drew's hand for a strong handshake and pulled him to a hug. The onlookers clapped.

Most of the crowd then dispersed to the gym, but Drew, Jason, Ray, and Dion stayed downstairs in the party room.

"Ray, we haven't heard much from you lately. What are ya planning for Christmas? What do you want for Christmas?" Drew avoided eye contact.

"Well, you can tell my mom I want a TV, Playstation games, a scooter and clothes, a lot of clothes."

"Whoa! That would be a pretty nice Christmas. I'll tell her. I wouldn't mind having that myself. Okay, you want Playstation games, and what else? Are you going anywhere? Have any plans to visit any special relatives?"

"I don't know. I wouldn't mind hanging out with my dad."

"Our dad usually calls right before Christmas to make plans to pick us up," Dion interjected.

Ray looked at Dion in disbelief, then paused before making eye contact with Drew. "Dion and I remember things differently, but I wish he *would* call. I wish he could have come to my games to see how good I am at football."

"And I just want to make sure I'm at home in time to catch my dad's call. My mom said he's supposed to call tonight when he gets off work to discuss Christmas," Dion said.

"Well, if you're not there you can always call him back, right?" asked Drew.

"Probably not," said Jason. "Man, if you're not there for the call, it seems like they sometimes use that as an excuse not to come. At least that's how it seems with me."

"I see. Then what are you going to do about it?"

Ray responded, "Well, I don't know."

"Ray, how do you feel about your dad?"

"I don't know, I guess he's alright."

"What do you do when you're together?"

"Uh, we fix cars. I spent a week with him in Virginia summer before last. We worked on his car together, we played football, and we talked, you know — about school and my family and his family and stuff."

"Has he ever been here to see you play football?" asked Drew.

"Yes, he came to one game."

By this time, a few more kids had gathered around.

"How did that make you feel?"

"Very good. Really great."

"Why?"

"Because he could see me and see what I could do."

Ray leaned forward and covered his face with his hands before giving each response. He appeared extremely uncomfortable. Drew asked him how he was feeling.

"I don't know. This is kind of hard."

"Ray," he asked, "why is this hard for you?"

"Because I normally don't talk about my father at all, at least not like Dion."

"Oh, then, do you think about him at all?"

"All the time. I think about my dad all the time."

"What do you mean by all the time?"

"Um, about 80 percent of my time," he said, glancing around the room to see if other kids were listening before locking his eyes with Drew's.

"How can you think about someone 80 percent of your time? Describe how that's done."

"Trust me," interrupted Dion, "he thinks about him 80 percent of the time."

"I believe you, Dion, but I want to hear it from Ray. Also, remember, we've agreed not to share confidential information discussed in this room, but we also don't want to bring confidential discussions into this room without first obtaining permission."

"My bad," said Dion, lowering his head while stealing a glance in his brother's direction.

"Do you think of him during your games?" asked Drew.

"I think of him during every game. I think of him during every play."

"Come on, every single play? How can you be thinking of him with every play?"

"I do think of him during every play because I'm wishing that he could have seen me make that play. I'm a receiver and get the ball all the time. I score touchdowns, and each time I score one, I'm wishing he could see me and be proud of me. I wish it so much that I just imagine that he's there. I pretend that he's there and watching me and cheering my name. I imagine him there in the stands. I look into the stands and notice my coach. His son plays on my team. The coach will run into the stands to say hello to his wife, my teammate's mom. Their dog is with them. They're a whole family, and part of me doesn't feel like I'm part of a whole family, a real family. And during the games, I'm reminded that my dad's not around when I watch other dads with their families and when the other kids ask me, 'where is your dad?' Then I have no choice but to be reminded. I also have no choice but to lie and say he's out of town or he's working late or that my mom went to pick him up."

"You don't have to talk about this if you don't want to," said Drew.

Ray's hands covered his face, but he peeked through his fingers and made full eye contact with Drew and conceded, "It's okay. I want to talk."

"Ray, what would you say to your father if you could say anything you wanted to him without his getting angry?"

"I would tell him that I want to spend more time with him. I want to see him more. I wish he would come visit more. He even asked me about living with him. He said that the schools are better where he is than where I'm going right now."

"Ray, what are the top three things that make you angry about your dad?"

Ray looked up as if searching for words. "The first is the lies. I wish he would stop lying and stop telling me that he's coming when he's not. I've waited for him and he's not shown up. The next thing would be that he's never at home when I call, and he doesn't call me much. I used to try to reach him but he was never home when I called. I always had to leave a message, and he wouldn't always return my call. So I stopped calling. But I want to talk to him every time I think of him."

"How often is that?"

"Every day. I just want to know he cares about me. I need to know he cares. I can't think of anything else." By this point, Ray was rubbing his watery eyes.

"It's okay, man — I cry sometimes." Drew walked over to pat Ray on the back. "It's okay. We don't have to talk about this anymore."

"But I want to. He said he wants me to live with him," said Ray, quickly wiping his tears.

"Well, do you want to live with your father?"

"Yes." Then he added, "So, are you going to tell my mother?"

"Not if you don't want me to. So how do you feel right now?" asked Drew.

"I don't know. It's hard to explain. I want to talk with my mom about all of this, but I don't want to hurt her feelings. I'm not sure what I want, but the reason I haven't asked my mom about living with my dad was I was afraid she would just say no. And … I'm not so sure that my dad was serious about the idea."

"Why do you say that?"

"I mean, it made me feel good and feel like I was wanted by my dad, but when we talked again after that he never mentioned it."

"Did you bring it up?"

"No."

"Why not?"

"I don't know."

"Yes, you do. Why didn't *you* ask?"

"Well, because I didn't want to give him a chance to back out of it or tell me it just wouldn't work. I would just make small talk and hope he'd say something, anything like, 'so have you thought any more about your coming here to live with me,' or 'Ray, I'd like to discuss this with your mother now,' or 'I found a really good school for you and I've talked with the principal about you.' But it didn't happen. We'd just talk about the weather, cars, school, the reason he hadn't come or called for months, and so on and so on. Nothing about the living plans. Nothing."

"Well, let me ask you — is living with your father what you really want? Or is knowing he wants you to live with him good enough?" asked Drew.

"Well, I really do want to be with him, but I know that would mean leaving Dion and my mom. If Dion came to live with us, she'd be all alone. So, I don't really know. I just know I need to be with him and with my mom," said Ray, oblivious to the rest of the group. They were hanging on his every word.

Even Drew was astounded that Ray's thoughts were always on his father.

"I would have so much to talk to him about, like things I couldn't talk to my mom about."

"Like what?" queried Drew, asking the question to which he already knew the answer.

"I don't know — life, sports, fixing cars, growing up to be a man — stuff my mom can't teach me.

"So, like guy things, including girls, right? Come on, it's no big deal to admit that. We can all agree that you'd rather get with a guy to talk about that than your momma, right?"

"Okay, yeah," answered Jason, followed by the rest of the boys.

"Well, it's true. There is a male perspective, a male persona, a male way of viewing and approaching life, and mothers don't have firsthand expertise. That's where fathers … and grandfathers, uncles, older brothers, godfathers, church leaders, and people like me come in," Drew said.

"The pastor of my church talks with us all the time," added Dion.

"Absolutely. Church leaders as well as the rest of us are here to help you along. Don't get me wrong. There's a lot your mom *can* teach you, and sometimes she's all you'll have. However, there are others, *and* there is your father. It's just that sometimes, there are barriers in the way, keeping you from each other, and you have a part to play to bring down those barriers. Just keep that in mind. Anyway, this question is for Ray or for anyone else who wants to answer, boy or girl. What would you trade to have your father here for Christmas?"

"Everything. I would trade all my Christmas presents to have him here," Ray said.

"Even your Playstation?" asked Dion.

"Everything."

The room was silent.

"Anyone else? What would you trade? Is anyone else going to see their dad or mom?"

"I'm going to visit my dad for Christmas," said Giselle. "Anything you want to tell me —especially something about how to handle the wicked stepmother and the new little prince who took our place in his heart?"

"Yes, keep your heart wide open. Forget about the stepmother. I mean, be respectful. Love the baby brother. He had nothing to do with this, nothing at all. I'm not saying everything will be perfect, but it'll be a step closer to patching up that relationship and keeping it tied," said Drew. "You may not understand what that really means right now, but at the right moment, these words will hit you."

"Anyone else having a reunion with your old man?" asked Drew.

"Well, my mom hasn't said it yet, but I bet she's going to tell me they're going to split me again this Christmas," said Tony. "I hate it when she says 'split me.' I mean, I actually feel split in two. The one holiday when a family is supposed to be together, I'm probably going to be split," he said, looking at Drew.

"Let me guess, that feeling is like being broken, not whole, not one, not united, not together — lots of nots, nots, nots," said Drew.

"Yes, that's exactly how I feel. How come they just don't get it?" Everyone else nodded in agreement.

"Maybe if she had said it differently, like, 'Hey, Tony, your dad shared with me that he really wants to spend some time with you and really catch up — really wants to spend part of Christmas with you. Your grandmother has been missing you so much and your cousins can't wait to see you. I heard they all have surprises for you.' Maybe if she had put it another way, it would have felt better."

"Well, we all know this is how most families do it, anyway — half the day with one parent and half with the other parent. Even the courts usually order that when they're deciding visitation. I know that doesn't leave you much to look forward to. But on the other hand, it'll be like having Christmas twice. Come on, now! You get two sets of gifts," Drew said, trying to stir laughter. "All of you *must* figure out a way to look at your situations with a different set of lenses. Root out the good that may be buried and not visible to the naked eye. And I know, the whole world is bustling and hustling to get ready for Christmas, and all you guys have to look forward to is the split. It's sort of like a constant reminder of *the* split, the horror of it all. But still, you don't have a choice, keep looking up."

"We have no say in it, but there they go again — on *our* day," added Giselle. "Christmas was supposed to be for the kids. Yet Christmas for us is a split just for us kids. Aren't we the lucky ones?"

"Well, if people ask what I'm getting for Christmas, I'm going to say 'a split,'" said Tony, weaving laughter through his words.

"I know that's right!" said Kalia.

"Hey gang, you're smart enough to know that is hurt talking. No need to be spiteful. Handle it with grace. Keep your cool and find the good," said Drew. "When we come back after the holidays, I want to hear about the *good* things that came of your holidays, or how you turned something that *looked* bad into something great."

When the evening was over, Drew wished all the kids happy holidays and he thanked each parent for their continued support — even Vicky, despite the concern she continued to express to the board over Drew's prying into the kids' personal lives.

DION AND RAY'S MOM had some news for them when they returned from the party. "Your brother called and he left his phone number."

Dion screamed, "Really?!? No way! It's been two years!"

Ray walked past his exuberant brother to the basement. Dion's heart was racing as he dialed his brother's number. Twenty-nine-year-old David answered the phone. The sound of his strong voice took Dion's breath away. He paused a few seconds, then said, "Hey, what's up! This is your baby brother."

"What's up, man? How's it going?"

Dion talked about his family, his life, school, and all his sporting activities. Dion then told his brother they were coming to the country for the Christmas holidays.

"We're going to have to get together," said David. "Where's Ray?"

Dion covered the mouthpiece and whispered to Ray, "He wants to talk to you."

"I'll talk to him later. I have to go to the bathroom," Ray had been standing in the hallway listening to the call. Dion and David made plans to meet on Wednesday. David said he'd bring their father.

Dion hung the phone up, and for the moment, he appeared to be the happiest boy on earth. "Ray, he said he probably won't recognize you because of how much you've grown."

"Yeah, and whose fault is that?"

"Why didn't you want to talk to your brother? Aren't you excited about getting together?" Ray's mom, Sharon, asked.

"Why should I be? Dion goes overboard for people who don't even want to be around us most of the time. It's embarrassing the way he reacts whenever they call. He acts like a dog chasing a bone. I'm not going to jump just because they say jump."

"That's your choice, but you know their situation. It's hard for everyone involved. You ARE planning to be there next week, right? I mean, this IS your family and you need to see those people," she said.

"Sure. It's just that Dion is so forgiving of someone who has stood us up over and over and over," he said as he turned to run upstairs.

For the next few days, Dion couldn't sleep or eat much. He lay awake at night thinking about the faraway stars in his life — his dad and his brother. For days Dion pondered what he would say to his brother. He imagined about one hundred possible scenarios for the rendezvous. On Christmas Day, Dion couldn't focus on Christmas events and activities. All his thoughts were consumed with Wednesday — the day he, his brothers, and father planned to meet. But Ray never spoke of the reunion. Instead he ate, played video games, and watched television all day.

GISELLE, SEVENTEEN, WAS about to spend the first Christmas with her father since she was ten.

"Giselle, don't forget to talk to your father about tuition. This is it. You have an idea of what you're looking at and you know I won't be able to cover it all, not even close. We need the help, alright?" asked her mother sternly.

"I know. I'll do it this time."

"Also, I don't want them getting into my business. They don't need to know what I'm doing or who I'm with," Giselle's mother commented as she parked in front of her ex-husband's house.

"I know, Mom. They really don't ask. We never talk about you when we're over there," she said reassuringly.

Giselle's mom leaned over to peer out the car window. "Look at her; she's not as cute as she used to be. He'll soon realize we ALL age and get a little fatter. Even his precious candy cane has put on a few, though she still has those chicken legs."

"Mom! Stop it," said Giselle as she and her sister climbed out of the car. Their stepmother was hanging Christmas lights on the shrubs.

"Hi, Candace," said Giselle as she approached the porch.

"Hey, girls. Your daddy's not here."

Instantly, Giselle cringed. She didn't want to hear that. Usually the phrase "your daddy's not ..." was followed by "home" or "coming" or "able to take you" or "able to pick you up" and so on. The last person she wanted to hear it from was her daddy's new wife. They had been married for about eight years, but Giselle always referred to her as "my dad's new wife." So as Giselle brushed by her father's new wife, she simply responded, "oh," though under her breath mumbled, "who are you to tell me what my daddy's not?"

"I'm sorry, did you say something?" asked Candace.

"No," snipped Giselle. "Where do we take our things?"

"Oh, you know where your room is."

"Oh, I just wasn't sure, you know, maybe you had other company staying with you." Giselle's father had already told her that no one else was expected to be there. Giselle also knew where to find the guestroom. As she made her way upstairs, she couldn't help but pause and notice the Christmas tree as if to compare it with her mother's artificial tree. The natural fir was eight feet high and full of decorations. Homemade angel ornaments adorned nearly every inch of the tree. The lights were white. The ribbons were gold and red velvet.

The girls finally made their way into the bedroom to plop their things down onto the floor. They looked at each other and with their smirks communicated the us-against-them posture. They giggled and snickered on their way out the door. Moments later, Giselle sat down in the den where she found her four-year-old brother. He was playing with his wrestling action figures. "I like the Rock because he's really tough. I can do those moves too," he proudly proclaimed.

"Wow," said Giselle. She allowed him to charm her, but she still struggled within herself. On the one hand, Giselle was thrilled to have a baby brother. "Look at those feet. Oh yeah, he's going to be lanky like me," she said quietly. She saw the things that connected her to this boy. Her stepmother could not take those things away. Neither could her father. Giselle began to speak, hesitated, and finally said in an almost inaudible voice, "So you're why Daddy hasn't called, huh? He was opening presents with YOU all those years. Speaking of toys, my goodness, I don't think I've ever seen that many toys."

The boy answered, "I always have a whole lot of toys."

"I bet you do," responded Giselle.

Well, he can leave our family, leave me, my sister, and my mother. He may never call, but we're bound forever by blood, a DNA code, genetic traits, Hamilton features, a shared ancestry, a shared history, and the same grandparents. We're both under the umbrella of prayers and dreams from common ancestors, and even if daddy, and grandma and grandpa leave us out of the bonding and passing of family traditions, we're still included. There's nothing anyone can do to deny us at least our name and the covering of those prayers, hopes, and dreams placed on us by those who came before this generation. When my great, great grandparents prayed for their children and their children's children and their children, they prayed for me.

Giselle could not believe the number of toys, educational items, and photos in this one room. She had also seen a full toy box in his bedroom along with a handcrafted bookshelf loaded with books. In the den she examined all the framed photographs. She was looking for one of her photos or one of her sister's. Perhaps there was a wallet-sized photo hiding behind the eight-by-ten picture of her brother. Giselle knew she had sent her senior photo to her father along with some wallet-sized ones. Giselle wondered whether her father carried her photo in his wallet. She stared at the family shot of the three of them — dad, stepmom, and brother.

"You can call us from time to time, you know," she said to the image in the picture. "One visit wouldn't deprive this boy of his lavish Christmases or your love, you know."

Her father finally returned home from last-minute shopping. Judging by the shopping bags, Giselle figured he had been at a teen clothing store. He rushed the shopping bags into the foyer closet and joined Giselle and his son in the living room.

"Mmmm, something smells good!" he said, looking toward the kitchen. "Candace, what's for dinner?"

"Oh, nothing special."

"So, Giselle, how's school? What grade are you in now, eleventh or twelfth?" he asked as he made himself comfortable in his recliner.

"Twelfth, Daddy." She folded her arms and looked toward her brother.

"I know that. I was just seeing if you knew," he said, chuckling. "And as smart as you are, I know you're going to college somewhere, right?"

"Yeah, Dad," she said, now focusing on the mission as charged by her mother.

"Well, be sure to start applying now and submit those scholarship, grant, and loan applications right away. I haven't heard from your mother about this, but … "

Just then, Candace abruptly called out, "Dinner's ready. Manny, come help me. I can't lift all this by myself."

"Excuse me, kids. We'll talk later."

After dinner Giselle pulled out the college applications she had packed in her suitcase and decided to request an audience with her father. After all, he had raised the college funding discussion first. As she prepared to venture out of her room, Giselle couldn't help but overhear the discussion seeping from under her father's bedroom door.

"By the way, a heads up, she mentioned her graduation and we need to make a decision," said her father.

"I still can't believe you promised her we'd be there when you hadn't even discussed it with me."

"What? I can't tell my daughter I'm going to try to make her graduation?"

"Let me remind you what you told her. You said you'd be

there for sure, but you keep forgetting there are things going on in this family. Let me put it this way, we're your family now. You have a little boy who needs you here. We're not rich. I'm working the job and the side business, bringing in the bulk of it until you get back on your feet. God only knows when that'll be. And … I'm sure I don't have to tell you her mother is probably going to ask us to help with tuition. You know it's coming, so get ready. We've already discussed what our answer is going to be, right?"

"Oh, here we go again. What are you saying, Candy?" asked Manny.

"Well, it's the truth that I'll be paying for the graduation trip and everything else is what I'm saying, and I'm tired of paying. I paid for their Christmas presents and I want you to realize that it's time to move on. Those girls are grown and this boy is little. Plus … " she stopped suddenly and clutched her slightly rounded belly. He glanced toward the belly, then his eyes zoomed in on his wife's.

"Are you, are we?!" he asked loudly.

In the adjacent room, Giselle's pen hit the floor as she gasped. "Oh God, not another one!" She threw the applications on the floor, turned the lamp out, and cried herself to sleep.

"WE'RE GOING TO SPLIT YOU this Christmas," said Tony's mom.

Tony didn't answer. He just walked to his bedroom. His parents had just finalized the plans for the split. All previous plans were abandoned. To soften the blow of the abrupt change in the holiday plans, Linda sought to assemble the best Christmas she could for Tony.

This year Linda was determined to have the air hockey game and the dual hoop arcade basketball set. So Tony's godmother purchased the items from Wal-Mart and had them shipped. Tony's mom was so excited to see the box when it arrived a few days before Christmas. Indeed, the love box came right on time. What Linda didn't know was that there was some major assembly required. The next morning Linda turned her attention to the toy assembly process. Not long after that the excitement of the delivery waned.

"These manufacturers must assume that Santa's little helpers *also* stick around to put these contraptions together. But they don't!" she huffed to herself.

Linda remembered her childhood Christmas mornings as a wonderful time. Bicycles, Easy-bake ovens, dolls, and tea sets for her and her sister and race sets for her brothers. Space ships and paint sets were everywhere. Linda and her siblings knew their father had stayed up all night assembling the toys and bikes. For Linda there was no daddy in the house to stay up all night long assembling toys. Fortunately, her brother Brian always came over on Christmas Eve to hang out with the family and assemble the toys.

Linda called home on Christmas Eve while shopping for last-minute Christmas items. Brian answered the phone. Linda directed him to look behind the sofa where she had hidden the basketball arcade toy box. "I got it. I got it. Don't worry; you know I got your back," he said confidently. An hour later, when she made it home, Linda saw that Brian had already assembled the air hockey game. He was proud of his work and Linda was thrilled. "One down and one to go," she said, beaming. Linda and Brian played a quick game of air hockey to test it.

"I better hurry and get started on the basketball set because Yvonne is ready to go home." Brian's wife and three small children were there. They were anxious to go home to prepare for their own Christmas. Brian went to work. Two hours later Brian hit a roadblock. "I think a piece is missing, or maybe two pieces I thought would fit together might not be an exact fit," Brian explained to Linda. It didn't help that there were fifty pieces and the instructions were in German.

"Maybe you lost your touch," she joked.

An hour later Yvonne called out to Brian from the den where she was napping, "Brian, how much longer? The kids are tired, and so am I. Plus, you know we still have to finish wrapping gifts. How much longer?"

Well beyond the breaking point, Brian stormed upstairs, poured himself a Pepsi, and served himself another helping of dinner.

"Is that your third plate?" asked Linda.

"Well, I eat when I'm stressed and I'm stressed, okay? Man, where'd you get that thing? I'm tired of it and can't seem to find where one piece is supposed to go. The instruction sheet, well, would you believe it's in German?"

Linda didn't answer.

"Look, it's getting late and Yvonne's tired. We still have to wrap presents, and I have to work tomorrow afternoon. Look, I can finish it up on the twenty-sixth."

"Wait. Don't go! I'll help. What do you want me to do?" Linda asked, panicking.

"It's no big deal. He has enough other toys. You spoil that boy anyway."

Linda's perfectly assembled Christmas was unraveling. She felt that somehow, her son's Christmas would be broken, incomplete, and a failure if she couldn't deliver the perfectly constructed scene for him to see when he woke up on Christmas morning. Without shame, she picked up the phone and called Jim, one of Brian's buddies, to ask him to help Brian. Jim was home assembling toys for his own son, Nicholas. This would be his first Christmas Eve with his wife and new baby.

Linda could not see past her desire to assemble the perfect Christmas for her fatherless child. Nonetheless, Jim agreed to try to come by later that night.

"I called Jim and he said he'll come by to help you with this thing. Besides, I blame the manufacturer. They shouldn't make it so hard to put these things together," she said.

Her brother went back downstairs to take one last stab at it.

"Maybe there's an all-nighter that has someone who can help. Are you missing a part? I'll go find it. Do you want me to drive Yvonne home? Maybe you can come back early in the morning. They can spend the night, you know." Linda prattled on as she saw her brother was giving up.

Brian shook his head no and said, "Linda, it's not going to happen tonight. Let it go." He put on his coat and ushered his family out the door with him.

TONY LOOKED AT HIS blue baseball clock the moment he woke up. It was already 7 A.M. *We have seven hours left,* he thought. He leaped to his feet and ran downstairs. Linda had yet to crawl from her bed. She'd collapsed into her bed at 4:30 A.M. after wrapping presents all night. She hadn't finished wrapping and she didn't much care either. At the sound of Tony's voice, Linda forced herself out of bed.

"Mom, thanks!" he screamed. "Look at all this stuff. Wow!!"

"Nice! An air hockey table! Mom, you really surprised me. This is a cool Gameboy game and clothes ... Wait — what's this?" Tony cast his eyes upon the biggest box under the tree. The cover featured the basketball arcade he had always wanted. "Mom! Look!" he said, leaning forward to grab the box.

This was what it was all about. This was the moment Linda had waited for. Christmas wasn't perfect — the tree was fake, the ornaments came six in a box from the dollar store, the turkey came from the church, and her big-ticket item was a picture on a box, at least for the moment. But, the thrill was there. Evidently the foreshadowing of what was to come satisfied him.

"Uncle Brian is still putting it together and it might take a few hours before he finishes because assembling a toy this size takes a while. But this is what it's going to look like," she said as she pointed to the box cover. That was Linda's great idea. They couldn't finish assembling it, but he could see the box. It worked. He was thrilled.

"Mom, it's great! I can't wait. It's so cool!" he said, hugging her. "Mom, I have an idea. But you'll probably say no."

"Try me."

"Maybe my dad can put the basketball set together when he comes."

"You're right. I don't think it's a good idea. We can manage on our own."

"Okay Mom, but we need help sometimes. It's okay to ask," he said. Drew had taught him that.

"Yes, that's why I asked Uncle Brian. Enough said, okay?"

"Yes, Mom. Anyway, everything is great. Hey, want to play air hockey? I'll cream you. I'm champ, you know!" he boasted. "Mom, this was the best Christmas ever."

"Honestly?"

"Yes Mom, really." He hugged her and Linda didn't want to let go.

So they played air hockey, although Tony asked what time it was every five minutes. It was already 9:00 A.M., just five hours before Christmas with mom was over.

"Is everything okay for you?" asked Linda nervously as she cleaned up the wrapping paper.

"Yeah! I'm happy, but … "

"I know you can't wait to see your dad," said Linda, probing.

"Well, it's just that I don't want to leave *you*. And, I feel cheated for you, Mom. Your whole time is spent rushing and getting ready for me to leave. That's your Christmas. Are you going to stay here by yourself after I leave?"

"No, we've been through all this and I thought you understood. I'm fine. You know Mommy likes her down time. Besides, I'm going to Grandma and Granddaddy's new house for dinner. That's why I made this big ol' turkey. Look, let's enjoy this moment. Let's have our time, okay?" Linda gently grabbed hold of his chin and turned his face toward hers. "Okay, sweetie pie?"

"Sure, Mom."

Linda kissed him on the forehead and returned to the kitchen. Tony had freezer waffles for breakfast since there was no time to cook breakfast with a thirteen-pound turkey to roast.

At 12:45 P.M., Linda peaked into Tony's room and asked, "Are your things packed? Do you have a dressy suit just in case?"

"Yes, Mom, I packed last night. Remember, I spent my Christmas Eve packing."

"Did you pack the long tie instead of the clip-on? You need to make your dad teach you to tie a tie, because I don't know how.

"Okaaaay, okaaaay!" snapped Tony.

By ten minutes of two Tony was sitting quietly in front of the tube watching college football. His mom tried her best to make conversation and inquire about all the fun things he would do with his dad.

"Yeah, Mom. It'll be cool, but I'll miss you. Do you want me to stay?"

"No, hon, I'm fine. Anyway, I'll see you on Friday night. I'm okay, really. You need to spend some time with the Kelloggs, you know."

Tony decided not to wait in front of the window. He waited

in front of the TV instead. When Tony heard a car pull up, he said as calmly as possible, "He's here." It was 2:30 P.M.

"Hey, Dad, what's up?"

"Hey, big guy. How's my son doing, huh, huh?" His dad grabbed him around the top of the head, drawing Tony into his embrace. "I love you, buddy."

Tony closed his eyes and hugged him back.

"Hi, Linda, sorry I'm late," said Nelson.

"No problem," said Linda. "Okay now, have a great time. I love you and behave yourself. Be respectful," she said as she put Tony's Redskins hat on his head.

"I know, Mom. I got it. I'm cool."

Moments after his dad drove around the corner, Tony rounded out his recitation of his Christmas gifts. " … and I got this really, really cool basketball arcade game. It's just that, well, Uncle Brian didn't have time to finish installing it. So my mom said he'll probably finish this week. I mean … "Tony caught himself, instantly realizing that he didn't want to betray his mom.

"What? You can tell me."

"It's just that Mom probably didn't want me to tell you that she didn't have the basketball arcade finished," he said, looking at his father and hoping his dad would offer to help.

"Oh. Are there any other things your mom doesn't want you to tell me?"

"No, Dad."

"Are you sure? You can tell me everything, you know."

"No, Dad, I'm sure. I don't know if Uncle Brian will be able to finish it. It looked really hard. If he does, it'll probably be after the holidays when I have to go back to school," said Tony. The fish weren't biting, so Tony stopped talking and turned his head to the window.

Tony and his father pulled up to his grandma's house forty

minutes later. When his dad knocked, Tony quickly stepped behind his father. But when his grandmother, dressed in a red knit sweater with embroidered candy canes, answered the door, Tony forgot his apprehension.

"Come on in, baby! Hello, angel, how's grandma's little boy? I sure have missed you!" She hugged him and squeezed his cheeks.

"Ouch."

"Oh, I can't seem to hug you enough. Your daddy never seems to want to bring you to grandma," she said, looking sharply at her son. "Come on in. Your whole family is waiting for you."

Tony immediately took in the distinctive aroma of a down-home Christmas dinner. As his grandma closed the door behind them, she announced, "Hey, everybody, Tony's here. Let me take a gooooood look at you!"

Tony made his way into the living room as his relatives continued to greet him. "He's looking more like Uncle Jack every day, isn't he?" said his uncle.

Tony smiled and began to look around his grandmother's living room. He immediately noticed the pictures of her grandchildren on the walls, on tables, and on the mantle. There were pictures of her children and grandchildren everywhere, and there were two pictures of Tony. One was taken when he was about five, and the other was a much smaller unframed photo of Tony leaning against a larger framed shot of all the other grandchildren together. Tony froze. *Why wasn't I called for that picture with the others? This is just how things are, I guess. No one said, "let's leave Tony out of this picture."*

Tony finally pried himself from that spot in front of the family wall and began to slowly move about. He noticed how the other grandkids roamed about the house with ease and obvious familiarity. Brandon, twelve, shot past him, "Hey, man, come on." Brandon grabbed a plate and prepared himself another helping of food.

"Oh, did you open your presents yet?" Brandon asked Tony.

"No."

"Well, come on back to the living room. I know we got you something and so did everyone else, I think. Oh, uh, did you eat yet? Make a plate if you're hungry."

"I ate with my mom," lied Tony. Then he heard his grand-mother calling for him.

"Tony, honey, come over to talk to your grandma, but first go over to the tree. I think there might be a little something there for you," she said proudly.

Tony opened all his gifts and hugged and thanked everyone. He tried to reassure everyone that they'd chosen gifts he liked and bought the right size.

Tony was starving. He didn't know if he should ask his grandma whether he could make a plate. "Dad," he called, "Can you come here a minute?"

Twenty minutes later, after gobbling down his last morsel of turkey, Tony made his way downstairs to hang with his cousins. They were joking about a past gathering. Dominique even said, "Tony, you were there, right?"

"I think so," replied Tony, but he knew he hadn't been there. He hadn't even known about the gathering. He never knew or heard because they never called or invited him.

"Do you want my phone number so you can call me the next time you guys get together?" he asked.

"Oh, my dad has it," said Dominique.

"Are you sure?"

"Well, if not I can get it from Uncle Nelson, right?"

Tony wanted to say something else, but instead he simply said, "Right."

Tony went straight to bed that night at his dad's house. During the next two days, Tony and his dad watched football, ate at

McDonalds, played Playstation, and watched a couple of movies. They managed to squeeze in a little talking. At least they were together. The bonding was underway, once again.

ON THE DAY AFTER CHRISTMAS, Sharon drove Ray and Dion to the Wal-Mart in Triangle, Virginia, the agreed-upon meeting spot. Dion saw his brother sitting on a bench out front and he hopped out of his mom's car even before she brought it to a complete stop at the curb.

Ray waited for his mother to write down all the contact phone numbers. He also watched his brothers' reunion. Dion ran right up to David and fell directly into his arms. He was in no hurry to let go. Dion felt like David had reached out and pulled Dion into his world. Dion thought to himself, *he didn't break up my hug — he hugged me back*. Dion's mom once said that God can make up the lost years — in no time he can restore what the locust ate up, and at that moment, Dion believed that's what that hug did.

Ray trailed behind.

"What's up, Ray?" asked David, reaching out to pull Ray into a hug. With his hands still buried in his pockets, Ray leaned his upper body over for a split second, then withdrew.

Journal

During dinner with Sharon, Dion, and Ray, Dion poured out his heart. I think the reunion with his brother finally validated him and welcomed him back into the family. "You can take back all my gifts so long as you don't take my brother from me. It didn't matter what I got or didn't get, I got him," Dion told me after dinner. It was as if he was no longer an exile — and it didn't come about because some judge forced "brother visita-

tion." *Unfortunately, Ray didn't have much to offer, except that, "Of course, Dad couldn't make it."*

The mothers had it tough during the holidays, too, though. They all had to wonder — will the kids go with dad or not? Will he show or not? Linda thought that if she was thinking about all this then her son certainly was too. So she constructed every step of the way. Even I was torn in different directions trying to assemble toys, bikes, racetracks, and dollhouses all over town.

Planning Christmas for the fatherless requires some assembly. These mothers carefully laid the plans — detected the landmines and ensured that they shielded their kids from daddymania, if necessary. But any attempt to eliminate the notion of father from the Christmas scenery is so unreal. I can't imagine the nativity scene without Joseph. Fathers are real, and each of these children has one.

Finally, we're mid-way through the school year. There's been progress. Still need to move Jason along. I'm sorry he didn't see his dad on Christmas, but hopefully the basketball tickets will bring them together.
— A.D.M.

CHAPTER FIVE

On the Outs

Mayra rushed upstairs from Springridge's basement lugging a large box of sodas. She dumped the box in the old nursery. She placed her hand over her heart and felt it pounding like a jackhammer. Her breathing was heavy. Tonight was "Girls' Night." Mayra slipped out of the nursery where she would host the all-girl gathering and into Drew's office down the hall.

"Anyone here yet?"

"No. Did you run up the stairs?" Drew asked.

"No. Has the food arrived?"

"No, but do you need any help?"

"Yeah, I'm kind of nervous. I've never done this before, you know, met with girls to talk the way you do during Keep It Real.

"You can handle it. I trust you, and remember, this was *their* idea. *They* asked for their own session so let them do the talking. You just draw them out. Now go get 'em, Dr. Spock."

MAYRA CONVENED ABOUT eight of the center's female members and friends to talk about the issues of life — boys, school, the future, drugs, sex, and, of course, fathers.

While the girls ate General Tso's chicken and fried rice, Mayra pulled out a flip chart and a thick black marker and wrote "Issue Board" at the top.

"Okay, tonight we're here to chill, eat, have fun, and talk about whatever you want to talk about," she said.

"Oh, this is like what Drew does," said Giselle.

"You name the issues and I'll be the scribe," said Mayra.

"How about boys?" said Kalia. "I think Jason is cute."

"We know you do," said Giselle.

"I think boys are a trip," said Digna. "They're always trying to get you over to their house after school."

"Or, trying to get into *your* house," said Mikala.

"Really?" asked Mayra. "I would think your mother or father would *want* to meet these boys."

"No. They try to come after school when your mom's still at work. My mom doesn't get home until around ten o'clock because of her second job," said Mikala. "My dad doesn't live with us so he's not there. So I have to babysit my brother until she gets home. So sometimes, a certain knucklehead knocks on my door and asks if he can come in so I can help him with his algebra. Like he ever even thinks about algebra."

"Do you let him in?" asked Mayra.

"No!" said Mikala.

"Well, if all you're going to do is watch music videos, what's the big deal?" asked Kalia.

"What do you see when you watch those videos?" asked Mayra.

"Half-naked women dancing like they're trying to do something," said Giselle.

"And you find that entertaining?" asked Mayra.

"Not really," said Giselle. "That's why I don't watch those videos."

"So what else is of interest to you ladies tonight?" Mayra asked, pointing to the issue board. "What's on your mind?"

"School."

"Boys."

"Boys? Okay, what else?"

"Being teased all the time because I'm dark-skinned."

"Yeah, the boys only like the light-skinned girls."

"Or they only like the girls who look like they just stepped out of a music video."

"Can we talk about dads?"

"Yeah, and how come they don't want to be with us."

"When did you last see your father?"

"A year."

"At least you know your dad. I don't even know my father. He left after I was born. I've never had a father, other then the four or five boyfriends my mother has brought to the house."

"How about my mother's boyfriend?"

"Or my father's girlfriend."

"I want to know why we have to have sex education with the boys in the class?"

"It's so embarrassing."

"My mom made me take the independent study class. It wasn't bad. It was better than learning about your 'monthly' with boys in the class."

"I know that's right," said Digna.

"I don't think sex-ed is so bad," said Kalia.

"Please!" said Márisol.

"Alright, so is it okay to kiss?" asked Kalia.

"Well, let me put it this way. It's not as easy as you think to stop," answered Mayra.

"The school gives us condoms and teaches us about safe sex," said Kalia.

"Wow! Good grief, you're only fourteen," said Mayra. "For me, at this point, I'm going to wait."

"I know, until you're ready or until you and the guy love each other."

"No, I'm going to wait until I get married," said Mayra, matter-of-factly.

"Well, some girls actually *want* a baby," said Kalia.

"Why on earth would some teenage girl want a baby?" asked Mayra, still writing on the board.

"They say it's because at least then they'll have someone to love them," said Kalia.

"Not me. I'm not having no babies and I'm not getting married, because all he's going to do is leave me and the kids. Then I'll be stuck just like my mom, raising kids with no help. The kids would all be miserable because they won't get to see their dad anymore. So, no — I ain't having kids and I ain't getting married," said fifteen-year-old Márisol.

"Well, not all dads leave their families, you know," said Alyssa. "My dad is still with us. He's pretty cool. All my friends like him and say he's a cool dad."

"Yeah, Alyssa's dad is the coolest," said Shanya.

"He comes to all my games and we take serious vacations every year. I mean, they are really tight."

"My father calls every purple moon and then never shows up," commented Andrea. "I never see him. When I was diagnosed with leukemia, I didn't even know how to find him. The doctors say I might need a bone marrow transplant, but I don't know his family and can't reach him to try and find a match. I'm really scared."

"Are you okay now?" asked Mayra.

"The cancer's in remission now but we'll know better in six months when I have my checkup."

"Sounds like my life," said Márisol. "I haven't seen my father since when I was real little."

"Is that why you're not planning to get married?" asked Mayra.

"Pretty much. It's the worst thing in the world to know he's out there and know that he knows I'm out here trying to make it, trying to grow up, and yet he won't help me, be a dad to me, love me," said Márisol, sitting on the floor and slowly rocking. "It's so wild because my mom said he named me after his mom because I was his sea and sun. But then he left me when I was three. He never married my mom. Instead, he married another lady and had kids with her. I saw him once on a soccer field. I saw him. He was playing on a team. There were a whole lot of people out there and I was sitting in the bleachers. Then I saw him. I recognized him from my mom's pictures. I couldn't take my eyes off of him. He looked at me from across the field. I figured he might have wondered who this girl was, but since I was sitting with my mother he must've known. He squinted his eyes. He even pulled glasses out of his duffel bag and looked at me. I'll never forget it. He smiled at me. He actually smiled at me."

"When was that?" asked Mayra.

"About five years ago, and I haven't seen him since."

"So what are we going to do about this father dilemma?" asked Mayra, hoping to lift the mood. "I've spent four years of high school and two years of college so far crying the daddy blues but I haven't done anything about it. And it sounds like you guys haven't done too much either. So what are we going to do about it? Anything?"

No one spoke up. Most of the girls had folded their arms and slouched even further into their chairs.

Then Kalia jumped up. "Hey, I want to do something. I want to call my dad."

"Me too!" said Márisol.

"Okay, now we're getting somewhere. When you guys get home and talk this over with your mothers, I'm sure they'll help to arrange a call or even a visit. That's all I'm really trying to encourage here," said Mayra, coming to life.

"I want to call my dad right now. I know his number. I've had it for a while," said Márisol.

Mayra extended her right arm as a stop signal. "Wait. I don't mean right now. I mean after discussing this with your mother. Not here and now. That's not a good idea."

"I call all the time," said Márisol. "I just hang up every time someone answers."

"You can use my cell," said Andrea, reaching into her pocket and pulling out a small cell phone.

"Girls!" pleaded Mayra. "This is not the time or the place for this."

"Mayra, if you're worried about getting into trouble, I'm not going to blame you. Besides, my mom knows I call. She doesn't care. She just keeps telling me that I'm wasting my time," said Márisol, standing up and reaching for Andrea's phone.

"If it'll make you feel better, I'll go to the gym." She started dialing the number while heading to the doorway.

"Ooh, I gotta hear this!" said Kalia, following Márisol.

Márisol and Kalia were followed by everyone except Mayra and Giselle. In the hallway, the girls congregated around Márisol. Her father's line began to ring. So did Drew's.

"Hello?" said Márisol.

"Si, hable," said a woman's voice.

"Uh, está el Señor Joe Contreras? Is Joe Contreras home?"

"No está aquí. Quién habla?" she said.

"Um, uh, pues, this is Márisol Contreras. Usted no me conoce, you don't know me, but … "

Meanwhile, Mayra reached Drew on speed-dial. "Drew, I have a situation!" said Mayra, trying to quietly scream into her cell phone. "Things have gotten out of hand. I told her not to, but Márisol is calling her father!"

"How did this happen? Where is she?"

"She's out in the hall. She said she was headed to the gym," said Mayra, moving to look out the doorway.

"Mayra — first calm down."

"I'm calm. We were talking about the best way to reach them and she jumped up and grabbed Andrea's phone and went into the hall. I told her she needed to talk to her mother first, but she said her mother didn't care and that she wanted to call now. Can you come down here?"

On the other end of Márisol's line, the woman spoke again. "I know who you are," said the woman. "I know your mother. How did you get this number?"

"I looked it up."

"I don't think so because it's not listed."

"Is my father there?"

"Can I ask what you want with Mr. Contreras?"

"I just want to speak to him for a minute. It's important."

"I know this must be hard for you but ya tiene su família. He has a family now. Debes hablar con tu mama sobre esta situación."

"I already talked to my mom and she said I could call him."

"Well you should talk to her again because you should not have called this house."

Márisol turned away from the other girls to face the gym wall.

"Ma'am, I just want to know him," she said with her voice cracking. "Just meet him one time. Just talk to him. Say hello.

Can't you just put him on the phone and let him decide if he wants to talk to me?" Tears were streaming down her face.

"Tiernita, please don't cry. No llore. Por favor, hable con tu mama. Please talk to your mama. I don't want to hurt you."

"But why can't you let him make his own decisions? Usted no es su mama."

"No, hija, I'm not his mother but he has decided already. That's what I'm trying to tell you. I must go now," said the woman before she hung up the phone.

"Please don't hang up!" pleaded Márisol. "I'm sorry! Hello?" Márisol dropped the phone on the floor and slid down the wall to the floor. There was dead silence.

"Drew, I have to go," Mayra rushed to Márisol.

"Girls, move, please! Mari, are you alright? Look at me," she said, kneeling to the ground beside Márisol.

"She said he's already decided."

"I don't know, honey, but I'm so sorry you had to go through this. This is what I was hoping to avoid. I should've never brought up this topic," she said, holding Márisol, trying to console her.

"It's not your fault my life is so messed up."

The rest of the girls returned to the meeting room. Ten minutes later, so did Mayra and Márisol.

"Mayra, we've all decided to do what Márisol did. If she was brave enough to reach out, so will we," said Giselle. "We're all in this together. We're not going to leave Mari to suffer alone."

"Well, after tonight, we all should agree it's not a good idea," said Mayra as she began to tear off the flip chart sheets.

"Are you with us?" asked Tiffany.

"No," she said, looking at Márisol.

Márisol wiped her face and said, "This is the worst day of my life so far. It just has to get better. I had to try. I think everyone should try. You'll hurt anyway, so you might as well try. Just maybe something good will happen for someone here."

Mayra sat down and sighed. She looked around the room for a kindred fearful spirit, for someone as frightened and father-shy as she was. The girls stood their ground. Mayra dragged her hands down her face and relented. "Alright, I'll try. We'll all try."

"Okay, so we'll all meet back after Father's Day, right? Let's make a pact. Everyone has to do something by the banquet. Then at the banquet, we'll tell all — the good, the bad, and the ugly. All of it. We'll hold each other's hands, deal?" declared Kalia.

Two WEEKS LATER JASON looked on the refrigerator to find the phone number held in place by a magnet and dialed a number he hadn't called since it had changed two months before. He had tried to hold out and wait for his father to call him, but he usually gave up waiting and called if he didn't hear from him for a few months. After the third ring, his father answered.

"Hello, Dad? It's me, Jason. How's it goin'?"

"Hey, young man, this is a surprise. How's life treating ya?"

"Good, good. What's going on with you?" asked Jason, not quite sure how to approach the visitation question.

"Not bad. Can't complain," he said, laughing. "How's school? How's your mom?"

"School's fine, Mom's fine."

Alright, now that we got all the pleasantries out of the way, what's on your mind? What can I do for you?"

"Hey Dad, I was just wondering if, uh, you know, if, well uh, when was the last time we hung out? You see, there's this new guy at the center and he talks about fathers a lot, and well, I think about you and all that."

"Oh, you think about me and all that, huh?" he said, chuckling. "Sounds interesting. So what else about fathers do you talk about? Anything I need to know about?"

"No, Dad. We just talk about issues and things. But that's not why I called."

"Does your mother know this guy is asking about family business?"

"Dad, it's not like that! I should never have told you."

"No, I'm glad you did. Okay, so this guy gets you thinking about me. I suppose that's a good thing, but I hope you love your old man enough to think about him without waiting for some busybody to get into your business, Son."

"DAD! Chill! I just want to hang out with you, okay?!" screamed Jason.

"Alright. Alright, I'm just messing with you anyway. How do you want to do this? Do you have some time frame in mind?"

"How about this weekend?" said Jason, pacing nervously in the kitchen. "Actually, I wanted to surprise you, but I guess I'll tell you — I have two tickets to the Wizards' game on Friday night at the MCI Center. The Wizards are playing the Atlanta Hawks and I want to take you to the game. We can even take the Metro, so when Mom drops me off, we can get right on the train and go. How's that sound? Then I could stay the weekend, if that's alright."

"It sounds pretty good. Where on earth did you get the tickets?"

"From Springridge Community Center where I play basketball. It's a long story. Can you come?"

"Sure, Son, but it's just that I don't have my car. It's in the shop. I'll have to get Gina to bring me. Do you want to meet at the Glenmont station?"

"You still with her?" asked Jason.

"Yes, I'm still with her. Don't tell your mother if she asks. So how's Glenmont on Friday around 6:00 p.m. That way, we can take the train and still have time to grab a bite before the game.

I can bring you home either late Sunday or really early Monday morning. This'll work. It's been some time since you decided to come about me, huh?"

"Yeah, Dad, but that'll all change this weekend. Okay, that works," said Jason. "So I'm going to call my mother to the phone now," said Jason as he walked out of the kitchen. "Mom," he called.

"What?" she yelled from upstairs.

"Phone, it's Dad," said Jason, his voice dropping. Although his mom didn't answer that last bit of info, she picked up the phone and began to speak.

"Gary?" she said. Jason immediately hung up the phone and began to walk upstairs when he slowed and then sat down halfway from the top.

"I'm glad you're on the phone because we've got to talk about this child support problem," she said.

After a loud sigh, he answered, "Vicky, your son wants to spend some time with me, so I think we need to put our differences aside for the moment and work this out. I'm going to pick him up from Glenmont Station Friday after work, but I need you to get him there. I'll get him home, but Glenmont works best for me."

"Uh, you haven't paid support in, what, six months? And now you expect me to spend more money on gas so you can see your own son? Forget it. You need to come and get him yourself!" she said loudly enough for Jason to hear. Predictably, Jason stomped up the stairs into her room, fuming.

"Vicky, you're getting petty. This is about Jason. It's not about me and it's not about you. I haven't seen him in a long time, no thanks to you, I might add. He called me, and I don't have my car. So I'm going to have to rely on you," Gary said.

Jason moved directly in front of his mother, his eyes burning into hers. She tried to ignore the imposing figure standing directly in front of her. "Jason, please! I'm talking on the phone," she said, turning her back to him.

"Mom! Tell him you'll take me. I mean it. Don't do this. I want to go with him. Mom!"

"Look Gary, fine, I'll do it this time, but you need to make a payment. I am tired of doing all this myself. That's all I'm going to say. I *will* be calling child support enforcement next week if you don't make a payment. Yes, fine — friday at 6 P.M.," she said before she slammed the phone down.

"Jason, don't do that again. When I'm on the phone ... "

"It was my father and you were talking about me, my life."

"I don't care who it is, you will not disrespect me like that again. I took it from him all those years. I'm not taking it from you. You're just like him. You think you can just bully me. Well, I'm not having it," she said, storming out of the room toward the stairs.

Jason followed her. "I can't believe you did that. You always compare me to him. I can't believe it. Whenever I do something you don't like, you say I'm like him — well, maybe I don't like that and maybe you need to stop disrespecting *me*!"

"Boy, that is enough! I don't care how big and bad you think you are, don't you talk to me like that. I'm still your mother. I brought you into this world ... " she said, turning to face him at the top of the stairs.

"Yeah, yeah, yeah and you can take me out of this world! Whatever. Fine," he said as he turned into his room, slammed the door, and turned up his music to drown out any other sound.

On Friday, Vicky pulled up to the house at 5:40 P.M., delayed by the heavy downpour that slowed traffic. Jason was waiting in front of the door.

"I'm gonna be late if we don't leave right now," he said, barely letting Vicky squeeze past him to come into the house.

"I just need to go to the bathroom. I'm tired but we can go in just a minute."

Meanwhile, Jason grabbed his Wizards duffel bag and his CD player, pulled his windbreaker hood over his head, and ran to the car. When Vicky returned, he was already in the front seat ready to go. She climbed into the car, and as she pulled away, she saw the mail truck in her rearview mirror.

"Quick, see if you can catch him to get our mail," she said, stopping the car in the middle of the street.

"Mom, I'm going to be late!"

"Just get it. I'm expecting something."

Jason jumped out of the car, ran to the letter carrier for the mail, and got back in the car.

"Oh, look Mom, we won a million dollars again," he proclaimed sarcastically. "I don't know why you keep sending this junk in. You know it's a scam. We're never going to win this stupid thing. I still can't believe you waited at home all day on Super Bowl Sunday. Uh oh, there are some pink ones. Looks like *something's* about to be cut off."

At 5:50 p.m., they pulled up to Glenmont station. "See, we're early and he's not here," she said. She reached for the mail and immediately noticed a certified letter. "What is this?"

"Oh, I signed it when I got the mail from the mailman," said Jason, looking behind him through the back window, as if expecting his father to pull up.

"You're not old enough to sign for that. Hmmm, it's from the family court," she said, ripping into the damp envelope. "Jesus! I don't believe this! He didn't say anything about this on the phone! There's a hearing. He's trying to get the child support reduced. Wait a minute … Hell, no!" she said, reaching for the car keys and restarting the car. "We are out of here!"

"Mom, calm down! I'll just get out now if you're upset. I'm okay. I'll just wait for him."

"I said we're out of here!" Vicky put the car in drive and suddenly pulled off.

"Mom! Stop the car and let me out, NOW!" he screamed.

"No! Your father's not going to get away with this. He thinks I'm some kind of fool. Well, I've got news for him, he will not treat me like this. I'm not taking any more of this. You're not going and that's all there is to it, not until that man pays the support we're supposed to have!"

"Mom! Let me out! I want to see my father! You are wrong. I'm old enough to go live with him if you keep doing this!" he shouted, unlocking his door.

"Yeah, well — you go right ahead but I promise you he's too busy with his slut of a girlfriend to let you live there! Sorry to disappoint you but there's no room at the inn, baby!" she said as she pulled up to a stoplight directly outside the station.

Jason opened the door and jumped out of the car. "Pop the trunk, Mom."

"Boy, if you don't get back in this car, so help me … "

"So help me what? You gonna beat me up? What — ground me? Man, I don't even care 'cause you are so wrong! Dad said the judge said visitation and child support have nothing to do with each other, so I can go and you know it. Pop the trunk, damn it!"

"What did you say? Don't you ever cuss at me! Get in this car; the light's about to change! Get back in this car! Now! You are in big trouble. That's all I've got to say!" she screamed, leaning toward the passenger window.

Jason began to walk down the street, appearing not to hear her. She followed slowly behind him in the car and pressed the button to let down the passenger window.

"I will call the police on you if you don't get in this car

right now, so help me GOD! This is your last chance. As long as you are under MY roof you will do what I say. Now GET IN THIS CAR! Have you lost your mind?!" she asked as the light changed. Cars began to beep as they tried to pass her. Soaking wet from the ongoing downpour, Jason stopped walking and cradled his head in his hands, floods of tears pouring from between his fingers and a rage-filled moan escaping from his mouth. He stood there, motionless for a few more seconds. Vicky was forced to put the hazard lights on before Jason flung the backseat door open, threw himself in the car, slammed the door, and said, "I hate you!"

Vicky didn't respond at first. After driving a few blocks, she addressed Jason's outburst. "I don't know what to do with you. You've become so awful to me. I don't deserve this and I hope to GOD you see the error of your ways."

At home Jason called his dad and left a message on his voice mail. "Dad, Mom said I can't come because you're taking her back to court. But we were there until she opened the mail. I'm sorry. I want to come live with you."

Then he hung up the phone and went to his room. This time, there was no music.

FOR THE NEXT SEVERAL WEEKS, Jason was a no-show at the center. He hadn't heard from his father after the incident. He suspected that his mother had erased the voicemail messages before he could get to them. She had done it before and told him of the call weeks later. Drew called a couple of times but his calls went unreturned. Finally, Vicky and Jason's phone was disconnected. Drew even went to Jason's house, but no one was home. Drew refused to believe that a cold, as Kalia claimed, was what kept Jason away from basketball and the center.

WHEN MAYRA PULLED into the center's parking lot during the first week of April, she was excited about round two of her all-girl session. Drew had convinced her that the Márisol fiasco was a fluke and possibly a good thing. Fortunately there was no parental backlash. Just as Mayra unhooked her seatbelt, her cell phone rang.

"This is Mayra."

"Sweetie, it's Mom. You need to call your father. I've got some bad news for you," said Brenda.

"What is it?"

"Your grandfather has died and your father wants you to call him," she said softly.

"Oh God, no!" cried Mayra. "Not Papa!"

Mayra turned around and went home.

"You're coming, right?" asked her father on the phone.

"You really want me there?" she asked sheepishly.

"Of course I do, why would you say something like that? Of course I want you there. The whole family is expecting you and your mother," he said, reassuring Mayra.

"Okay, I'm coming, but you'll have to give me exact directions."

"Your mom knows exactly where the church is. She's coming too, right? You know she was like a daughter to my father even after we broke up. He always talked about her. Always had such good things to say about her."

What I want to know is whether he had anything to say about me?! Obviously not, since you didn't mention it, thought Mayra even as her father spoke. *Stop it, Mayra!* she told herself. *I don't want to be angry right now. I really don't. I am always filled with so many things — but anger is the one feeling that's always with me when my dad is on my mind. How can I be so self-centered on the day my dad lost his dad? Now, maybe he will know how it feels to be fatherless.*

Three days later, Mayra was en route to the funeral with her mother.

"Mayra, are you listening? You seem a thousand miles away."

"It's nothing."

"Tell me."

"I'm just daydreaming about how things are going to be," said Mayra.

"Well, honey, just keep the faith and hope. Try and see the best in people. It took me a really long time to forgive and move on, but we have to do it. Just trust that things will be the way you want them to be."

"Nah, I'll do one better. I daydream about how I wished things would be. I'm a realist, Mom. I haven't dared to hope, because my hopes were always dashed. After a while I learned not to hope. No, I learned to just dream it and live it in my dream. From the dream in my fantasy world, I live it the way things are supposed to be lived out. Each day brings a new rendition of the right way my reunion is supposed to take place."

"I'm not so sure that's healthy, but I'm not gonna argue with you because I know you're upset."

A few minutes later, Mayra and her mother Brenda pulled up to the cottage-lined street where the tiny community church was located. Mayra remained in the van, looking for familiar faces.

"Are you ready?" asked Brenda as she focused her eyes on the rearview mirror to touch up her hair and makeup.

"No, I'm just trying to collect myself and figure out how I'm going to answer all the questions people might ask me — like where have I been or even who am I," she said with her voice escalating.

"Well, you've been busy. That's all they need to know, honey."

"Mom, you KNOW why I'm never with them. They don't call me. They never invite me to family events. Is that what I should say?"

"Well, I'm sure there's a nice way to say that."

"Huh? I'm not so sure I want to be nice. The few times we did get together was because you insisted that I call since I was going to be in the area. When I did go, I'd go to Grandma's house or Aunt Didi's house. I'd see cousins, uncles, and aunts. I would always get the usual polite pat hug. It's required if you're related. But there was never much feeling, no love. The real hug says, 'I missed you,' or, 'I've been thinking about you.' I never got those hugs. You know, the 'you're family' hug."

"Mayra, honey, relax! Whew! I see you still have the same issues you've always had, but did it ever occur to you that you might actually be wrong about them? Perhaps there are family members who actually do care for you," continued Brenda. "Just maybe there is not a vast Taylor family conspiracy to disenfranchise you from the family, huh? Just chew on that for a spell."

"Fine. Maybe I've incorrectly presumed that no one wanted to really know me, who I am, or be a part of my life. But if so, they didn't make it clear."

"You'll be fine," said Brenda as she unlocked the car door and grabbed her purse. Mayra looked around for familiar faces as she stepped out of the van.

"Look, there's your cousin Sirina. See if you can catch her."

"Mother, please! Like I'm going to chase them down. I'm not going to force myself on anyone. I'll let them spot me and see if they reach out to me. Don't call anyone, Mom, 'cause that'll just make us look desperate to be a part of them and I'm not desperate."

People looked curiously at Mayra and her mother as they walked through the parking lot.

"I shouldn't have come," said Mayra.

"I still think you should've called your grandmother and arranged to be with your family instead of coming separately."

"Why didn't they call *me*? Besides, that's why I wanted to

come a little early so that if any of Rick's family sees me, they can do the right thing and invite me to be with the family instead of me forcing myself upon them."

"You need to stop calling him Rick."

As she stood in the vestibule looking for familiar faces, someone tapped her on the shoulder and said, "Don't I know you?"

Yes, yes, of course you do. I'm Rick's daughter!

"I'm your cousin, Alba," continued the young woman.

"Oh, hey Alba!" *At last someone knows who I am. Someone knows that I am his granddaughter and that I'm grieving too. Mayra sighed within herself.*

"When did you get here?" asked Alba.

"We just got here. My mom came with me."

"Wow, it's really been a long time, hasn't it? It's good to see you. Anyway, see you inside."

"Are you going in now? I can walk in with you."

"No, I'm not going in yet. I'm looking for Mother. If you see her, tell her I'm looking for her, but I'll see you inside." Alba gave Mayra a short pat hug and walked away.

That's it? Why didn't she walk me in? Consent to being related to me? She knows I'm Rick's daughter and that I'm probably hurting more than she is. After all, she had her father.

The rest of the family had yet to arrive. An usher was guarding the empty row reserved for the family. Mayra considered herself an immediate family member, but she just didn't have the courage to approach the usher and ask to be seated.

"Honey, there's a spot right behind them. We can squeeze in," said Brenda.

"Not this time," said Mayra. "I've been trying to squeeze into a place in this family for far too long. They should've made room for me long ago. I'm always the one contorting myself and my life just to be close to the front row."

"Where are we sitting then? It's up to you."

"Over on the left side. You go first," Mayra said to her mother with the smile that told her that this whole visit had to be carefully choreographed.

Brenda faintly smiled back, telling Mayra she understood.

The organist gracefully moved from one sad song to another as Mayra and her mom squeezed in the third row from the front. The row, along with the church, was nearly filled. Brenda entered the row first and seemed ready to sit toward the outside, but Mayra asked her to keep moving over, further toward the inside, where Mayra would be able to see her family — and where they could see her. Moments later the family filed in and filled the first two rows.

"Oh, my God, I can't believe this," Mayra whispered. "Gwen is here! Somehow, they made sure to inform her and include her in the family."

Mayra's heart sank. "Mom, how can you include one daughter and not the other one? What do I do? Should I go over there?"

She began to weep, and Brenda pulled her closer.

"I know how you felt about your grandfather, though you weren't able to see him much. Sweetie, I know you loved him."

"It's not just him; it's like I lost all of them," said Mayra softly.

The pastor stood up. "Next in the program for this morning's homegoing will be the singing of the *Lord's Prayer* by Tiffany Dawson." After the song, the pastor directed the attendees to read the obituary recorded on the back of the program. Mayra lifted her head and put the program back in her lap. Brenda's eyes instantly zoomed in on the "survived by" section. Mayra's name was not listed as one of Richard's granddaughters. Before Brenda could slam the program shut, she noticed Mayra's disappointed expression.

"I'm not on it, am I?"

"No you're not, sweetie."

"That's it. I've had it. Why am I here? I'm not family? I'm no one, huh? So why am I here? I'm leaving," she grabbed her purse and began to stand.

"Mayra, wait. Let's just wait, maybe it was a mistake," whispered Brenda as she grabbed Mayra's arm. But Mayra broke loose and climbed over the others seated in the row and walked out. She turned for one last glance in her father's direction to see whether he even noticed she was there or that she was leaving. He didn't budge from consoling his mother.

On the ride home, Mayra pulled out her cell phone and left her father a voicemail message — after she had screamed, ranted, and raved to her mother.

"Daddy, I just wanted to let you know, I was there. Talk to you later."

BY MAY, GISELLE HAD passed several months without speaking to her father.

"They're here!" yelled Giselle's mother when the mailwoman delivered the graduation announcements.

"Let me see them!"

"Okay, okay — can we look together?" asked her mom.

"Mom! Let me see — they're mine!"

"Well, if you wanna be technical, I did pay for them," her mom teased.

"Okay, fine!"

"Here, Giselle. Let's look together."

Giselle's grades and SAT scores had earned her a spot at Spelman College, St. Mary's College, Boston University, Howard University, and of course, the University of Maryland. She'd chosen Spelman College. The tuition question remained unresolved.

"They're nice. What do you think?" asked Giselle.

"They'll do. So ... are you going to invite your father? I know you've at least told him already, right?"

"I will, but I haven't called him yet. You know Dad," said Giselle.

"I do know him and that's why I told you to tell him weeks ago. You could have sent a card or a letter. I know how you like to write. You've never had a problem writing me a letter when I've ticked you off. Besides, you don't know what Spelman's going to do about a scholarship. You must talk to him about tuition. I've told you this over and over."

"I know, Mom, but the part that gets me is that he knows I'm going to graduate. He knows he has a daughter in the twelfth grade. How can he forget? I reminded him about graduation at Christmas. I said 'Dad, you know I'm graduating.' I told him my graduation date. He knows I'll need help with college. He sort of brought it up when I was there, but his new wife kinda got in the way," said Giselle, studying her mother's expression.

"Kinda, sorta? What does that mean? Did that woman say anything to you about this situation? You didn't tell me about that!"

"She just interrupted him when we started to talk about it, that's all. She didn't say anything to me. We never had the chance to finish because she was always around and I was afraid of her. Yes, I could've called back and reminded him. But I hoped deep inside that he would want to come and talk about tuition on his own, not because I kept calling and not because I kept reminding him, but because this was something important to him. I need to know that my big days are of value to him — and not because I forced it on him. The truth is, I was waiting to see if he was going to call me first and ask."

"Listen, you need to learn to go after what you want in life. Sometimes you're so passive. You retreat into your journal, and you suppress what's going on inside. But it's going to have to come out. You can't let every little wind blow you away. You also can't just sit back and wait for all that's good and right to just plop into your lap. You've got to go after the good. Chase it down. Take chances. You might be frazzled when it's all over, but at least you would have found or even recovered what was trying to get away from you. Ask him. He might say no. You made sure of that, but ask anyway."

Sounding defeated, Giselle responded, "Alright, Mom. I'll call him now, but it almost doesn't matter. It does, but it doesn't. Whether I called one hundred times or three months earlier. The real thing I need from him is missing."

"Well, now, let's just wait and see, he may be coming. Don't give up yet. I still think you should've called. I'm sure, I mean, I know he loves you and cares about you, but you know, people get forgetful and they get so busy. Your dad was never one to remember things like that. He comes by it honestly — his own father was like that. Not much real personal attention from him. It's really not his fault. I always had to remind him of special events — even things like his own mother's birthday. Now if a man can't even remember his own mother's birthday, and we know he loves his momma, right? Right!"

"Mom, stop making excuses for him," she paused and then added, "but maybe you're right. Though he should understand that this is the most important day of my life! He must know this. I'll call him. I'll call him now."

Giselle went up to her bedroom, closed the door, and lay down to bury her face in a pillow. *Why can't he ever initiate? Doesn't he care at all about me? Don't I mean anything to him? I have always called you — remembered you — thought of you —*

remembered your birthday — called you on Father's Day — sent you a card.

She was in no condition to call her father and she knew it. She took the address book next to her bed and threw it across the room as hard as she could. Then she cried herself to sleep.

It was another week before Giselle worked up the courage to place the call.

"Hello, Candace, this is Giselle. Can I speak to my dad?"

"Well, hello, Giselle," she said. "I bet I know why you're calling, but your daddy's not … "

"Just tell him I called," snapped Giselle.

"Oh, wait a minute, I hear him coming in. Hold on."

Moments later, Giselle's father came to the phone. "Hello."

"Hi, Daddy."

"Hey, how's it going! How's school? Aren't you graduating this year? It should be coming up soon, right?"

"I'm fine, Daddy, and actually, I'm graduating in two weeks. Are you still coming?"

"Huh, uh, well, when is it? You were supposed to call me!"

"I'm calling you now. But I told you at Christmas, remember? Well, anyway, it's in two weeks." Giselle could hear her step-mother talking to her father in the background.

"Whoa, well, okay — wait a minute – um, well — that's gonna be kinda hard — you should've told me earlier — you know how I am about flying and I probably couldn't get a good price anyway — I'm sorry. But hey, make sure you take lots of pictures. Get your mom to videotape it. You know I'll be with you in spirit. What does Daddy always say, huh? Let me hear it."

Giselle could barely speak.

"Hello, are you there? Hello? Come on now, what does Daddy always say?"

"I'm here. Daddy's always with me in spirit," she responded, almost robotically. Suddenly, she was in a big hurry to end the call, "Okay, then, I gotta go now. There are a lot more people I have to call and invite."

"Okay, then, I'll be sure and send you something, okay?"

"Okay, Daddy," she said. "See you later."

"Bye, Giselle."

She hung up the phone and grabbed the journal at her bedside. She wrote as if she was writing to her father.

> *You could drive. We drove there at Christmas. We always drive. You could drive. You didn't even try and I cannot believe you. I don't want to cry — I'm so angry, but I don't want to cry. And, okay it's my fault! Great. Mom is going to say I told you so. Fine. She was right but there's no excuse. There are just no excuses. And I know it's because of the baby.*

Journal

When we move to Father's Day discussions, I plan to step out on a limb and challenge these youngsters to take the initiative and reach out. We've talked all year but I think it's time for action. The school year is winding down, but we've not really made the progress I had expected we'd make by this time. These kids, especially Jason, need some contact with their fathers. Or at least they need to try. I'm going to ask them to create cards, even download some off the Internet. I'd like them to write letters and tell their fathers how they're feeling. I think by now they're ready. — A.D.M.

CHAPTER SIX

Preparing for Father's Day

On a warm Friday evening in the first week of June, Drew opened the Let's Talk discussion by congratulating Giselle on her graduation.

"Everybody, let's give it up for our girl, Giselle! A high school graduate! Soon to be a college student!"

The group cheered, clapped, and some even stood up.

"I enjoyed the graduation and was honored you invited me. I felt like my own daughter was graduating."

"My father didn't come to my graduation," Giselle lamented in the war room.

"Okay, well how do you feel about it?" asked Drew.

"I don't know. Okay, I guess. I mean, I'm mad but I'm better about it now. Besides, my mom is the one who's been there. Why should he be able to just show up and get all the glory as if he did anything?"

"Wait a minute. Is this the same Giselle who said my dad has tried to be there and has done some things right? Why are you all of a sudden so hard on him? Do you think if he had come he'd be trying to get all the glory or would it be that he was just trying to share in one of your joys?"

"What difference does it make? He wasn't there."

"And when did you invite him?"

"Two weeks before graduation. My sister thinks I didn't give him enough of a chance," she said, looking at Jason for support.

"Well, did you? I mean, is two weeks really enough time?"

"But he already knew before I called him. He knew I was graduating and, just once, I wanted to see if he was going to take the lead on something important in my life. He could have called my mom. He could have called me. He could have called the school. He could have remembered. There is just no excuse. I'm sorry."

Drew wanted more. "So what if you had called in plenty of time. Then what?"

Giselle slowly lifted her head and wiped her tears. "I think I didn't call because I was afraid that if I had called with plenty of time and he still hadn't come, then that would have been it. It would have meant he really doesn't care or even love me, and I couldn't take that. This way, I had a part to play, some control even, over his not coming. Besides, if he had really wanted to come, then I had the power to deny him the way he has denied me all these many years."

"Okay," said Drew, "so you're the one with the power now. And how does that make you feel?"

"Pretty good," Giselle said, laughing and looking around the room.

Everyone stared at her, but no one spoke.

"You know what, when I get married, they're *both* going to walk me down the aisle. My mom's the one who really has to give me away. I belong to her. I'm not really his to give away, because he has made it clear he doesn't want me," Giselle was on a roll now.

"Yes, you are his and yes, he does want you," Drew commented.

"How can you say that? You don't know anything about this. You don't know how I've been made to feel all these years. I've defended him and held out and tried to understand but he hasn't been there when I needed him. And now I'm grown and it's too late. This graduation was his last chance and he missed it. It's over," she stood up and headed for the kitchen.

"Wait, don't slam him and then leave. Stay and listen."

Giselle stopped in the doorway.

"It's never too late while you both are still alive. Never give up on that relationship. That's what relationships are about. You've shared good memories with us, and so I know that you know that he cares. I mean, have you let him know how you feel?"

He paused to look the room over, connect with the eyes of all his attendees. "That's the question I've been asking all of you all year. Are you all that afraid of your fathers? Don't you realize that's what communication is all about? There can be no relationships without communication. People must talk or write or email — something! Giselle, you're a writer — write him a letter. Dion can talk, so pick up that phone. Do something. Send a postcard, reach out somehow. Leave a sign, drop a line or a note saying — hey, I haven't heard from you, hey would love to see you — anything! You guys are hurting, but you're not giving your fathers a chance. I'm not saying they won't fail you. They will; sometimes they will. I'm not saying it won't hurt. But some of you guys won't even give them a chance to do that. What's wrong with YOU being the one to reach out? Even if you have to do it more than once or twice or even more than that. I just wish you knew what I knew. I'm trying so hard to spare you."

"Spare us?" asked Ray.

"Just trust me. The window of opportunity doesn't stay open forever," he said as he pulled out a cart overflowing with paper, scissors, markers, and other artsy tools. Giselle sat back down but didn't say anything more.

"Hey guys, I thought we'd use this night to make Father's Day cards and write letters to your parents. It's up to you. We also have some pretty cool gift packs you can choose from to go along with those cards and letters. The gift packs have a nice club brochure listing the events for the rest of the year, including individualized sports schedules, team and individual photos, two tickets to Kings Dominion, two movie passes, and coupons for two free pizzas. Together with your letters or cards, I think this will be really nice for Father's Day. We also have stationery, stamps, boxes, card-making kits, and you can use the computers if you want. After you finish writing, you can read your cards to the rest of us. You can also get help with your poetry for inside of the card if you need it."

"Poetry?" asked Ray.

"Oh, come on now, you guys write rap songs all the time. Rap ain't rap unless the lyrics are rhyming, so don't go all blank on me now. So, like I said, it'd be nice if the card could rhyme. You know. It doesn't have to but I know you've got it in you."

"If you say so," mumbled Ray.

Drew caught Ray's indifference but ignored it.

The kids went to work. The art was the easy part. At a loss for words, Jason looked up and noticed Dominick Turner just sitting there — no paper, no marker, no card kit. Drew noticed him too.

"What's up, man?" asked Drew.

"I don't know my father and I feel nothing."

"Well, you don't have to write only mushy stuff, man. You can write a letter telling him what's going on inside. You can talk to him. Is there anything you want to know, to ask him?"

"Fine," he flipped his chair around and sat down again. "I'd want to ask him, 'why weren't you here? Why'd you name me after you if you weren't going to stick around?'"

"Slow down," said Drew who had picked up a pen.

"I want to punch him in the face. I'm angry."

Drew wrote furiously.

"Tell him how you feel, talk to me as if I were him."

"You want to know how I feel? My life ended the day my father was born. I feel dead!" said Dominick.

"Talk to ME!" said Drew. "I'm your father today."

Jason dropped his marker and turned around. The creative buzz in the room ceased.

"Okay, then, I died when YOU were born. You haven't been there and I'm now supposed to just tell you how I feel. How do you think I feel? Why don't YOU tell ME how I feel! You left me. I want to ask my mother why, if you knew you couldn't handle the stress of raising me, why did you have me? Why should I take the first step? It's not my job. It's yours! I won't open myself up for more rejection. My defenses stay high. Even if I saw you on the street, like last time. I wasn't crushed. But inside, it hurt. You hurt me. But I had to suck it up, not let you see what I was feeling. My biggest fear is opening up to you just to be rejected again. I know I told you that you have nothing I want. I remember telling you that you're not my father, that you're nothing to me. Well, the truth is that I'm filled with anger and fear."

Drew kept writing.

"I was numb after you left. I was so angry and didn't know why. I was just a little boy. I hated you. I cried. I broke toys, dishes, anything I could put my hands on. Later I medicated myself with whatever worked. You were supposed to teach me about manhood, how to survive, what to look for in life, how to look, how to think, how to make it in this world. It's funny, I know that you had a time of it yourself. Maybe you just didn't know this stuff and had nothing to teach, but you should have tried — my life and my future depended on it.

"What you did show me is that when the going gets rough, leave, quit, throw in the towel. Do I blame all my failures and problems on you? No, but you're at the root. You were right there at the starting block." Dominick stopped when he couldn't hold back the tears. He turned his back to everyone and wiped them with his tee shirt, then he walked out of the room.

At the next table, Ray's letter read, "*Dear Dad, I sure wish we could more spend time together. I love you. I always really miss you when we're not together. Can you call me more? It really is hard to try and call you. I don't know how to dial all those calling card numbers. It's hard for me. I don't have your cell phone number. I wish there was something we could do.*"

"Wanna hear my letter?" asked Dion.

"Absolutely," said Drew. "Everybody, listen up. Dion's kicking this thing off right. Go ahead, Son."

"If I had to complete the sentence that begins 'dear dad,' I would say, 'I love you, Daddy, and I really wish we could be together. Dad, we used to do a lot of things together. We'd go to the mall and to the movies. We used to go shopping and hang out together. It was really cool. We used to talk about loads of things. So Dad, I hope I see you again soon so we can hang out again. I know you're busy, but I understand.'"

"Excellent! said Drew. "How many times DID you see your dad last year? This question is for everyone."

"Uh, I can't remember, but maybe three times," said Dion.

"We did all those things, I think, the week I was with him in the summer."

Drew turned toward Jason and asked, "Anyone else?"

"About once every three to four months for like, half a day, no more than two days," answered Jason.

"Kali?" said Drew.

"Did I even see him last year? Not really, like maybe once."

"Okay, here's a tough one — how many times is enough? Every day? Once a month? What would work for you? And after you've thought about it, then tell me if you've ever told your dad, 'I'd like to see you once a month or every day or I'd like to just talk to you once a month' or whatever the case."

"I think if he just called even when he can't come, I'd be okay. You know, just to hear that he's there and that he's thinking about me," said Dion.

"Shoot, man, I don't know. Before my parents split, you know, he was there every day and he knew what was going on in my life. It was like he was all interested and stuff, like in my basketball and school work. He made me do my homework. Of course, I didn't like it then, but at least my grades were pretty good because he made me do the work. He made me stay in to study. He took me to the doctor when I was sick or got hurt from sports. It was pretty cool to have my dad do all that. It was like he cared, you know, loved me or something. I don't know. But now, shoot, it's like all that just stopped. My mom ain't never home, so it's just me for the most part. I don't know what I'm supposed to do other than just watch TV all the time and play basketball. That's all I do, at least that's all I did till I started coming here all the time," said Jason.

"Yeah, man, where you been lately?" asked Dion.

"Huh? You can't even imagine. I've just been buggin' out over everything. Just buggin'. I've been trying to see my dad and my mom's been trippin'. It's like she's lost her mind. She won't let me see my dad. But I need to see him every now and then. I need to talk to him and have him be interested in the things in my life. I just don't know what to do."

"I'm feeling you, man," said Ray. "I just want to know that he's thinking about me, that he hasn't forgotten about me, that I'm important or something. I get so mad because he won't come. I think he might be embarrassed or something like that."

"When my dad doesn't call or come, I can't believe it when he says he loves me because I've heard that love is an action verb. When we lose too much time, it's kinda hard," said Kalia.

"Yeah, my dad lives far away now and now that he has a new family, it feels like he thinks he can just throw us away now," said Giselle.

"This is heavy, y'all. I see everyone's perspective. Maybe they *are* embarrassed after not calling for so long. And each day that passes makes it all that much harder for them to call. It doesn't mean they don't want to. Maybe they don't know what to say if they did call. Maybe they're paralyzed. Maybe they believe they've lost you and there's nothing they can do about it, that nothing can restore what's already lost, that nothing can make you respect them again. Maybe they believe you don't love *them*. Maybe they believe you don't *need* them. Has any one of you actually told your father, 'I really love you. I really need you. I can't face this life without your wisdom. I won't know the road to take without your guidance. Let's get together regularly. Can I still be a big part of your life? What can I do to make that happen?'" Drew probed.

No one responded.

Drew continued, "Something has to change this situation, and I firmly believe that you, the children, the sons and daughters, have a part to play.

"If you want once a week, work toward that. If you think

once a month is good, ask them, ask your moms. You know how to beg your folks for everything else you want. Now's the time to realize what you need and go after it. Anyone else want to join in? Do you miss your fathers?" Drew asked.

To everyone's surprise, Ray spoke up. "I do. I miss my father. I had to teach myself how to fight, how to protect myself, about life in general, and what it's like to be a man. I'm going through puberty alone. I have to be responsible and protect my mother. And there's no point in starting up again if he's just going to drop us again. That's worse than never trying at all. Little by little would work because I can't handle big promises he can't keep. I know I make it hard for him, but I want to see if he'll keep trying. That let's me know that I'm worth fighting for. I need him to tell me I'm worth it, show me I'm worth it, just be there. I'm not going to open up for a while, but I need him to hang in there. I need to know and see that he really means it this time. The only proof of that would be if I remain closed up and in spite of it, he sticks around and keeps trying."

The room was silent.

"I think dads are good," said Dion. "I like the movie *Big Daddy* because of all the boy stuff they do together. You need a dad to have someone who cares about important stuff like school and football. It's important to have someone to teach you things — like how to shoot a three-pointer. My dad taught me how to shoot three-pointers."

"Well, my dad taught me how to fish. He taught me and my brother how to play pool. There are some things moms can't teach," said R.J., joining in for the first time. "Dads know boy things. He talks to me about things I don't want to talk with Mom about. My dad is the greatest. He even does my baby sister's hair. He takes us camping and fishing. He comes to school to meet my teachers and he cooks. He's so cool."

"Yeah, that's because you live with him and not your mom. My only problem is not seeing my dad often enough. So when I do finally get to see him, I have to get to know him all over again — almost like I'm meeting him for the first time. We never really pick up where we left off," said Tony.

"Well my dad coaches my football team and takes us to swimming lessons. He does everything a dad and a mom are supposed to do," said R.J.

"Well, my mom is like that. She does everything. She takes me to my scout activities and takes me everywhere. She even plays basketball and baseball with me. She's cool, at least most of the time," said Tony. "But I have two moms. But she's not really my mom. She's my stepmom. She's far, far, far from being my mom."

"But Tony, stepmoms can't replace moms," said Dion. "No one can ever replace your mom. So, don't even worry about that."

"But still, it's just weird when I go there to see him, and I come back here to see my mom, then go there, come here, go there … it's crazy!" explained Tony.

"Tell me about it," said Giselle.

"Listen up, guys, I want you to try and make contact with your dads for Father's Day. Invite them; let them know you want to see them. Tell them you have presents. If they can't come, be sure to send them. Ask for their addresses. You guys should have your father's address and phone number. Buy a present if you already planned to do so. And let me say this, it may not turn out the way you had planned, but you will have tried. You have everything to gain and just a little hurt to risk. Trust me, I know what I'm talking about."

AFTER THE FATHER'S DAY session, Jason decided to try and reach his father one more time. His mother advised against it. She even told Jason she was going to write a letter to the center's board of directors complaining about Drew's constant interference in the personal lives of the children. Jason left a message on his father's voice mail, and two days later, Vicky delivered the glad tidings that his father had called while Jason was at the center. The message said he would come by for Jason sometime – either Friday night or Saturday morning. Jason was willing to cancel all his plans with friends to spend time with his father. He had promised to join Drew, Ray, Dion, and Kalia at Tony's baseball game but pulled out for the chance to be with his father. On Friday night, Jason's father was a no-show. He didn't come Saturday morning either. Jason left messages and sat around the house all day. That night, when Vicky returned home from shopping, the rap music told her that Jason was in a self-imposed lockdown in his bedroom.

"Jason!" she yelled. "Turn that stuff down!" *What is wrong with that boy?* No sooner than scolding him did she remember that his father hadn't come the night before.

Vicky went downstairs to the kitchen, grabbed the phone, and called her friend Sharon. "I'm really scared about Jason. He said to me, 'Mom, I've been down for so long, I don't know if I can get back up.' His grades are falling in every subject and he has no motivation at all. But my son is not stupid. Can you tell me why a child would not turn in schoolwork that he's already completed? He's doing his work. Then he puts it in his backpack, but when the teacher asks for it, Jason doesn't turn it in. I asked him why and he simply said, 'I don't know.' You explain that to me. I even took him for psychological testing. Now they say he has mild A.D.D. He just can't find a way to do the things he needs to in order to succeed or to keep from falling as far as he has. Thank God he's not on drugs, but it's as if he's forcing himself to face this train head on."

"Are you sure he's not on drugs?" asked Sharon.

"I'm pretty sure, but he's really in a bad way and I don't know what to do about it."

"I don't know what to say. I'll keep praying for him. Maybe we can find someone to talk to him. When was the last time he saw his father? Is there anyone else who can talk to him?"

"Well, it's been a while since he's seen his father, and frankly, until that man pays, I'm not letting him see Jason," she said vehemently.

"Are you sure that's a good idea?"

"I know what I'm doing. It's just too bad there's no one else to help him. I've already talked to all the would-be father figures in my son's life and asked them to talk to Jason. They all ask, 'What's wrong, Jason? Is it your dad?' Then they'd say, 'Maybe you and I can hang out from time to time.' And they would — from time to time. One after the other would call to check on Jason. They might even follow up with an outing, a guy thing. Jason would have a little fun. They would talk about things in general. Mostly, they'd go to the movies or the video hangout. But those men go home to their real families and their real obligations. So that's nothing Jason can really count on because no one is really obligated to him.

"The time they spend with Jason usually tapers off after a few weeks. Jason is their charitable work and he's always been aware of that. Jason doesn't need a man here and there, to come around once in a while, and give a lesson or two in life. Jason needs someone who is tied and bound to him. He needs a connection to someone in it for the long haul. None of the father figures, counselors, psychologists, and even ministers can put Jason back together again. It seems like his issues are too deeply rooted to get any kind of healing from a short-term investment. Worst of all, he knows that. He's not stupid."

"Well, I like Drew. He seems committed. Maybe he can help — spend some time with Jason. It looks like he'd be in it for the long haul," said Sharon.

"Not if I can help it!" screamed Vicky. "Surely you don't believe the hype. He's just using them to get ahead. I think they're just the case studies or the clinical portion of his school studies. He doesn't care about these kids. I think he's causing more harm than good."

"How could you think that?" asked Sharon.

"Ever since he joined the club, Jason can't stop talking about his father. Jason can't stop trying to see his father. Jason can't stop calling his father."

"Vicky, you assume that out of sight means out of mind and that if no one mentions his name or utters the word father that Jason isn't missing his dad. Is that what you think?"

"Pretty much," Vicky answered smugly.

"Well, I think you're wrong. If you think basketball and all those after school enrichment programs are going to keep that boy from thinking about his father, you are wrong," said Sharon.

"All this talk is doing is leaving him crushed and broken-hearted every day. He can't think or concentrate on anything else. But don't worry about it. I'm going to put a stop to this mess," hissed Vicky.

"Oh Lord, what you trying to do, girl?"

"Like I said, put a stop to this."

At 7:05 A.M. Monday morning Vicky called up the steps for Jason. It was time to take him to the school bus, but he didn't answer. Vicky had prepared his favorite breakfast but he hadn't come down to eat.

Instead of yelling again, Vicky walked up to his room and noticed the sound of the shower running. *Oh, he's okay. He's just running late.* Vicky decided her son was entitled to be a tad bit late for school. She was grateful that he was up and around — that was a step up from Sunday. Vicky knocked on the bathroom door.

"Jason, are you all right? You okay?"

Vicky heard the sound of sobs. She slowly opened the door and saw her sixteen-year-old boy in his school clothes on the floor of the shower. His hands were crossed and folded over his legs. He was crouched, rocking himself.

"My father doesn't want me. He doesn't love me. Nothing else matters."

"Jason!"

"Mom, go, leave me alone, please."

"Jason!"

"Please, Mom, please!"

Stunned and terrified, Vicky closed the door. She slid down the door to the floor, sobbing, and she began to pray. After a while, Jason stopped crying. He looked up and noticed the water pouring on his head. The soothing droplets of water felt like a soft blanket, covering every inch of his being. Jason sensed he was not alone. He felt something he had never felt before. A still small voice suddenly captivated his attention and whispered, "I'm your Father and I love you. I'll never leave you nor forsake you. I have heard your cry and I've bottled your tears."

"God, are you there? God?"

Jason's disfigured countenance began to return to normal. He began to sense the presence of a force greater than the rejection and anger that had put him in this pit in the first place. His earthly father had been a no-show, but his heavenly Father showed up that Monday morning before Father's Day.

FRIDAY, THE SEVENTH OF JUNE, nine days before Father's Day, the schools began incorporating Father's Day themes into their lessons. Tony's fifth grade teacher, Mrs. Gillespie, asked the class, "What does your father do for a living?"

"My daddy's a bus driver!"

"My daddy works for the Navy!"

"My daddy wears a suit and drives to a big building every day!"

"My dad works at the Pentagon."

Many students, including Tony, sat quiet and still. As the other kids in his class proudly announced their father's occupations, Tony drifted inward to solve his dilemma — what to say when the teacher called on him.

She's almost at my row! Oh man! What am I going to say? Do I even know what he does? He told me once but I don't remember. Dang it, Mommy. Why didn't you tell me what he does for a living? You know they ask this in school before Father's Day. You know all of this. Oh God! I know I'm not supposed to tell a lie, but I don't want to say I don't know. Oh God! Please don't let me cry. That'll be the worst of all! Uh oh, she's on Nathan, then Gabriella, then me! Why doesn't anybody say they don't know? I KNOW Marcus and Mario don't have a daddy at home. So how come they had an answer? Maybe their daddy told them and they actually remembered. COME ON, TONY — THINK! Try and remember what ...

"Tony, it's your turn. What does your father do for a living?"

"Um, I don't really remember exactly, yeah — I don't exactly remember but I think he's a teacher or something," said Tony with minimal confidence. *Whew*, sighed Tony, believing he had dodged a big one.

From the back of the classroom Marcus taunted, "How can you not remember what your dad does for a living and then all of a sudden remember?"

"You're so stupid. You think you know everything. Well, you don't know anything, just that you're stupid! Not everybody lives with their father, dummy. So I don't remember. Big deal. Where's your daddy, huh?"

Mrs. Gillespie abruptly interrupted, "Okay, okay, there's no need to insult each other or question each other's experiences. We all have different experiences."

Tony listened intently, desperate for redemption.

"Class, some families have a mommy and a daddy, a sister and a brother, and … "

Tony immediately tuned out. He didn't want to be reminded of his second-class status. He knew that when Mrs. Gillespie began to describe the various family structures, she began with the first class family — mommy, daddy, sister, brother, and dog. Everything else was the consolation prize. As she spoke, Tony rewrote the script in his mind. He rewound the day's events and imagined other children admitting they did not have a father around.

"So class, are there any questions? Tony, is there anything else you want to add to this discussion?"

"No," replied Tony as he continued his doodling, avoiding eye contact with anyone.

When Tony's mom Linda arrived at the day care at day's end to pick Tony up, she was immediately flagged by Mrs. Campbell, the day care director. "I don't know what's bothering him, but he was a little disrespectful today. In fact, he's been full of himself all week, agitated and on edge. I put him in time out yesterday. I forgot to tell you, but I thought you should know."

Five days before Father's Day, Mrs. Gillespie's class began its Father's Day gift and card-making workshop. Tony's project momentum ground to a halt when she directed the class to begin by addressing the envelopes. Tony was not really concerned about what to make or what the card should say. Tony was worried his dad would never see his gift.

Tony walked to the front of the room and said quietly to Mrs. Gillespie, "I don't know how to mail this to my dad or how to take it to him. I don't have his address. I don't know if my mom has it either. And sometimes she's mad at him and won't let me go to see him. I don't know if he's coming for Father's Day or if I'll see him to give him this present. Do you have his address?"

Mrs. Gillespie, who had been writing on the blackboard, sat down to listen. "Hmmm," she said, "um, I'm sure your mom has it and, uh, you just go ahead and make the gift and card and I'll send a note home. Yes, I'll send a note home and I'm sure your mom will help you get it to him, okay? Don't worry, alright?"

She pulled a sheet from her note pad, wrote a brief note, folded it, and handed it to Tony. "Now put this in your backpack and get back to work. It'll all work out," she said gently, turning him around and nudging him in the direction of his seat.

After school that day, Tony's mother picked him up and took him shopping. Even though he was making a gift in class, Tony had been pleading with her to take him shopping. They started off in the drugstore where Tony began to search for cards. Tony asked, "Mom, do you have Daddy's address?"

She didn't answer.

He grabbed a card.

Far back as I remember, you have always been right there,
Every dream, hope and truth you most willingly did share.
With every word and every deed,
and with your faith you sowed a seed
of joy in me that grows to let me know you truly care.
HAPPY FATHER'S DAY!

The poem filled the right inside portion of the card. On the outside was a sailboat and the words, "To My Dad, You're the Best."

"That's a nice one, Tony."

"No, Mom, I just want to look at some other ones."

"I found it," said Tony.

HAPPY FATHER'S DAY
May this day be all
You hope it to be.

"Mom, this is it," Tony said, smiling with a sense of satisfaction.

"Tony, it doesn't even say daddy or father or dad, something that recognizes who he is. Here, this one says, 'To My Father,' she said, handing him a card.

Tony sighed, and after looking at her pick, a card with a father and son on the front, he answered, "Mom, I want the one *I* picked."

As they walked to the register, Tony noticed people smiling as they read the cards. They were obviously trying to find the best and the sweetest. Tony's idea was different. He sifted through the maze of tender messages and deep expressions to find the one card that just barely satisfied the minimal and mechanical requirements for a Father's Day greeting. He succeeded.

In the men's department of J.C. Penney's, Linda strolled through the racks of summer shirts and shorts and picked out a prospect.

"Here's a nice shirt."

"I don't like the color," said Tony, looking past the shirt to the others on the rack.

"Here are some matching shorts. They look good together, don't you think?"

"I don't like it," said Tony, wandering toward a display of electronic items.

"One minute you're all gung ho about this and now it's as if you've cooled off. What is up with you?" she said.

Tony didn't answer. Strolling through the store aisles, he

noticed a sun-powered radio on the counter. The packaging featured a family at the beach. Tony was glued to the picture.

"This is it," he said.

Noticing how Tony stared at that beach picture, Linda smiled and asked, "Is that you with your dad in the picture?"

"No, Mom," he said, as if she should've known the answer. "We've never been to the beach together." He grabbed the box to stand behind the next person in line at the register.

"Sorry. Anyway, it's a nice gift," she commented.

As Tony and his mom climbed into the car, Tony asked, "Mom, do you think he'll come on Father's Day so I can give him the gift? Should we call him again? Do you think he'll call? It's been a really long time."

It had been six months since Tony had seen his dad who lived about an hour away. His dad picked Tony up after school and treated him to dinner for his birthday, and they had spent a couple of days together at Christmas. Linda always had the quick answer, right or wrong. She was accustomed to making all the decisions concerning Tony — and each day presented new decisions. Go to the doctor or ride the fever out? Go for stitches or bandage it up? Fight over a grade or let it go? Pressed for time between work, helping him with homework, and taking him to practice, Linda routinely made quick unilateral decisions. But not this time. This time she said, "Just call him and tell him how you feel."

At home she said it again. "Just call him and tell him how you feel."

"Yeah, that would really work — 'hey dad, you need to do better.' 'Hey buddy, how 'bout a visit or a call now and then.' I don't think so," he said sarcastically.

"Tony, I don't have all the answers. I wish I did. But you have to try. I don't know. Just try. Do you want me to dial the number — tell him how you feel and tell him what you want?"

Linda was silently praying that her child wasn't being set up for a big letdown.

Tony reluctantly took the phone.

What am I doing? Linda suddenly thought. *Why should HE have to call his own father? Why should a child have to initiate contact and be the one to reach out and touch? It seems so unfair.* But she knew something had to be done.

"Okay, Mom," he said quietly.

She turned off the kettle, made her tea, and disappeared upstairs.

"Hi, Daddy, this is Tony ... I'm fine ...Yes ...Yes ... I'm in fifth grade ...Yes, we get it in two weeks but I already know I have five *A*s and the rest *B*s ... uh huh ... Everyone is fine ... Daddy when am I coming to your house? It's been a really long time ... okay, I'll ask her. Daddy, my church is having something special for Father's Day. Can you come? Uh huh ... yes ... okay ... I'll ask her ... okay, bye. I love you too, bye."

When Tony hung the phone up, Linda came back downstairs.

"So, what did he say? Are you going to see your father? How do you feel?"

"Fine. He said he might come for Father's Day and that he would call you about me maybe staying an extra day. We don't have anything going on in school that week because it's the last week of school, so it's okay, Mom."

She answered, "Yes, it's okay."

Linda expected Tony's dad to be a no-show. She daydreamed about taking Tony to Florida or the Bahamas to make up for it. She actually found a package deal to the Bahamas and called a travel agency for more information. Naturally, the total price was more than the rate advertised in the ad.

Linda called Sharon to commiserate after Tony made plans to see his dad.

"Girl, now you knew the chances of boarding a jet with these kids for the long Father's Day weekend on such short notice was next to nil," said Sharon, moving Linda to laugh along with her.

"I know, but I just want to believe I have the power to carry out the Hail Mary rescue mission, if necessary. I just don't want Tony sitting around waiting all day or thinking about his father. He's watching everyone else go places or do things on Father's Day. He's had to deal with it in school and hear about Father's Day all week and all weekend. I'd rather be far away if he's going to be a no-show. He's had ten fatherless Father's Days. Since I can't magically produce him, I'd rather just make the day go away."

"Oh, I am SO there. Well, we can do something together if their dads don't show. We can take them somewhere."

The women began to work on Operation Father's Day: Plan B.

KALIA HAD DECIDED THIS Father's Day would be different. Her only connection to her father was through her grandmother. Kalia treasured and prized her grandmother's phone number because it was her only real tie to him. According to her mother Joanne, this allowed her father to keep her at bay, keep her mother at bay, and of course, keep child support enforcement at bay. But Kalia decided to call her Grandma Lois anyway.

"Hi, baby, how's grandma's girl?" as if they saw each other regularly.

"Hi, Grandma. How are you doing? How's your knee?"

"Oh well, you know 'ole Arthur is wearing on my knee but no sense in complaining 'cause it don't help none, now does it? And if it did, I'd be the first in line."

Kalia thought, *why do all old people call arthritis* Arthur? She stared at a wallet-sized picture, her only picture of her with her father as she listened to her grandmother's small talk.

"So, is my daddy there?" probed Kalia.

After a pause, Lois answered, "Well baby, you know, I haven't seen him lately. He called the other day. I think he has been out of town for a while — I did tell him the last time you called. He said he was going to call you."

Kalia was embarrassed to admit that he had not called her but merely answered by asking, "Grandma, do you have his pager number? It's really important that I reach him."

"Is everything all right? Are you okay?" asked Lois. "I'll try to find it, but I'll have to call you back. Honey, your grandmother is lying down trying to rest this old knee. You wouldn't want me to put too much pressure on it, would you?"

"No, Grandma." Kalia's heart said something else. *Why is she making this so hard? Why should I have to beg my own grandmother to help me reach my dad? She has obviously taken his side. If anything, she should make him come see me — she is his mother, right? Why won't she help me? I thought that even when parents don't always do right, at least grandparents step in. A lot of my friends even live with their grandmothers. Their grandmothers take better care of them than their own parents.*

"Grandma, I have to write a paper for my social studies class on what our fathers do for a living and then do research on how to enter that profession. That's why I need to speak with him. Today is Monday, but the assignment is due Friday. I don't even remember what my daddy does for a living or where he works," she pressed.

"What did granddaddy do for a living?" she asked, luring her grandmother to more freely engage in the discussion. She knew her grandmother couldn't resist the bait to boast about her deceased husband.

"Oh, your grandpa was a carpenter. Could fix and build any-thing he put his hands on and your daddy's the same way. He learned from his dad all the same things. His company is called Kings of Carpentry, and it's over on Georgia Avenue. I'm not sure exactly where, though. And one more thing … " said Lois as she put the phone down, shook her head, and wiped her slowing forming tears.

Lois decided to stop enabling her son's irresponsibility. She had found her greatest worth in her maternal role and she was no longer going to let her son or anyone else discredit her successes.

"Just one more thing … I think this will help you, baby. Take down this number … "

Kalia wrote that number on the back of the picture she still held in her hand and in three other places around the apartment she shared with her mother and sister. It had all culminated in this one call. It was as if all was forgiven. All the pain and all the anger momentarily dissipated. It just didn't matter that he had not given her that phone number himself and that she had to extract it through her grandmother's clenched teeth. Neither did it mat-ter that he had clearly instructed his mother not to give that number away. The more than 365 days of no contact just didn't matter. Her unending love for her father was all-forgiving and unconditional.

"Hello, sorry I missed your call. Leave a message and I will call you back, you can count on it. Beep."

Kalia's eyes grew wide as the sound of her father's unmis-takable voice. She was stunned, disappointed, yet almost relieved all at once. She had to think quickly, but she froze and said noth-ing at all. Beep.

"Oh, man! I blew it."

Kalia called back. "Daddy, it's me, Kalia. How ya doin'? Um, uh, can you call me? My number is 301-555-1244. Can you come to my church on Sunday? It's Father's Day and I have a present for you but I don't have your address to send it to you. The address to the church is 21212 Greathouse Lane in Rockville. Plus, there's a special Father's Day service. Please call me and please, please come. I have a surprise for you. Bye, I love you." Beep.

She began to wait.

For the next six days, Kalia waited with anticipation. She had taken all her allowance and bought a delicate heart-shaped crystal picture frame to hold her ninth grade picture. This was her first high school picture. Instead of the normal strawberry melon lip gloss she was allowed to wear, her lips were painted "unforgettable red" with her mother's lipstick, which was usually forbidden to Kalia. She'd worn eyeliner and mascara, and her hair was swept off her face and shoulders and held in place atop her head by a brown barrette. A part of Kalia thought that perhaps her father didn't want to deal with a small child. She believed that was why he had been an absentee father. When Kalia was only five years old, she heard her father say, "Children are a hassle and just get in the way." Kalia' mother was pregnant with her younger sister at the time. *But I'm in high school now. I'm not a kid anymore. I'm grown up, so there's nothing to stop him from being my father now.*

Her father did not call on Tuesday or Wednesday, but someone did call on Thursday although the caller didn't leave a message. Kalia knew someone had called because the caller ID displayed a call from "unavailable." The time of the call registered about 5:30 P.M. Kalia was normally home from school at that time and her mother was still at work. Since the call came in at that time, Kalia figured it must have been for her. Since her father didn't call on Friday or Saturday, she concluded that the Thursday call was probably her father. She wouldn't allow herself to consider the alternative — that he didn't call at all and was not coming.

She used the situation as an excuse to call Jason. She left a voicemail message. "Jason, it's Kalia. I think my dad called me back. I think he's coming to church on Sunday. Is yours coming? Anyway, call me when you get a chance. Also, are you going to Orlando's party Saturday night? I heard everybody's going to be there. I need a ride, so if you're going, maybe you can borrow your mom's car and come get me. Call me. Oh, and uh, I'm supposed to remind the church youth that we're supposed to do a tribute to fathers during the Sunday school brunch and to tell you to bring your father. Peace out."

Journal

The newspaper circulars are filled with ideas for ways to spend money. Merchants are using TV ads to prod and bait consumers to remember their fathers by purchasing gifts from their establishments. From fishing rods to lawnmowers to ties to chainsaws to Hawaiian shirts, everything is on sale so that moms, oops — uh, kids, yeah kids can show those deserving dads how much they are appreciated. Even the schools were abuzz with Father's Day discussions and gift-making workshops for the many deserving fathers all around us. And the fatherless? Well, they were not sure just what to do. There is no Father's Day for Dummies out there. Neither is there a "Father's Day for children of divorce," or a "Father's Day for children of single mothers." Some assembly is definitely required.

But what if they reach out to their fathers and their fathers don't respond, don't come to church, or don't even call back? Will they feel that their efforts have backfired and will it jeopardize the trust I've developed with them? I know my presence at their games, plays, and other events has helped somewhat, but I know I'm no substitute for their fathers. —A.D.M.

CHAPTER SEVEN

Father's Day

"Mom, what time did he say he'd be here?" Jason asked his mother while rummaging in his drawer for ties.

Vicky had lost count of how many times he had asked that question that morning.

In bed the night before, Jason had imagined the scene at church. He pictured himself sitting in the pew. The service had already begun. Jason glanced upward just in time to see a well-dressed man politely acknowledge an usher. As the usher led him to his row, the mystery man anxiously glanced across the room. He lifted his head to peer above the people, just to find his son Jason. Then their eyes met or, perhaps, he noticed Jason first. He dreamed it over and over. Every time their eyes connected, his dad's face glowed with love and sheer joy at seeing his son ... then Jason fell off to sleep.

"Mom, what time did you say he'd be there? What exactly did

he tell you? No, what were his words? I just want to know what time I should begin to look for him, that's all."

"Remember now, he said he *might* come if he can get off work. He also said if he didn't make it, he'd be sure to make it up to you. So please, honey, don't get yourself worked up over this."

Moments later, Jason asked, "Mom, do you think he's coming? What should we do if he doesn't come? Have you made any plans?" They hadn't even left the house for church before Jason began to doubt and contemplate Plan B. Nevertheless, Jason was now acquainted with a different type of hope. This hope had taken root during that unforgettable shower and drew Jason to church on Father's Day.

WHEN JASON AND HIS MOM pulled up to the church, Jason noticed Tony lingering by the playground.

"What's up, Tony? Why ya just standing there?"

Before he could answer, Vicky added, "Does your mom know you're outside in the parking lot? Isn't church about to start?"

"It's okay, she knows I'm waiting for my dad. He's supposed to be here by now."

"Alright, man," said Jason. His cynical expression suggested that he knew the end of this drama before it began. Jason had been there so many times. He turned to glance at Tony once more. His own anger wanted to blurt out, "HE'S NOT COMING, TONY! JUST FORGET ABOUT IT!" But he also didn't want to crush the little guy's spirit. *Maybe he'll deflate little by little, like a slow leak*, Jason thought. *That's gotta be better than the big blow.*

Tony waited and watched others go by him as they entered the building. He noticed Michael, his Sunday school classmate, climb from his parents' car, his mother and father in tow. Tony waited in the parking lot 'til the last possible moment. Friday night, his father had assured Tony he'd be there for church. At least, that's how Tony heard it. In fact, Tony's dad had promised he'd come Friday, then changed the ETA to Saturday morning, then called back to say he would be there for church. Tony was determined not to show his hand, so he continued to wait.

As he did so, Tony asked God the question of the day — *why does that kid get to have his daddy and I don't? What did I do to deserve to be punished like this? Okay,* thought Tony, *if it's not my fault, why do I have to pay the price for my mother and father's mistakes? Is that fair, God? Is that fair?* Tony was jolted from his prayers by an approaching automobile. It was a black Ford XLT just like his dad's. *My prayer's been answered!* Then he realized that the driver was not his father.

Tony heard the soulful stirring of the opening hymn and decided to go in. He headed straight for his safe haven — the back row. He found his crew already seated — Kalia, Ray, Dion, Jason, and a few kids whose dads and moms were seated rows ahead.

Out of the corner of his eye, Tony noticed Jason glancing in his general direction. Jason was trying to steal a full glance at Tony to learn how the story was progressing. Jason knew from his own experience not to ask. Besides, Jason could see that Tony's dad didn't come in with him. But he kept looking Tony's way because he wanted to see the pain. He could relate. He was not alone. Although Tony didn't want anyone to detect his pain, he nonetheless looked in Jason's direction. He needed comfort from somewhere, although he didn't appear to.

Jason noticed how different things were that day. On any other Sunday, they were all full of energy, usually running around in the parking lot until told to come inside. Then they'd line up in the back in their own little world — giggling, teasing, passing notes, and drawing pictures. Nothing distracted them from catching up on a week's worth of fun.

Today was different. There was no parking lot football. Instead their hands were buried deep in their pockets. They were reminded that before man and in their hearts they were fatherless. Tony sat in the pew and thought, *I bet he makes it to work everyday. I bet he makes it to see his girlfriend or whoever is in his life. I bet he manages to arrive at the movies on time when he wants to see a movie. Funny, he just can't seem to get to me. Why is that? God, won't you tell me why that is?*

Tony recalled that his father once asked him to try and understand that in the adult world, things come up and they have to be tended to. The job calls in. The car breaks down. Tony heard his father's words and tried to select a plausible excuse from the repertoire since the alternative was unacceptable. *He forgot me. He just didn't care enough to call me or to come. I'm not worth his attention. How could he do this? This is Father's Day. He is a father only because of me. Has he forgotten that he's a father? How do you forget that you're a parent? Could I ever forget that I have a mother? Could I forget that I have a father? How does anyone forget he's a father? Is that the problem?*

Tony's thoughts drowned out the hymn and he began to shout in his head. *What is wrong with you? What are you thinking about? Where are you? Are you watching TV? If you're watching the NBA finals, they'll mention that it's Father's Day. At some point today someone will probably wish you Happy Father's Day. And I'm the reason why. So when they do, are you going to think about me? Are you going to remember you told me you were coming to church today? Is it going to make you want to call me or to try and show up? If you only knew that I loved you and I have a present for you today. All you have to do is come. Just come. Are you lost? Call the church. I gave you the phone number. Stop at the gas station and get a map. Do what it takes to get to me. Is there something wrong with me? Did I say something disrespectful at Christmas, the last time you saw me? Are you ashamed of me? What if I did better in school? Would you be proud of me and want me around more then? Maybe if I grow taller and look more like you, will that do? Just tell me what I need to do.* Tony's eyes began to well up.

Tony sensed someone was looking at him. He instinctively turned his head and noticed Jason looking his way. Jason quickly turned his head away but then turned back. This was no time to allow Tony to save face. So Jason gestured by nodding upward as if to say, "I know about it, I understand, I've been there, I'm there now, and it's okay." Jason wanted to ask Tony if he was okay but he didn't want to expose a brother's vulnerability. Nobody broke that cardinal rule. Jason didn't ask. Tony nodded back.

"Will all fathers please stand?" said the worship leader. The men rose to their feet in a sea of amens, smiles, and applause. Nearly everyone looked with pride at their church's fathers. These men were married. These men attended their children's basketball and soccer games and recitals. In fact, they pressured all their friends and families to attend. These dads brought their children to church. These dads joined the men's choir and sang on the first Sunday of every month. These dads cooked every year for the annual church fish fry. Some of them even taught Sunday school. They showed up week after week, bringing their little ones with them like appendages. And despite the obstacles that hold others back, these men were there for their families. Jason knew these men were different from his father. They were also different from perceptions offered by girls at school, by his mom, by her friends, and by what he saw on TV.

Jason smiled at Randy's dad and whispered, "Soccer dad." Jason remembered how Randy's dad would always ask Jason, "Do you want to come to one of Randy's games? If you want to come, we'll pick you up and drop you back and you know we're gonna stop and eat something along the way. You guys are human garbage disposals." Jason mustered a little smile. At least one father in this world tried to reach him, even if it wasn't his own.

As much as Jason resisted his mother's attempts to correct him, he envied kids like Randy, whose fathers were there to enforce the judgment they handed down. "You know how lucky you are to have your father? Do you know how great your dad is?" Jason had said to Randy one day. "Man, don't you know I'd give anything to have my dad come see me play?"

"Where is your dad? Is he alive?" Randy had asked.

"Yeah, man, he's around. But I've stopped asking him to come. And my mom can't really share in what I'm doing like my dad could. She's supportive and she tries to help but it's just different if your dad is there, trust me."

Jason remembered that conversation and honored the faithfulness of Randy's dad. *I'd gladly endure a month inside with no Playstation if I had my dad. I would listen and obey his rules. I would listen, God, I promise I would. And I would be so proud if he came to my basketball games.*

"You may be seated," announced the worship leader to the fathers and worshippers who stood for the morning scripture and praise songs. Pastor Carey emerged and Jason watched as he entered the pulpit. The pastor looked past rows and rows of people to rest his eyes directly on Jason. The pastor smiled and offered the same nod that Jason had offered Tony. How did he know?

Tony had tuned it all out. When the worship leader had called for the fathers to stand, Tony had pulled his Gameboy from his pocket, reserved for that precise moment.

Tony was determined to ignore everything going on in church — until the left door opened. Someone was about to enter the sanctuary. Tony stretched his neck to see past the other kids. Kalia did the same. She was dressed in a floral print dress. She wore stockings. She also had sneaked a spritz of her mom's Jes-

sica McClintock perfume. She was ready — just in case. In the
doorway was a tall black man. His suit coat was draped over his
arm, and his body and head were turned away from the back row.
Kalia gasped. But when he finally turned out, they saw the truth.
He was not Kalia's dad, not Tony's, and not Jason's. Kalia and Tony
leaned back in the pew.

Mrs. Thompson leaned toward their row and whispered,
"You kids keep looking every time this door opens. Are you
looking for anyone in particular?"

"No," said Dion, turning away from her.

"Nah," answered Kalia.

"They're just curious," said Jason who never looked up. He was
a veteran of the "failure to appear," or, as a judge would say, FTA.
He knew the odds were in favor of an FTA rather than a surprise
visit. Jason chose to accept the former with resignation.

Yet this time it was different. His father's FTA did not issue
a fatal blow. This Sunday he didn't opt to stay in bed and blast his
gansta rap CD. Last Monday Jason had arrived at the place he had
attempted to avoid — the bottom. The nightmare he had lived
for years had progressed to a crash landing in the shower. Jason,
to his great surprise, had survived. Six days later Jason was in
church and actually listening to the words sung by the choir and
anticipating what the preacher had to say about fathers.

"If you believe in God, keep praying, keep trusting, believing,
he won't fail you … " sang the choir. Jason looked back to his own
D-Day as he listened to that song. While he was not motivated
to join in — others stood to join in the singing of the song's
refrain, "keep believing, keep trusting GOD … he will never, ever,
ever fail you." Jason listened to the song and remembered the
moment where he thought he actually met God. *Did he actually
talk to me? Did God himself actually visit me on that shower floor?*

After the choir finished singing, the pastor stood up to face the waiting congregation and announced his sermon title, "A Father's Greatest Hour." *Oh, this ought to be good,* thought Jason. *Well, I guess I'll find out if God really talked to me. You told me you were my Father. Is this your greatest hour in my life?*

"It's a good thing that we honor deserving men," said the pastor. " … Honor to whom honor is due." Jason slouched in his seat and smugly folded his arms. He couldn't help but think, *Hmmm — I'm the judge today and on trial is you Daddy. The question I must determine is whether the evidence supports your case to receive honor this Father's Day. Well, Dad, I can say that your case doesn't look too strong right about now.*

"I want to remember those fathers to whom honor is really due," said the minister.

This really WILL be good, thought Jason.

"If you haven't abdicated your role in the husband-wife relationship or if you have not failed to assume your position and responsibility in the home, then we honor you today."

Oops! Well, Dad, since you told me you didn't love my mother any more — strike two! Dad, I wish I could help you.

"The test rules out abandonment," argued the preacher.

Abandonment? Jason remembered overhearing his mother discuss the divorce case. His mother had used that word when she began to discuss the grounds for the divorce.

"If you raised your children in the fear and the admonition of the Lord … "

Whoa, Dad! Now I know you're in trouble of advancing to the lightning round. If we think about it, you never came to church with us. I don't even really know if you believe in God. Well, I believe. Because He was there for me when you weren't. Jason's brows relaxed and his scowl melted into a look of sadness and vulnerability. He uncrossed his arms and reached for the hymnal to clutch it to his chest. He realized he did, in fact, believe and even know in his heart that God met him that previous Monday morning. Nonetheless, Jason carried on with his one-sided tongue lashing. *Since you won't give me the chance to tell you anything, good or bad, happy or sad, then I'll have to judge you this way. One way or another I'm going to say how I feel about how you're treating me ... one way or another.*

Tony had also tuned in and was grading his own father. For Tony, it wasn't fatal for his dad to come a little late. Tony didn't care if his dad even walked in after the benediction. It would be okay even if he saw him walk in as the people were gathering their things and preparing to depart. *That would be alright. I know you're late, Dad. But you can still come. Please come, Daddy, please ... ignore what my mom said, Dad, and just come.*

Tony remembered his mother's instruction to his father. She said not to come if he was going to arrive too late. Tony wondered why she couldn't realize that he didn't care what time his father arrived. Tony didn't care if his dad pulled up in the parking lot as he and his mother were pulling out. Tony visualized defying his mother, demanding that she immediately stop the car, release him, and allow him to get in his father's car.

Tony snapped out of his daydreaming and realized the pastor was about to close his sermon. He began chewing his fingernails. There's not much time left. Tony remembered there was a telephone downstairs in the fellowship hall and he decided to slip out of the service to call his dad's cell phone. But it occurred to Tony that he didn't have the phone number. He had left his jacket locked in the car. Oh, God. I have to get her keys and get my jacket. I'm sure he's lost, and I need to call him and find him. Tony knew it was now or never. Tony really didn't want her to see his anxiety. Tears began to well up in his eyes. He felt like the chance would be lost forever if he didn't call his dad now and steer him in the direction of the church, as if he could feel his father wavering and pulling away. Tony grabbed his dad's gift bag and leaped to his feet and made his way to the end of the row, squeezing past Jason and the others.

"Where are you going? Tony, you're going to have to sit still now. The sermon is almost over. You know we don't walk around during this time. Now, sit back down," ordered Mrs. Thompson.

"But I gotta go to the bathroom really bad, Mrs. Thompson."

"You kids really need to learn how to go before service begins. You can hold it. I asked all of you if you had to go and you all said no. So hold it," she snapped.

"Please!" begged Tony.

Mrs. Thompson was determined to prevail. And she did.

With the reality of her dad's no-show sinking in, Kalia folded her arms and pouted. Her brows drew together as her anger grew. But then she slowly began to grin as she allowed her thoughts to drift to a place where she felt empowered, her imagination. Kalia was a superstar, a singer. She had just accepted her award for best female vocalist at the American Music Awards. Now, she was starring in a Spike Lee or Stephen Spielberg movie, and who should be interviewed in advance of her Oscar night? Her father. She then pictured the *coup de grace* — her *Entertainment Tonight* interview where she was asked to comment on her father's interview about her and his desire to reestablish their relationship.

Kalia recorded the script in her mind.

"Well, I last recall leaving a message for him to come see me on Father's Day. I was fourteen years old and I had a gift for him. I had spent all my money on that gift, but he didn't come, he didn't call – so, in reality, I don't know who this man is because I don't have a father. He determined that years ago when he decided I wasn't worth visiting, caring about, or loving."

Kalia then imagined her father watching the interview and finally experiencing just a tinge of her unrelenting pain and rejection. Kalia refused to pray for her father. The daydream felt far more satisfying. Then she cried.

Meanwhile, Tony was fenced in. The preacher began the invitation to join the family of God. He initially directed his call to come to the altar to receive Jesus, prayer, or to rededicate their lives to God or their families.

"Today, I'm calling on the men of the church — we need to rededicate ... " While the choir softly sang *I Surrender All*, the pastor directed his invitation to all the men. "Humble yourselves under the mighty hand of God. Even our young men, you ought to come and receive God's blessing in your life now."

At this point, Randy's dad and the other dads proudly turned and motioned for their own sons to join them as they stepped out into the pews and slowly turned and walked down the blue carpeted aisle toward the altar.

"If you wish your husband was here — right where you are, pray for your man, your husband."

One by one, most of the men and fathers made their way to the altar. The women also bowed their heads and began praying. Jason listened as the pastor urged his flock on. Pastor Carey motioned the deacons to come close to him. He leaned over the pulpit and quietly spoke to them. They then dispersed through the congregation.

"Bless now the sons of us fathers ... "

But what about me, Lord? Is my daddy included? Can he be blessed? wondered Jason. *Lord, can I be included in this prayer? Is it only for those sons whose fathers are here and doing right? What about us sons whose fathers have flunked the honor test? Is there room at the altar for their sons? What about the sons whose fathers didn't come? Is there room for us? For me? My dad's not here to take me up. I want to go up, but I want my father to take me. I have no one, God. If you want me, you have to come get me. I can't move, but I'm dying to come to you. I need a miracle. I can't take it. I miss him so much. I need ...*

"If your wives or children are here, go to them right now. Come on, love somebody!" urged the pastor as the choir vigorously sang, "We say, YES, Lord!"

Jason prayed on. *Help me, Lord, I can't do this! If you are real, if you are really here for me, then please do something. I know it probably won't happen, but this is it.* Jason cried. He gripped his pockets and tightened his fists. *I tried to meet you today. I thought you were my father. I thought you would meet me. I thought ...*

Suddenly a hand grabbed Jason's shoulder and a man's voice called out, "Jason."

He looked up and there stood Deacon Rosemere, summoning Jason. "Jason, come to the altar, God is calling you."

With tears streaming down his face, Jason lowered his head into an embrace with this fatherly deacon and Sunday school teacher. He tearfully whispered, "Thank you, God. You answered."

The two of them walked to the altar, and Jason felt that same presence that was with him that Monday morning in the shower. It was as if the arm wrapped around his left shoulder was the arm of God himself. Even then, Jason heard that same voice that had spoken to him on Monday. "I am your Father. Even when your earthly mother and father forsake you, I will take you up."

Jason openly wept. His prayer had been answered. He now knew that God was there and that God had found the *via dolorosa* leading to Jason's heart.

THE PASTOR SAID, "AMEN," and it was over. The father-directed thoughts, prayers, confessions, discussion, acknowledgment, bulletins, sermon, and praise had come to an end. For most, this was a delightful service.

The service ended, but the back row crew stood there, watching the others as they gathered around their fathers. Even Jason made his way back to the familiar row after wishing Happy Father's Day to Pastor Carey, Deacon Rosemere, and others. Tony was still trying to slide by the other parishioners. *Mom was right. I should have left this stupid box in the car. She's really right. I shouldn't have even brought it out of the house. For that matter, I shouldn't have bought him anything. I better get out of here before someone asks me who this present is for.* Finally he managed to squeeze his way out of the church.

"Man!" he exclaimed as he struck the car's side window with his hand. He'd forgotten the door was locked. Tony decided to place the present on the top of the car and leave it there. He reached deep within himself to muster all the apathy and indifference he could. *I don't even care if someone steals it.* He planned to walk to the side of the church to hide from the departing churchgoers and pull himself together.

"I don't care," he muttered under his breath. "It just doesn't matter and I really don't care." Tony leaned his head on the car and said, "Oh, Dad. Oh, Dad, why does it have to be like this? What am I to you? Am I anything to you?"

He glimpsed Randy getting in the car with his dad, stepmom, and baby sister, and he wondered if his own father felt guilt, whether he had a conscience. Filled with anger, Tony pushed himself from the car and began to pace. With his fists clenched, he stopped, looked to the sky, and took a deep breath. He folded his arms and fell back against the car. "I'm so tired of this, God, why do I have to think about him all the time? The preacher said you can do anything but fail — well, can you make me forget my father? Can you do that? Huh? Can you make all this just go away? Why does it have to be like this? What have I done wrong? I came here fatherless."

Crying, he whispered, "Dad, I can think of fifty things, easy things, you could do to be there for me without it really costing you anything. I know that is probably why you won't come around – money — but it really doesn't take much." Then he said, "Maybe you just can't help it. I could help you."

Tony began to see his father just as he was — imperfect — filled with faults and sins. Needy. In this near role reversal, Tony thought, *WOW! I need to help HIM!*

As he wiped his tears, a black pickup zoomed right by him. "Dad!!" he yelled as he ran through the parking lot. "Dad!" shouted Tony as he ran up to his father's window.

"Hey, Son!" his father said joyfully.

"Happy Father's Day, Daddy!"

KALIA CONJURED UP an excuse to go downstairs to the fellowship hall to stall for time before leaving church. She waited around in the fellowship hall in the church basement as long as possible. She didn't want her emotions to be visible to onlookers. She had believed her self-generated hype. Kalia thought her father would come.

Kalia sat down on the edge of the stage and began to swing her legs back and forth. She noticed an inscription on the Sunday school wall. "A father of the fatherless ... is God in his holy habitation," — Psalm 68:5. It prompted her to wonder, is this just another day? Kalia didn't want to admit that Jason was right about that. She had heard her friends at school utter those same words all week long. She had been the lone hold out, refusing to give in and diminish the day set aside for honoring fathers.

The drafty air in the hall caused Kalia to think of her life without her father — cold and hollow. It was not an option. The rejection she feared was a small price to pay for the reward of having her father. Then Kalia remembered what others told her about that. "You'll get over him. You'll get tired of trying to reach your father. You'll eventually come to see him just as he was, not worth the heartache."

But Kalia refused to give in to those words. *Maybe I will give up one day and maybe I will be so hurt that I quit trying. But right now, I want my father. This is where I am. I need my daddy.*

After a while, Kalia heard footsteps approaching. It was her sister.

"Mom's been looking all over for you. It's time to go."

"I'm ready, let's go."

When they pulled up at home, Kalia didn't make a move to get out of the car. "Come on, honey, it's time to come in. It's over. He didn't come, and he didn't call," said her mom. "I'm sorry about how you feel, but I've been telling you for a long time now to get over him, move on! I'm sorry, but I can't hold it in anymore because all this daddy stuff gets on my damn nerves! It upsets me, it upsets you, and it upsets your sister." She slammed her car door.

"MOM! Just let it go. I wasn't even thinking about him," said Kalia as she climbed out and wiped tears and mascara from her face.

"I'm just tired of it. Honey, I don't mean to hurt you, God knows that. I want to help you look to me, look to God, look to life for your joy. The whole world is not wrapped up in your father, although you walk around here like it is. I'm just trying to help you so you don't get so hurt."

Kalia tried to storm past her mother toward her bedroom, but her mom was obviously not finished.

"Kali, come here. Sit down. We need to have this talk. This has gone on way too long," said Joanne, shaking her head.

"Mom, I'm okay. Really. I just want to go to my room. My stomach hurts." Kalia was hunched over as if she was cramping. "Mom, I just need to lie down."

Joanne stood up, grabbed her child, and pulled her close. "My sweetie. Do you know how much I love you? But even more than me, do you know how much God loves you? You're such a pretty child, although you deal with your stress by eating. But God loves you and can be that father to you."

"I know Mommy, but I want my father."

Joanne answered, "I know how you feel … "

"NO, YOU DON'T!" shouted Kalia, suddenly withdrawing from her mother's embrace.

"No, you don't know how I feel. You had your father all your life. You don't know what this feels like! You can't know! I want my father. I need my father. Everybody needs a father, Mom."

"God is a father to the fatherless."

Kalia instantly pulled away, leaped to her feet, and screamed, "Aaaaaaaaaahhh! You just don't get it! I know, Mom, God is a father to the fatherless. But I want someone I can see, someone who can see me! Someone I can hug! Someone who'll hold and hug me! I need someone who'll come visit with me, tell me I'm important, tell me he loves me, tell me I'm pretty, BE IN MY LIFE! I want a REAL father. I want MY father, flesh and blood, Mom. Flesh and blood!"

Kalia's face told the story — it said her mother had missed the boat. She had failed to grasp her daughter's real, immediate, and unimagined need for her father.

"Mom, I believe in God and I pray all the time. Mom, I pray *all the time* that he'll send my daddy back to me. But he hasn't done it, okay? How long am I supposed to wait?"

"I don't know, sweetie, I just don't know."

With that, Kalia walked away, but her mother followed her into the bedroom.

"Please, leave me alone. I don't want to talk to you."

"What do you mean, talk to *you*? You act like this is *my* fault! I know you're upset, but you seem to forget that *he* left *us*! He left me and he left *you*! Hey, I've had to be your mother and your father. So whatever he's made you to feel right now, it's not my fault! Don't even try to put this on me!"

"No, no! You're not my father!" she screamed, loud enough to be heard outside the apartment.

"You're just my mother, and I want to scream every time you say that. You can never replace my father! And yes, this IS your fault! You made him leave! You drove him away! You could've been nicer. You yelled at him all the time. You called him stupid all the time. But if he was so stupid, then why'd you marry him? Huh? If he was so stupid, what did that make you?" screamed Kalia.

"That's enough! You've crossed the line, little girl, and you need to watch your mouth!"

Joanne turned to walk out, but then turned back to watch her broken child. She walked over and sat back down on the bed to hug Kalia.

An hour later, Kalia tiptoed into the kitchen to call Jason.

In a subdued voice, Jason answered the phone. "Hello."

"Jason, it's me, Kalia."

"Oh, hey, what's up?"

"Nothing. I'm chilling."

"You got a cold?" he asked. "You're all stuffy."

"No."

"So, what's going on?"

"What you doing? Is your mom home?" she asked.

"No, she went to see my grandma for a while. Why?"

"Well, maybe I can come over. I can get on the bus and be by in about an hour."

"Uh, I'm kind of tired and really need to chill out alone for a while."

"Well, I need to chill out too and my mom's driving me crazy. I just need a place to hang out and talk."

"Kalia, your dad didn't come, did he? I know how excited you were about the whole prospect of him coming."

"No, he didn't. So, can I come? I still have on my church dress. Did you like it?"

"Kali, you're my girl. You're like my little sister. You only want to come by because your dad didn't come. You don't realize how really cute and smart you are. But I've been meaning to tell you. You don't have to chase boys, not me or anyone. Drew told me that sometimes girls who don't have their fathers around want attention from boys."

"Jason, that's not true. This is embarrassing. I don't chase boys. I just happen to think it's okay for girls to call boys. I called you, so big deal!" she snapped.

"Well, a guy will never tell a girl this because we can be dogs sometimes, but when a girl calls a guy, he thinks she's fast and easy. And boys talk, Kalia. Trust me, they talk. Look, I think of you as my little sister, and I just don't want you to make some bad decisions that might hurt you later. You know, there are a whole lot of girls getting pregnant up at that school."

"I'm not like that! You're so wrong."

"I hope so. You're special, very special, and I don't want you to think you need some boy to tell you he loves you in order for you to love yourself." Jason stopped when he heard Kalia's whimpers on the other end of the phone.

"Well, since my dad doesn't love me, I need someone who will! God, I'm so tired of crying and hurting. I'm just so tired of it.

What's so wrong with me that he won't come see me or love me or remember me? Jason, am I so ugly and fat that no one will love me? What's wrong with me?"

"Nothing at all. Everything is right with you. You're smart and cute, and if you ask God to help you, He will. I'm not saying that everything is going to be perfect starting right now, but you'll begin to feel better. Stop looking for love from boys, Kalia. That's not the kind of love you need anyway. So try something different. I'm here for you, though, okay?"

"Okay. I'm going to lay down now."

"Are you sure? We can keep talking."

"I'm okay. I feel a little better … and Jason? Thank you." Then she hung up.

TONY WAS THRILLED when his dad pulled up to the church, but after the first few minutes, the reacquainting chatter stopped. The rest of the day included dinner at a trendy restaurant, an NBA playoff game at home on the widescreen TV, and late night movies with popcorn. His dad loved his Father's Day gift, and Tony went to his room with a grin.

He sat on the bed and looked around the room. He was surprised to see so many toys. Then he remembered he'd received them for Christmas but had to leave them at his father's house. They wanted him to play with the toys during his visits, but the visits never happened. He opened the dresser drawers and discovered clothes he'd received for Christmas. He noticed that the price tags were still on most of the items. He tried on a pair of jeans, but they were already too small. He decided to just go to bed.

The next morning, he had just made it to the bottom of the stairs when he heard his stepmom call him for breakfast. Tony walked into the kitchen and said, "Good morning."

"Hey, buddy, did you sleep well? You know that's your room whenever you come, and I'm hoping to be able to get you more often," his father said.

It had been almost six months since his father had picked him up for a visit, and now in his father's kitchen, Tony tried to build up the courage to speak freely. He began gobbling his breakfast of scrambled eggs, sausage, and toast. As he smothered his toast with grape jelly, Tony looked like he expected to be scolded. His mother never let him put that much on.

"So, Tony, how's school?" asked his stepmom.

"Good."

"So, what grade are you in again?" she asked.

Tony looked at her and paused before he answered. He wanted to see if she could remember on her own. Every time they picked him up, they had the same discussion. There was no opportunity to preserve the information and build upon it. They always pretended like there was no distance between them, but Tony knew they had to start from scratch.

"So, who's your favorite basketball team now, Tony?" his father asked eagerly.

"I like the San Antonio Spurs. I think Tim Duncan is cool."

"Maybe I can get you tickets for a game, if you think you'd like to go?"

No kid could resist the offer to attend a basketball game. No kid could resist brand new tennis shoes. No kid could resist Dave and Buster's. No kid could resist McDonalds every day. Tony was only a typical boy — he was not going to resist any of that, but even at age eleven, he knew there was something missing and he didn't know how to tell that to his father.

"Cool," answered Tony.

As he ate his breakfast, Tony decided to tell his father that he had been playing baseball to see whether his dad would take an interest.

"That was delicious!" he said as he cleared his dishes.

"Tony, hurry up and get dressed — we've got a lot to do today. We have to get moving because I do have to get you back home for the last couple of school days," said his dad.

In the car, Tony decided to throw it out there. "Dad, I play baseball. Do you want to come to one of my games?"

"What? You play? Well, of course, I do. You're going to have to get me a schedule. Are you any good?"

"DAD!"

"You're my son. Of course, you're good."

IN THE SCHOOL CAFETERIA, Kalia tried to eat her pizza in peace. "So Kali, how was Father's Day?" asked Justin. "Did he come like you said he would? I'm not trying to start nothing. I'm just curious," he said, trying not to snicker.

"Leave her alone," said Jason.

Kalia looked up and rolled her eyes at Justin. "Loser," she said as she turned back to her cold pizza.

"Hey, you're the one all gung ho about dads and how you spend all this time with your father and how they're good and all that. So, you know, I'm just trying to keep the faith as you told me."

"Leave me alone!"

"Man, I said leave her alone," said Jason again. "What's your problem, man? You have a problem with your dad? Let's talk about your dad, how about that?"

Justin climbed off the table and turned to face Jason. Suddenly, a figure appeared and said, "I believe the young lady wants to be left alone, and I know you don't have a problem honoring her wishes, do you?"

"Daddy!" screamed Kalia as she jumped out of her seat to yank him into an embrace.

"Hi, daddy's girl!"

"Dad, what are you doing here?"

"Well, I did get your message and it made me feel pretty good and pretty bad. I mean, I didn't realize how long it had been. I wanted to come to church but it had been so long, I just figured God would strike me down or something," he said jokingly.

Kalia and Jason laughed. "*And*, I talked to your mother. But I knew I needed to come see you even *before* your mom called to say how upset you were yesterday. So I knew I better get over here." He held her gaze as he spoke.

"This is your dad?" asked Jason.

"Dad, this is my friend Jason."

"Hello, sir," said Jason, reaching out to shake his hand.

"How you doing, son?" asked Kalia's dad.

"Good."

"You looking out for my baby girl in a good way?"

"Yes, sir. She's my buddy. I'm not gonna let anything happen to her."

"Okay. You guys aren't giving Kali a hard time, are you?" he boldly said, looking at Justin and his friends.

"Aw, no sir, just having some fun."

"See you, man," he said to Jason as they walked away. Turning to Kali, he said, "Well, I just came to have lunch with my little princess."

"Dad, don't call me that," she said, giggling.

"Okay, honey. That's right. You're in high school now. Isn't that what that message said to me? Anyway, what time do you get out of school today?" he asked, reaching to break off a piece of Kalia's pizza.

"We have a half-day Dad, and, anyway, Wednesday is the last day of school."

"Well, let's go have lunch and celebrate Father's Day."

"That sounds good, Daddy."

Even as they walked out the door, Kalia remembered previous reunions and the disappointment that always followed. *When would the next visit be?* She decided not to allow herself to get too excited this time. She figured she'd get the post-visit phone call two weeks later and then all contact would taper off again.

Then Kalia heard her name called. "Kalia! Kalia!" her teacher called out. "Wake up!" Startled, Kalia lifted her head from the desk in her World History class. When Kalia realized her father's visit was just a dream, she turned her head to the window and stared out of it for the rest of class. She skipped P.E., her last class of the day, and began the two-mile walk home. Outside school grounds, she untied the black windbreaker she customarily wore around her waist and tossed it into a garbage can. Moments later she ran back to the trashcan and scooped it back out, saying, "I'm sorry, Daddy."

Journal

The big day finally arrived, and for every sleeping and waking moment, children and adults all across America had daddy on their minds. I know I did. Dr. Jackson invited me to spend the day with him and his family. I chose to stay in and stir my own father feelings. I'm no different than anybody else. Whether he was there or not, whether he came or not, whether they know him or not, whether they hate him or not — people woke up this morning with their minds on dad. Young and old; those from all ethnic and racial backgrounds; male and female; rich, poor, and middle-class alike; all found themselves at the same place — Father's Day.

And for the fatherless? I'm learning only God can make up the difference. That's the one thing I have yet to teach these kids — that when all else and "everyone" else fails, try God. — A.D.M.

CHAPTER EIGHT

Father to the Fatherless

"I don't believe this!" said Drew.

Dear Mr. Miller:

Please be advised that the Board will convene an emergency meeting on June 24, 2002, to conduct your annual performance review. As you know, that review was originally scheduled for August 1, 2002, but in light of the attached letter, we felt it was imperative to advance the review date in order to properly address the matter raised in the attached letter, as well as address other matters of board concern. We plan to first conduct a closed session. You will be expected to participate once we have met.

Mr. Miller, we are confident we can and will resolve these and other matters professionally and cordially. Please call me to discuss this letter, or if you wish to discuss the board's plans.

Very truly yours,
Bruce Conrad, Chairman
Board of Directors,
Springridge Community Center

The phone rang, interrupting Drew's thoughts.

"Drew, line one," said the receptionist.

"Drew Miller," he answered.

"Hello Drew, this is Jim Goodman. I wanted to give you a heads up on ... "

"I got the letter," interrupted Drew.

"That was quick! We just mailed it Saturday! Anyway, I'm awfully sorry about that. I was hoping to reach you first."

"It's cool, Jim. I don't know, I kinda sensed something coming down the pipe."

"Well, try not to worry about it. You have supporters on the board. They don't speak up or dominate the meetings, but when the vote comes down, I'm sure they'll come through, at least that's the sense *I'm* getting. You're still our guy, understand?"

"Thanks, Jim," said Drew, with a voice of resignation.

"Hang in there. You're doing a good job. Besides, you know what they say, 'no good deed goes unpunished!'"

"I got you. See you next week."

Drew hung up and read the letter attached to the chairman's.

May 15, 2002
Board of Directors,
Springridge Community Center
Rockville, Maryland
Re: Andrew Miller and "Let's Talk"

Dear Board of Directors:

I am writing this letter to express my concern over the way Andrew Miller, Executive Director, delves into the personal lives of the youth that attend the center. My son Jason is a regular there and he has told me that Mr. Miller conducts weekly talk sessions. During the sessions he asks many personal questions and demands that these children reveal the most personal details of their lives. In particular, my son has shared information from our private life.

Most disturbing of all, Mr. Miller has encouraged these kids, my son included, to call, hound, or chase their absentee fathers and demand attention. I don't agree with his methods and believe that my son has suffered for it. My son has had emotional problems all year as a result. He's made repeated efforts to reach his father — as directed by your employee — but those efforts have failed. As a result, he's become difficult, hostile, and moody — all because of his failure to reach his father.

Finally, Mr. Miller has forced his personal religious views onto these children, promising them that God will somehow miraculously make their lives all better and "be a father to the fatherless." He tells them to forgive people who are walking all over them. His methods are unrealistic and misleading.

I ask that you admonish this behavior or take other

action to remove him from the center. As an employee of
the Malden Foundation, I trust I will not have to raise this
matter as an issue when Malden conducts its proposal
evaluations.

Thank You,
Mrs. Victoria Phillips

Drew immediately turned to the computer, pulled out a disk, and
began a document search using the keyword *resume.*

JUST BEFORE THEY GOT TO SCHOOL, Tony mustered the courage
to ask his dad to come camping with him. Tony realized that
there was a limit to the degree of involvement his mother
could offer. While he was able to attend some of the scouting
events and outings, he missed out on many. He reflected on
how in her frustration, his mom would occasionally say, "I
can't do everything, and I can't be everywhere at all times!"
Tony couldn't help but notice the involvement of his friends'
fathers. With three or four exceptions, all the kids in their
pack had their fathers to share in their scouting adventures. But
camping was an altogether different story. And the time had
come for Tony to sign up for the overnight camping trip. His
mother clearly was not first on his list of invitees.

Tony wasn't really sure whether he was ready for his mother
to share in that with him. The thought of sharing a tent with his
mom while all his buddies had their dads wasn't hitting the spot.
So Tony had to think of something quick.

"Dad, the Cub Scouts are going camping this summer and,
well, can you take me? It's really not a trip for moms. All my
friends will have their dads there."

"When is it? I'll look at my calendar when we pull up to the school," replied Nelson.

When they arrived, Nelson pulled out his Palm Pilot and navigated to the calendar.

"Now, when is it?" he asked.

"It's in a few weeks. Mom already paid and we already have a tent. But she says if you want to go, you can take her place."

"Well, let's see. When did you say?" he asked, looking at June on his calendar.

"Two weeks from now," answered Tony. "Mom said she already mentioned it to you."

"That's right, your mother did give me that date. We had talked about it a few weeks ago, and I told her that I should be able to make it. There are some things I have to get out of, but let's just say I can make it. I doubt there'll be a problem. I'll go. Don't worry about it, I'm going. Boy, we are going to have some FUN!"

"Oh, and Dad," said Tony as he reached for his suitcase in the backseat, "Don't forget, I left my baseball schedule on the kitchen table. We have a game Friday and the last game of the season is Saturday. You're coming, right?"

"I'm sure I'll be able to make at least one. So, we'll see. Okay, now — see you later."

That Saturday was a beautiful and hot early summer day. Tony's team was playing for first place in the division. The team bench was ten feet from his mother's chair. Tony sat there staring, waiting for his dad to show up. He was lost in thought when Peter's father said, "Hey, buddy, you're third at bat. Let's work on that swing." He sifted through the bats to find just the right one for Tony.

As he rose from the bench, Tony looked past the backstop toward the parking lot. When the game began, his father had not yet arrived. In the first inning, with a count of two and two,

Tony whacked the ball past the first baseman, bringing in two runners. He was headed for third.

"Slide! Slide!" yelled Peter's dad to Tony. The league rule required the runner to slide into the base to avert collision and so the umpire could see the play to make the call. Tony slid into third, sending dust into a swirl.

"But they didn't even throw the ball to the base," said Linda, unsure why Tony needed to slide.

"That's not the point," said Peter's father, without taking his eyes off the field or loosening his grip of the coiled backstop wires.

"It's more important for them to learn to listen and act on what we tell them. Following the coach's instructions and doing what we teach is the important lesson."

In the fourth inning, Tony was playing shortstop. The score was tied six to six. The batter came to the plate.

"Strike one," yelled the umpire.

"Tony, get ready, he's coming to you!" yelled Tony's coach.

Linda yelled too. "Tony, get ready, here it comes."

Linda was thrilled as she watched her young son serve such an integral role on his little league team. Tony was adored by his teammates as well as by his coaches.

Linda looked around and noticed all the fathers fully engaged in this business of baseball. One dad was the head coach and the rest served as assistants. Some dads helped the boys put the catcher's uniform on. The team captured their complete attention. The world seemed perfect. Then Linda did the unthinkable. She counted to see if any dads were missing. Only one was — Tony's. Linda felt ashamed, guilty, and then paranoid.

Do others notice this too? Does anyone else notice that Tony is the only boy out there whose dad isn't here? Are they wondering where he is? Do they realize he's never been here? Linda began to wallow in the pain she harbored for her son. *Oh God*, she thought. *Why is my son the only one? What has he done to bear such a burden?* Linda had always wondered just how God would be a father to her fatherless son. Tony saw his father only two or three times a year, and less than that during some years. She remembered the divorce recovery group meetings at her church. She recalled hearing how God would be a father to the fatherless. She had always believed that would be the case. However, time passed, and as Tony grew older, there just didn't seem to be any sign of that happening. She had the same struggles as all single mothers. Linda had two grown brothers, but she felt neither made a conscious effort to make up the difference for their nephew. They were too busy with their own lives as they busied themselves with their own families and careers. Linda always believed that they should put forth more of an effort and sacrifice more. She wished the men's group at church would do something to reach out to fatherless boys. Year after year passed and her frustration grew.

She looked around the ballpark and just as she was about to buckle under the weight of the pain, she heard the voice of God. *Wait, no. Stay up there. Don't sink. It was me who opened your eyes. I have allowed you to see that your son was the only one without a father today. And I did that because you didn't notice at all. My dear daughter, that's the point. You hadn't noticed. For two baseball seasons, practices, games in and games out, you relished in your son's thrills and his accomplishments. You watched him laugh and sport as a warrior. You watched these dads and coaches, scores of them, encourage and teach your son. And you never even noticed he was fatherless. You never noticed because I have been here all along. I have been the Father to your fatherless child. I've come, not in one but in many. I had to open your eyes, not so you could see his suffering and his lack, but so you could see Me.*

When she really began to think about it, Linda realized they — fathers — were everywhere. Several days each week they were with Tony, giving lessons in sportsmanship, character, teamwork, individual responsibility, discipline, fitness, attitude, camaraderie, commitment, perseverance, and fun — all in three months. Not bad for an eighty-dollar activity fee, she thought. All I had to do was get him here. Linda realized these fathers give time, resources, energy, reputation, and pride.

There were times when the coach saw things — strengths and even vulnerabilities — that she hadn't. All the dads took an active part, calling her child by name, encouraging him, egging him on. "Hey, Tony, good play! Way to go ... move a little to the left ... tighten up on the bat ... step a few inches away from the plate ... that's it ... don't worry about it ... you'll get it next time ... you're a hitter ... just relax ... hang in there, buddy."

Linda was so caught up in this revelation that she hadn't noticed her two younger brothers arrive to cheer Tony along in his game. "Hey, Brian. Hey, Jedediah! Thank God you made it!" she said as she finally saw them.

"Oh, you know we weren't going to let the whole season pass without coming to see the boy play. Come on, now!" said Brian.

That evening at his grandparents' house, Tony sat next to his grandfather to watch *Jeopardy*, a ritual they shared whenever they got together. They also loved to discuss current events. Suddenly Linda realized how priceless these times were. She even realized that the occasional "talks" her younger brother Jedediah would have with Tony were a valuable contribution to her son's developing manhood. His sleepovers at his Uncle Brian's house and trips to the beach with his uncle were also incomparable — standing in the gap was a collective effort.

DAYS BEFORE SPRINGRIDGE'S annual banquet, Drew and Mayra were busy calling parents to ensure a large turnout. "I'm thinking about calling Jason's father. Ever since his father wasn't able to go to the Wizards' game with him, Jason seems to have lost interest in everything. But I've seen his resilience. I know he can recover from this. We've made too much progress during the year to let it slip away because of one more no-show," said Drew.

"Are you sure you want to do that?" asked Mayra. "I mean, did Jason ask you to call his dad?"

"No, and I'm not calling as a counselor, nor will I break any confidentiality. I'm calling him like I'm calling all parents to provide information. He's no different."

"Yes, he is. You know he is. Why would you ignore the situation with his mother? Have you forgotten that your job is on the line here? This call could put you in the unemployment line."

"Mayra, I'm not afraid of all that, and I'm not afraid of these fathers. They're people just like us and they have issues too. Let's take Ray and Dion's dad. He's a lawyer. I know he travels for his job and that can explain why he doesn't see them. And there's always, always more to the story than meets the eye. There's always some sort of barrier or breakdown in communication that hinders the relationship. Sometimes it's guilt. But I refuse to just dismiss them all as deadbeat. That's too easy. It's gotta stop. It seems to me that no one wants to reach out, ask the hard questions, investigate what's at the root of the problem."

"Drew, I just think you keep overextending yourself. And you cross the line sometimes. I know you've helped many of these kids, but you've also ticked off some people."

"People?"

"Okay, parents. I've just heard mumbling about how you've missed some activities when you promised to be there and that it is the same as what they had before – no-shows."

"Well, at least I'm trying," he said defensively. "And I'm calling

Jason's dad. This call could also turn things around for Jason." He dialed the number.

"Hello, may I speak with Mr. Gary Phillips?

"This is he."

"Mr. Phillips, I'm Andrew Miller, director of the community center where your son Jason plays basketball. He was also tutored here for a while during the first part of the year," said Drew nervously.

"Is there anything wrong? Has he done anything? Was he hurt?"

"Oh, no, no, nothing like that. He's great and everything's fine. He's a great kid, very bright when he applies himself. I'd say he's a natural-born leader."

"Yes, he is. So what can I do for you?" asked Gary.

"Well, uh, I'm calling all the parents to remind them of the end-of-season games, parent night, and most importantly the year-end banquet scheduled for June thirtieth."

"So, uh, why didn't Jason call me about this? When are these events?"

"Well, the last game is this Friday at 6:30 P.M. and parents night is immediately following from 8:30 P.M. till 10:00 P.M. that night. The banquet is June thirtieth at 6 P.M. at the Holiday Inn Conference Center in Silver Spring."

"Well, I don't know about Friday because ... "

"Jason is some ball player," interrupted Drew, attempting to catch Gary before he said no.

"I know," said Gary, slightly agitated.

"Have you been able to catch him this season? Did you see the game where he scored twenty-two points? Man, he was amazing!"

"I know he's amazing, but I have to work on Fridays. Jason understands. We have an understanding."

"Are you sure about that? Are you sure he understands?"

"Excuse me? I think you don't know what you're talking about. And, who are you … " Suddenly the phone clicked. "Wait a minute, I have another call," said Gary.

Drew covered the mouthpiece with his hand. "He says he has another call. I bet he's just trying to get rid of me."

"Hi, I'm sorry. You were saying?"

"Um, I hope you can at least make the last game because Jason looks for you at his games. So I just wanted to know if there was anything I could do to help you make it to this one game or parent night or even the banquet."

"Did Jason's mother ask you to call me?"

"No, she didn't."

"Did Jason ask you to call me?"

"No, I'm just calling because I know how your son feels," said Drew.

"Really, what's your name again?" asked Gary, his voice growing louder.

"Drew."

"Well, Drew, I'm sure you mean well but what's between my son and me is none of your business. You don't know how he feels. If we need help, we'll ask for it."

"He's asking. In fact, you might say he's begging and he has been doing so all year. He needs to see you. He needs to spend time with you."

"I'll ask it again — Jason asked you to call me? 'Cause if not, I think you're probably out of line. What is the name of your manager or director?"

"Sir, I don't mean to upset or offend you, but … "

"Well, you did. So as I said, this is none of your business!" There was a long pause before he continued. "Look, I don't mean to come off so hard. It's just that I'm pretty used to never getting my side out, and I always end up looking like the bad guy. I'm always wrong, no matter what I do and no matter how hard I try! I'm sure Vicky has you believing I'm a deadbeat dad who doesn't care about my son. She has the world thinking that — the judge, the lawyers, her mother, our friends, the school — to them all, I became a monster, the enemy ... "

As he listened intently, Drew dropped his mouth and looked at Mayra. His eyes grew wide before he dropped his head and turned his swivel chair around to face the wall. He knew he couldn't interrupt and needed to let Gary air obvious frustrations that had lain dormant for some time. Gary continued.

"I love my son, whether you or anyone else believes it. I work extremely hard, partly to be able to pay $878 in child support."

"How much?!"

"That's right, $878. That's $439 drawn from my check every two weeks," he said.

"And I still try to buy my son things at Christmas and for his birthday. That's about all I can afford, so I look like the bad guy. Look, I'm not a Disney dad who shows up once a year for the big event or the big trip. I'm working day and night trying to do the right thing and meet my obligations. I even put $100 aside every month in savings bonds for his college education — I just hope he decides to go. Vicky doesn't know that and I hope you don't tell her."

"I won't."

"Anyway, I do pay her. I don't know what she's told you. I just got behind a couple of months and now I'm playing catch up. But I'm trying. So, what did she tell you?"

"Nothing. We've not talked, certainly not about you."

"Well, I don't know what she's doing with that money. I did see a new car the last time I saw them, but it's cool, I'm not complaining. My son needs to ride in a nice car. I'm just saying there's more to the story than what most people think. I'm not even saying it's too much, but in order to pay my rent, gas, food, car note, insurance, and bills I have to work two jobs. Since I just started the part-time job, I have no seniority. So I gotta work Friday evenings and Saturdays. But the whole world just assumes I don't care and that I'm living it up. But I'm not. It's not even like that. My mistake is telling Jason that I'll try to be there. I know the chance is slim, but I don't have the heart to just tell him flat out no. I just can't. So I give him a maybe and he's let down when I don't show.

"My evening manager threatened to cut my hours in half the day I was supposed to go to that Wizards game. It was either go to the game or have the money in the account for when child support enforcement snatches the payment. It tore me up," he said, as his voice softened. "So give me the information. I can't make any promises because I'm scheduled to work on both days."

"Gary, I'm sure Jason appreciates whatever you can do. Do you have a pen?" asked Drew so he could give Gary all the information. They even exchanged cell phone numbers for emergencies.

When he hung up from the call, he looked at Mayra without speaking. She didn't say anything. Finally he said, "Here, take this list. I'll finish with the fathers and you hit the mothers and the community leaders. Then I'll call the churches."

Mayra went to an adjacent office to place her calls. When she got tired of talking to strangers, she took a break to call her voicemail for messages. There was one from her cousin Alba. She gasped in surprise and immediately returned Alba's call.

"Hello," said Alba.

"Alba, this is Mayra."

"Hey girl, it was nice to see you. I can't wait till the reunion this weekend — what time are you going to get there?" asked Alba.

"Reunion? What reunion?"

"Yeah, you know, Grandma's. Anyway, I'm sure she tried to

call you. I guess you need to call her. It's this weekend – it's a Father's Day celebration even though Grandpa is gone."

"Oh, right, okay, I guess I can be there. When is it?" asked Mayra.

"Friday evening, though the big picnic is Saturday. You need to call your father or Grandma or someone to get all the info. I need to finish getting ready because I'm going to leave tonight to get there early, so I'll see you there, right?" said Alba, suddenly in a hurry to hang up.

"Um, we'll see. Later."

Mayra was stunned that she had not been invited to the gathering and decided not to put off making a phone call.

"Grandma Taylor?" she said. Her voice grew softer. "This is Mayra. How are you feeling? I'm so sorry about Grandpa."

"I'm fine Mayra just tired, you know, losing my sweetie of the last forty-seven years. I suppose I'll be alright after a while. I'm taking it one day at a time. What's up with you, honey?"

Mayra paused, hoping her grandmother would mention the reunion.

"Grandma, I'm fine but I'm so sad for you and for my dad. I heard there's a reunion tomorrow?"

"Oh yes, there is. I'm sorry I forgot to mention it. Didn't you know about it? I really wasn't involved in the planning, but I think because they never see you they just assumed you wouldn't be able to come — especially since we didn't see you at the funeral. I know I'm going to see you at least this time, right?"

"I was there!" interrupted Mayra.

"Oh, you were?"

"Yes, I was there but, well, we'll talk about that later. I do want to come if I'm invited."

"Well, of course, you're invited. You're a Taylor. Come on up girl."

Thirty minutes later, Mayra gathered her things and prepared to leave the center.

"Where are you going?" asked Drew.

"Actually, I'm going to a family reunion. So I'll be gone for a couple of days."

"What? This is new. When did this come up? Whose side of the family? Your mom's side? Tell her I said hello."

"Actually, on my father's side," she said with a slight grin.

"What!? Whoa! That's heavy. And, uh, when were you going to tell me?!"

"Would you believe I just found out? It's an after-Father's Day reunion in honor of my grandfather and I just happened to find out by accident. No one invited me, and it was like everything was happening all over again."

"And you're still going after all that?"

"Yeah."

"Who are you? And what have you done with my Mayra?" he joked.

"Ha, ha. I'm going because, after all the times I've been stabbed in the heart, I am still alive. I sat in the kitchen during your Father's Day session and cried. I cried all the way home and decided to fight for this relationship. I have to fight back. I'm not fighting them. I'm fighting fear and hurt and rejection. I'm fighting pride. I have to forgive and reach out or else I'll go crazy. So I called them and invited myself."

"Now, that's what I'm talkin' 'bout! Hey, do you want me to go with you and hold your hand?"

"No, I gotta do this by myself. God is with me. You know, I've realized that He was there all along. I wouldn't have made it this far if He wasn't. He's leading me now and won't let me go in there alone. I'll always have Him. So even if they do drop me cold again, like my girl Whitney says, 'when there's no where else I can go, I can go to Him.'"

"Whoa, don't ever forget, you have me too," he said.

Mayra didn't respond.

"Oh, it's like that, huh? I mess up one time and now you can't count on me?"

"Drew, you're going to stand here and act like you haven't let me down your fair share of times? You're going to try and act like I didn't have a good reason to break up with you? Come on, now, you were like him in many ways. You never were there when I needed you. You were too busy trying to be nice to everybody, including the lecherous girls like Ariana. So, no, I don't need you now. You're a good friend and maybe sometime in the future, things can change, but as a boyfriend? Not now."

"Mayra," he said, looking at her with an expression in his eyes he'd never used before. "I'm sorry for everything I've put you through. You were right. I was like him in a lot of ways. I said you were needy. Now I know we all are somewhat needy and that's okay. I didn't respect you and I put others before you. I was selfish. I'm sorry. I hope to grow into the man you deserve. You're my girl and I do love you," he said, holding her gaze. "I always will, all my floozy ex-girlfriends notwithstanding, you're the one."

Mayra opened the door and walked out, turning back to wave goodbye.

JASON ARRIVED A LITTLE later to help with the phone calls. He slammed the door as he entered the office, and Drew immediately knew what was wrong.

"I can't believe you called my dad! I didn't say you could do that! You're going to blow it for me! Last thing I need is someone to give him an excuse to be mad at me!" shouted Jason.

"Calm down, you're upset, but there's no need ... "

"I can't believe you!" said Jason, waiting to hear something reassuring.

"It's okay. Really, we had a good talk. We really did. Your dad is cool. Man, we hit it off. Come on, was he mad that I called? Did you talk to him?"

"I don't know. My mom told me he called her and told her that you had called. I left right after she told me that. She didn't tell me anything else. But you just don't realize that's not the point. You had no right to call him. Did I ask you to call him?"

"No, you didn't."

"I can't believe this! You don't have all the answers. You think you know everything but you just don't. You think you can just pick up the phone and make it all better, just say a few magic words and it'll all go away. It just doesn't work that way."

Drew was stunned and finally realized that Mayra was right. He had overstepped his bounds. So, he just stood there and let Jason vent his feelings.

"Man, don't you see, I'm scared and nervous. I'm tired of not seeing him. Okay? I don't want him to use this against me. It almost seems like any old excuse will do. Don't get me wrong, you've helped a lot. Inside me things are better. I also know that I really do need the old man and I don't want anything or anyone to ruin it, not even you."

"I know how you feel," said Drew.

"No, you don't. You have no idea how it feels to grow up without your father and have everyone around you think they can fix your life. I've been trying so hard to get to him and NOTHING WORKS!"

"But I *do* know and I'll prove it to you. Let's just wait and see what happens, okay? He probably won't make it to the banquet but he's doing his best to get back to you. Trust me," said Drew as he patted Jason on his back, leading him into the office where Mayra had been placing her calls. "Here. Here's a phone. Let's get some people here for the banquet. If he can make it, he will. If he can't, I'm here, and I'll be your father guest, okay?"

"It's not the same. He wasn't there for Father's Day or anytime I needed him. I can't handle it anymore. I quit. It's just too late now."

"Jason, if you've not taken anything away from what we've done here the past ten months, take this with you — it's never too late as long as he's alive. It's not too late. But trust me when I say, it WILL be too late when he's gone. And when that happens, if you've not reconciled, if you've not made your peace, you will regret it, possibly for the rest of your life. I speak as someone who knows."

Jason could see something in Drew's eyes.

"Besides, you think Father's Days weren't rough for me? I had a lot more anger than you do," added Drew.

"Nah, man. No way."

"For real. I once punched a hole in my mother's wall."

"You're lying! You never told us you didn't have your dad."

"No. I'm for real. I was so mad I just couldn't take it anymore. I'll tell you all about it, but it's all good now. Just trust me, it was cool between me and your old man."

Still scowling, Jason mumbled, "Sure, whatever."

"Jason, let me just say this. You can't walk on eggshells around your dad. You're going to have to learn to speak your heart and to not be afraid that he'll get mad and never come around again."

Jason followed Drew into his office and closed the door.

"Have a seat," said Drew.

"You remember Derek? It's been almost six months since we talked about him."

"Yeah, I remember. You said he made it to his dad's house and they worked things out."

"Well, yes and no. Things were going fine until Derek accused his dad of beating on his mother. That started a horrible fight. Derek accused him of hitting his mom, which caused her to fall down the stairs, but his dad told him a different version of the events. Derek didn't believe him and they argued some more. Finally his father left the house to cool off and Derek went to find his weed. When his dad came back, Derek was smoking out on the porch. Man, his father flipped out. He called Derek a drug addict and told him to get out. He said he was a disgrace. The thing was, Derek was trying to smoke that weed in the middle of an asthma attack. His father went inside when he was done yelling. Fortunately his dad looked back out the window, because Derek had collapsed.

"His dad called 9 1 1 and then gave him CPR. By the time the paramedics got there, Derek was sitting up and coughing. They gave him some oxygen and wanted to take him to the hospital, but Derek refused. He also refused to stay at his father's house. When his father went to the bathroom, Derek grabbed some change and left for the bus stop.

"By the time Derek got home, there was already one message from his father. He left messages for weeks. Derek didn't return one of his calls. Then one day Derek overheard his mom talking to his dad. He could tell his father was getting ready to come over to the house to catch up with him. So he slipped out early for his spring break trip to the beach.

"Five days. I was gone for five days with my friends. Drinking. Smoking, like an idiot. Trashing my father. All the while I knew he was trying to apologize, make things right with me. I figured I'd make him beg for once, see what it felt like to look for me and have me not be there. But I really planned on catching up with him after he had suffered a while.

"When I finally got home, I went into the kitchen for some food. I ate a bowl of cereal and reached for the newspaper. I opened to the Metro section. I turned to the obituaries, and I saw my father's name. Do you understand what I'm saying? My father's name and picture were in the newspaper obituaries. He had a heart attack. He'd tried to apologize. He must have known he was going to die. My family was out looking for me. They had called everyone they knew. The funeral was that day. It was going on as I read the obituary. I missed my chance to say goodbye. I didn't give him the chance to apologize. He wanted to make things right and I was too selfish. I thought I was too hurt. Well, I didn't know hurt until then."

"You?" asked Jason.

"Yes, my name is Andrew Derek Miller. I'm Derek."

"You are Derek? You are Derek! I knew it!"

"That's right. It was me. I am Derek. All the drugs, the DWI, the juvenile jail, the near death asthma attack, everything. I made a mess of my life."

"So you DO know what it's like. I'm so sorry about your dad. What did you do when you realized the funeral was going on?"

"I called a cab and made it as they were rolling my dad's casket down the church aisle. Everyone stared at me like I was some sort of freak. I looked awful. I was high. My sister called me stupid when she walked by with the rest of the family. It was as if I had failed in every way. I just followed behind her and slipped into the limousine with them. No one said a word, except my stepfather who told me everything he had done to try to find me. He had even called every hotel at Ocean City. The problem was, we changed our plans and went to Virginia Beach instead. My mother said, 'you don't need to tell him all you did, you don't owe him anything. He's the one with the owing.' She was right," said Drew with his arms now folded tight across his chest.

"I'm so sorry, man. How do you handle it now? How did you turn it around?"

"Well, at the grave sight, the minister was about the only one to come talk to me. He made sure I sat right up front with my family. When it was over, I couldn't move. I just couldn't move. I dropped my head and cried. Everyone else, except him, walked off and left me. I didn't care. I just kept saying, 'Daddy, I'm sorry. I'm so sorry. I love you.' That minister stayed there until I could collect myself. He said, 'It's okay. He loves you too. He told me so right before he died.' It's when he said those words that I finally heard him. I wiped my tears and stood up. He walked with me afterward and later told me to come visit his church. He had something for me. So I went. He offered me a job at the church's counseling center. I began to sit in on the group sessions just to take notes for him. That was my job — taking notes, working the video camera, all the audio work. He paid good money. But it was the note-taking and the sessions that finally got me. Soon I joined in. Soon I poured out my own heart. The minister gave me all kinds of good words that, I can't explain it, but they were like medicine. He told me God loved me no matter what I had done. All I had to do was be sorry and try the Lord. So I did. I began to change. I wasn't perfect but God made a difference in my life, helped me to pull it together. It took some time. I'm a work in progress, but I went to school and I'm now in this Master's program. Not bad for a former juvenile delinquent, huh?"

"Wow, not bad at all."

"These days, I do all I can to get people like you back with their fathers so they don't make the same mistakes I made. Because then, it IS too late. So give him another chance. I know you're hurting. But what do you do when you get hurt playing ball? Do you let your team down, knowing they need you?"

"Well, I stay in the game anyway and put my pain out of my mind."

"Exactly. Your team needs you now. You and your dad are a team but the team needs help. You're also hurt right now and although you're not in the game, you need to get back in. Get in there and take the punches, but keep shooting. If you miss, take another shot. If you miss, you might get leveled by the opposition. Of course, it still hurts and I get disappointed sometimes — just like I disappoint others. I disappointed you. I let you down when I called your father without your permission.

"But get up, dust yourself off, or even go to the bench for a while, get some water, and recover. Talk to the coach who can reassure you, give you strategy, and let you know he believes in you. Consider God your coach. Consider me as one of His assistant coaches. I'm telling you to get back in there. Your team needs you and you'll make the difference in the game. For God's sake, don't wait until it's too late. Don't wait."

Then he leaned forward, looked directly in Jason's eyes, and said, "Know this — you have nothing to fear. God didn't give you that fear. You have the power to overcome this and all the obstacles in your way."

"Okay," said Jason. "Okay."

Journal

Well, my defining moment came. I came clean and exposed the real me to Jason — the drug addict and delinquent. I hope it doesn't diminish his perception of me. I think I had no choice. What he does with the information is up to him. Hopefully he'll go after that relationship before it's too late.

I hope this revelation isn't one more misstep. I think I've even made some missteps as far as some parents are concerned. Dr. Jackson was right, but I had to try.

The real challenge I see is to help them cope when there's no "big brother," or when the mentor had to cancel, and when there's no one there to help them cross into manhood or womanhood. In other words, there's something about finally reaching out and laying it all on the line … with your OWN father. No "big brother" or "mentor" or "club" or "village" or any other group can replace the incalculable value and vitality their own fathers bring to their lives. I firmly maintain that this is where the emphasis should be placed — on reconciliation, not replacement.

So, my secret is out. Jason suspected all along anyway. I confess my hypocrisy only to myself, that of accusing Mayra of not opening up when all along I've been afraid to divulge my deepest wounds. I now question everything I know to do. I'm thinking of resigning. It's better than being fired! God, I pray for one more chance to make a difference. — A.D.M.

CHAPTER NINE

Their Hands Are Stretched Out Still

Giselle's decorative keepsake box was filled with letters, including a twenty-page letter she'd started at the Father's Day session. The letters spelled out all her concerns and feelings. The box also contained old photos of her and her dad, her sister, and the entire family taken before her family broke apart — even a few photos of her grandparents. Up until her parents' divorce, they were normal doting grandparents — ones who called, stopped by, and showered her with Christmas and birthday presents. But after the divorce, they never called her or her sister. Never. When Giselle called them, it seemed as if they never had much to say. Because of that, she also had a letter written to them. The box held the two birthday cards, the one Christmas card, and the one letter from her grandparents that she'd received since her parents divorced ten years earlier. The box held all she held dear. The words *My Essence* were written on the box in scarlet ink, traced with lace, and dotted with pearls. With her last pre-adult summer underway, Giselle was ready to mail the letters.

She borrowed her mom's car to go duplicate them. When she finished, she placed the letters and their copies back into the keepsake box. She left the office supply store and went to her car, placing the box on her car roof. There was a crack of thunder and Giselle jumped into the car, flinging her backpack onto the back seat, and took off. Just as she crossed the train tracks, Giselle heard a swooshing sound. Her heart froze. She looked into the rearview mirror and saw the contents of her box flying and twirling in the air behind her along the busy road. Her *essence* was scattered to the wind.

She slung the wheel to the right and pulled over into the first parking lot she saw.

"Oh God! No! This is not happening! No!"

She leaped from the car and without thinking rushed after the papers as cars flew by her. Pages were everywhere. Photos were everywhere. Words were everywhere. Feelings were everywhere. She tried to stop traffic and each time the traffic light changed, she had just a few seconds to retrieve a few more pages or pictures. There were about 100 pages in all.

Then Giselle heard a train approaching. Giselle gasped. Without looking, she knew. She just knew. Words that had taken so much courage to write were on those tracks. Sure enough, she looked up and saw several pages. Giselle instinctively looked left toward the train, judged the distance and the time it would take her to rescue the pages, and leaped onto the tracks. Drivers waiting at the crossing signal were afraid they were about to witness a suicide. It seemed like the last page was stuck to the track as the train drew closer. But as soon as Giselle crumbled the last page into her hand, she leaped off. One driver had already begun to dial 911.

Giselle stumbled back to the car. She smoothed the pages as she flipped through them and cried. One page, now marked with a tire tread, said:

Daddy, can you at least tell me now where you were all my life when I looked for you and you weren't there? Can you please reassure me of all those times you wanted to be there. If you thought of me, or even bought me a present for my tenth birthday. Tell me about it. I want, no, I really need to know that I was loved after all.

Daddy, all my life I just want to nestle in your arms and rest in your protection the way I did when you carried me from the car to Aunt Maisie's house in Chicago that snow-covered day when I was seven years old. You were my refuge from the cruelty and the harm in the world. I could have known without a doubt that I was protected, even worthy of protection like a person guards a fine jewel or a fine car. I would, from you that is, know how to recognize respect and genuine love from lust and abuse.

Even prom night. This night took me back to all the other dates. I needed you then. I wish you had been here to tell him that I'm someone special, that he must honor me and respect me. But Daddy, what does that even mean? What does it look like? I wish guys could know that there's someone there who will hold them accountable if they do wrong by me. They need to know not to cross the line. Hey, I need to be told not to cross the line. I need the boundaries to keep me in line. I know I sometimes act like I don't want that type of attention. But I do. Otherwise, I won't know how to handle myself. When you used to say, "it's going to be alright," I believed it. I really did. When you put that band-aid on my wounds, it stuck and made the

*pain go away. When you said you would keep the bogey-
man away, I really believed it. I could trust that. I could
sleep at night.*

Giselle sifted through those pages, trying to place them in order.
Since she had not numbered all of the pages, she compared lines
at the bottom of the pages with lines at the top of the next.

> *From you, Daddy, I needed my confidence to face this
> life because this world sometimes just seems overwhelming
> for me. And at times I felt worthless — worthless —
> worthless. But I'm doing better now. I truly am because I'm
> trying to learn that my value as a person can't be wrapped
> up in whether someone else accepts or rejects me. I know
> God loves me even if nobody else does. For that, I know I
> can make it. But Dad, I still do need you.*

Strangely, Giselle's tears slowed and the content distracted her
from the more mechanical task of rearranging the letters.

> *When my best friend talked about how her father sets
> a curfew and how he was at the door when she walked in
> past curfew — if she only knew how good she had it. All
> that harassment really just shows that he cares and wants
> to protect her. Daddy, don't you realize I want to know that
> you want to protect me and keep me safe from harm? A girl
> is looking for her hero, her knight in shining armor. Don't
> you know it's you until the prince comes?*
> *I used to really wonder if you cared about whether I
> lived or died. Is that an unfair question or do I have just
> cause to make that an issue? There's so much danger in
> this world and there's so much I don't know — things*

that would protect me from danger. Safety measures such as making sure my home is secure and what to do if my life is threatened. Do I run, do I scream — do I fight? How do I fight? If you cared, you would teach me something — at least one thing that I need to know to stay safe, to keep alive.

Your giving me words like, "be careful," or, "be sure and lock your doors," and knowing that you are ready, willing, and able to defend me, come to my rescue, and protect me would have given me the confidence to go forth in this world. I would know that if I fell — you'd pick me up — that if I was offended or harassed — I could run to you. I would want to know that my daddy would come with haste to defend my life and my honor. But, Daddy, despite all the distance and time we've lost, I still love you. Always have. Always will. I'm not mad at you anymore. I need you and I really want to get to know you — have a relationship with you. Yes, there are things I know you missed from my life but I believe it's not too late. I've even tried not to think about you, but you're a constant presence in my life. So, can we try again?

Dad, I'm preparing to go to college now. I tried to ask for help, but we never seemed to get around to finishing that conversation over Christmas. Maybe you can still help me, although I know you have "Candace" issues. (Please don't read this letter to her!) Although Spelman offered me a full scholarship (did Mom tell you?), I'll still need help. I'd be lying if I said I wasn't disappointed you didn't come to my graduation, but I'm willing to admit I had a part to play in that. Truthfully, I had figured I'd be stood up anyway but maybe you would've surprised me. We'll have to wait until my college graduation, I guess.

Dad, I hope this letter (or any letter I send) doesn't turn you away from me. I need the freedom to open up my heart to you. I gotta go now, but I'm growing up now and I realize that we'll grow further apart if we don't do something now before it's too late. I choose to grow closer with you and my little brother ... and the baby. Yes, I know about the baby. I admit I had some mixed feelings about the baby (even the boy, for that matter), but I'm better. I adore him and I know I'll adore the baby. Please know that it doesn't have to be either / or, them / us, that family / our family. There's enough love to go around. You can love all of us — you don't have to choose. So, please don't.

Dad, call me or write or send a card or even pictures of the kids. I'll do my part, too, if you give me a chance. You can even come visit. Let's be there for each other. I'll even give Candace a chance, honestly! Anyway, I better hurry up and mail this before I change my mind. I'll be fine no matter what happens. I know that now, but a girl needs her daddy (even if she's almost eighteen) and, finally, I have no problem saying that. Please write back.

Your daughter, Giselle.

Satisfied that she had found what she needed, Giselle drove off.

JASON DECIDED TO MEND the disconnect. He was going after what he lost when his parents divorced. If Drew could reach out and confront the issue, then so could he. Without saying goodbye to Drew, he grabbed his backpack, hoisted it over his shoulder, and was out the door. He dug in his pockets for cash and found fifteen bucks, more than enough to catch the bus from Aspen Hill Road to the Glenmont Station where he'd ride the Metro to his father's apartment in Gaithersburg. He'd have to take one more bus after that, but he figured he knew the route. He had ridden with his dad once before and was pretty sure he remembered the way. Jason stopped home first to grab some food. His mom had gone to look after her mother. So she wasn't expected to be home for a while. Jason left for his father's home around 7:00 p.m.

He walked out of the Shady Grove Metro Station around 8:16 P.M. and caught a glimpse of a bus pulling out of the depot. He ran after it, but the bus got away. So Jason returned to the stop to look at the schedule. The next bus wasn't due until 8:46. When it finally came, he climbed on board and instinctively gravitated to the back of the bus. He plopped down. The summer sky was almost dark. Jason noticed the street lights turn on even as the bus passed by. As the bus drew close to the complex, Jason began nibbling his fingernails.

Jason buzzed his father's line at the apartment complex and waited. There was no answer, so he made himself comfortable on the steps of the complex as if settling in for a long wait. A moment later, Jason heard shots ring out followed by the sound of feet running. Jason jumped to his feet and leaped toward the shrubs to duck. When he didn't hear anything more, Jason lifted his head to peer from above the bushes.

"There he is!"

Gunshots were fired toward the bushes. Jason rolled out of the shrubs, stumbled to his feet, and took off as fast as he could. Two assailants chased him, firing as they ran. Jason ran back toward the parking lot, weaving between cars. Bullets shattered the windshield of the car directly in front of him. Then, one assailant slowed to a stop, took aim, and fired one last shot.

"I got him!" screamed the shooter. "I saw him go down. Let's roll!"

"Make sure you got him!"

"Let's roll. I ain't going back to Seven Locks."

Both turned to run away from the scene. Jason lay motion-less between two cars. Moments later, a crowd gathered.

"Somebody, help! Call 911! It looks like a boy's been shot."

"I see blood!"

"Somebody call an ambulance!"

"He's not breathing!"

SEVEN OF THE BOARD MEMBERS arrived at the center and began their meeting in the all-purpose room. Drew waited in his office for the signal to join the "emergency" performance review. Mr. Conrad finally came to Drew around 9:10 P.M. and said, "We're ready."

The board members greeted Drew and got right down to business.

"We know you're busy and the hour is late. Let me just thank you for agreeing to meet with us on such short notice. We felt it was important to be able to talk with you immediately following our meeting to share with you any decisions that would come from the meeting. You understand, don't you?"

"Certainly," said Drew.

"Well, Drew, we definitely want to commend you on many of the accomplishments you've achieved this year. Giving to the center has not dropped following 9/11. Considering the decline in giving to local organizations nationwide, we're holding our own and we want to keep it that way. As careful and astute as you've been with the books this year, you, of all people, know what even a ten percent decline in giving would do to operations. We'd probably have to lay off a couple of people, maybe drop one of our sports programs, or even reduce the number of weeks we're open during the summer.

"Drew, if that happened, do you know what that would mean?" asked Bruce Conrad, the board director.

"Sure, Bruce. If we couldn't offer the full ten weeks of summer camp, our clients would go elsewhere. They'd choose another summer program."

"Precisely. And if we lost our summer group, we'd lose the $50,000 grant given exclusively for the summer operations. We'd have to close during the summer. And if we closed during the summer, we'd lose a great portion of our yearly clientele. Drew, you see the ripple effect, don't you?"

"Of course," said Drew, matter of factly. "Let me guess, this has to do with Mrs. Phillips and her perceived influence over the Malden Foundation."

"Well, I don't know whether it's perceived or actual. Here's the point — she's upset over what she feels is an invasion of her and her son's privacy. There's a little too much personal involvement in her son's life, Drew."

"Bruce," interrupted Drew.

"Just hold on. You don't have to say it. You're not violating any performance rule or ethical canon, and we're not saying that. We're not saying you've not done a good job. We just want you to lay low, back off a little, let this thing die down. We've also heard a lot of good things about your work here. But you know how it is. It just takes one apple. We're prepared to support you if you agree to work with us. We'd like to secure some assurances from you — that you'll stay out of their private lives. No more personal talk. No more God talk, or at least tone it down."

Drew bit on his tongue to keep from saying the wrong thing, but the phone rang and interrupted things anyway.

"I need to get that," said Drew.

"I think it should wait, Drew. Besides, it's after hours now. Let's finish this meeting," said Bruce.

"I need to get this," said Drew. He hurried to his office and snatched the phone before the caller hung up.

"Springridge," said Drew.

"Drew! This is Vicky Phillips. Please don't hang up! Jason's been shot."

Drew fell back against the wall.

"I'm on my way to Shady Grove Hospital. I don't know much. There was a message on my voicemail from the hospital saying something about a shooting and how Jason was asking for someone named Drew. I know I've caused you a whole lot of trouble, but please … "

"I'm on my way."

Drew ran back to the board meeting and said, "I have an emergency. I have to go."

"Family?" asked Mrs. Ferris.

"Yes," said Drew.

"Well, just remember what we said. You agree to keep the work impersonal, even suspend Let's Talk for a while, and we'll consider not ending your contract early," said Bruce.

Twenty minutes later, Drew stormed into the emergency room.

Vicky rushed to meet him. "Drew."

"How is he? Where is he?"

Before she could answer, Vicky broke down into a wail and fell into Drew's arms. He held and consoled her while he looked around the ER for someone who could provide information.

"Mrs. Phillips, it's okay. Tell me, please, tell me!"

"I'm sorry. He's going to be okay. I'm so relieved, but this is unbearable just the same. He doesn't want to talk to me. He only wants you."

"Okay, where is he? Where was he shot? Was he hurt bad? What happened?"

"He's okay. Some boys evidently mistook him for someone they were after. They shot at him but only nicked him on the ear. They did have to stitch it, though. The blood loss came when he went down. His face landed on a rock, which caused a bloody gash. He also suffered a concussion. They're going to keep him overnight for observation. He's just shaken up, though not as much as I am."

"He's talking to the police right now. Let's see if they're finished."

Drew followed her to Jason's bed in the ER. The police officer had just finished his questioning.

"Okay, if you remember anything else, let us know. And when you do talk to your father, please have him call us. Since he lives there, he may know something about the troublemakers." He turned to Vicky, "Mrs. Phillips, can I have a word with you?"

"Sure," she said, and they strolled toward the waiting room.

Drew took a deep breath as if searching for nerve. Then he pulled the ER curtain back. Jason lay there, covered to his neck by a white sheet. The gauze on his forehead overshadowed the facial lacerations. Blood stained the bandage. Another bandage was taped all around his right ear, covering it almost entirely. Drew pulled a chair over and sat down, inadvertently waking Jason.

"Shhh," said Drew. "Relax, you've probably been sedated."

"No, I'm okay. They did give me a painkiller, but I'm really not supposed to be sleeping because of the bump on my head," he raised his hand to feel the gauze on his face and head. "Do you know what happened?"

"Yes. Your mom told me everything. Why were you there? What were you trying to do?"

"I just wanted to see my dad. I was just trying to hang out with him, let him know I really wanted to try. I just got tired of waiting on my mom to take me. She kept trying to stop me anyway, so I decided to go on my own. I was just in the wrong place at the wrong time. No matter what I do, I fail at finding my father every time. I fail." He turned his head away from Drew, but continued to talk. "I know it was stupid, but I just figured he'd be home by the time I got there."

Jason turned his head to see Drew dialing a number on his cell phone. Drew pulled the phone to his face and said, "Hello, yeah. Okay, you're on."

He handed the phone to Jason. "It's for you."

Confused, Jason reached out with his right hand and took the phone, whispering, "Who is it?"

"Talk, boy!" demanded Drew.

"Hello?" Jason heard a voice on the other end.

"Dad?"

The small boy vulnerability became apparent. He turned over in the bed, curled up to the phone, and began to whimper. Drew slipped out and pulled the curtain to give Jason privacy.

"Drew!" called Jason.

"Yeah, Jason?"

"He's on his way. Thank you."

"I got your back, Son. Now, talk with your old man." Drew set off to find Vicky and make things right.

"What time did she say she'd be here?" Mayra's father Rick asked his wife as he pulled his mother's lilac lace curtains back. He was referring to Mayra, who was scheduled to pull up to the family reunion that morning.

"What do you think she wants to talk about?" Rick asked his wife as they washed the breakfast dishes. "She said she wanted to come and be a part of the reunion and she said she just wanted to talk about something," his wife answered. Even surrounded by his mother, sisters, cousins, and wife, Rick was a little anxious. There was something about the words, "talk about something" that worried him. Rick had a gut feeling that the one thing that hadn't happened with her all these years — talking about that something — was about to happen. When Mayra had called and spoken with Rick's wife yesterday, she had politely informed Barbara that she was coming to the reunion.

Distressed, Rick glanced toward the living room window with each passing car. He walked nervously out to the deck to smoke a couple of cigarettes. Ding-dong rang the doorbell. "She's here," called Barbara. "Hi, Mayra, come on in."

"Hi, Barb, how's it going?" said Mayra as she reached to politely hug her stepmother. Mayra never referred to Barbara as her "stepmother."

"Hey, baby, how's my sweetie?" said Rick. "How was the drive? Did you have any problems? How long has it been since you've been here? Whew, I know it's been a while since we really spent any time together." Rick was chattering to loosen her up and feel out her mood.

"Are you hungry?" he asked, trying to lead her to the kitchen. "You know we have the works here. Barbecue chicken, Barbara's potato salad, your grandma's greens with turkey meat, your Aunt Helen's tuna salad, and Uncle Bobby is outside grilling."

Mayra sat down at the oblong kitchen table. "No, I'm okay."

He placed a cup with soda on the table. "Here's some Sprite. I know you like Sprite," said Rick.

"Daddy, can we go somewhere to talk? I don't want to talk around everyone else."

"Well, except for Bobby and your grandmother, it's just us. Everyone else is at the park trying to play baseball. This really is the best time before everyone comes back," he said, hoping that the rest of the family would indeed come back. They talked for a while about Mayra's college year, her subjects, and possible majors. She was torn between Economics and English. But after an hour of catching up, Mayra raised the real issues.

"Dad, we need to talk about us, about you being my father and about how we can make this relationship better — that's if you want it to be better. I know Mommy told you I was mad at you for just about everything," she searched his expression for clues about how he was feeling.

"I know, I know, honey. I haven't been the best father in the world … "

"Wait, Dad, I wasn't going to say that. That's the problem. You never give me a chance to say what I want to say to you."

"Come on, now, sweetie … "

"Ugh!" she sighed loudly as she dropped her head and tensed up. "Dad, will you listen to me?! That's the problem. That's always been the problem. The few times I've had to really talk to you and tell you all that's right and all that's wrong, it's like you don't want to hear it."

"Mayra, I can't change the past. I can't change all I've done, and I know I haven't been there all the time, but I did try."

Mayra wondered whether her father was going to listen to her at all or simply trod the same denial path he had always walked with her.

"Yeah, yeah, I hear you," he said calmly as if to suggest he understood. "But let's try and move forward."

"Rick," interrupted his wife. "She's speaking from her heart and you need to listen to your daughter."

By now, Mayra's face was wet with tears. The room grew silent. The air was thick with pain. The buzz of family voices grew as relatives came in through the doorway but Mayra heard her grandmother whisper something to them and then the voices toned down. No one came into the kitchen. Rick leaned against the counter with his arms folded across his chest. He looked at her.

"Alright, Mayra. Talk."

Mayra knew that his heart was not open to receive her words, and so she wept. Mayra had always willingly devoured the morsels of affection that her father casually tossed her way. She had always tried to decipher the meaning of his every word and action in an attempt to learn what he really felt about her.

Dad, I want to ask you why you didn't give me my grandfather? Why weren't you in my life? What kept you away? Do you love me? She had always wanted to ask these questions — but she never did.

"Go ahead and cry," he said. "I want to hear and I will listen, but only if you promise to listen to me, only if you agree to hear me out. I have enough guilt. I know you think I don't think about you and that whole situation. But I have and I do. I want to hear, but I can't help but feel like I'm being condemned. I did the best I could with what I had to work with."

"No, you didn't," said Mayra. "I don't think you did," she said angrily, making direct eye contact with her father. Her demeanor grew fierce. "But I'm going to speak my mind today and come what may. You're going to hear what my life was like without you, what it was like on those days you didn't show. I've been afraid all these years that if I *did* speak my heart, you'd turn away from me. Well, you never turned *to* me, so there's nothing to turn away from. You've already locked me out, so it can't be any worse."

"I'll leave," said Barbara.

"You don't have to go," said Rick, standing to grab his wife's hand.

"Oh man!" sighed Mayra. "Rick, we need to talk alone!"

"It's daddy to you, Mayra," he said, looking at her sternly.

"Maybe when you act like it," she fired back.

"You need to be respectful no matter what has happened."

"Oh my God, I don't believe this!" she said with a look of surprise. "Let me get this straight. You haven't been anything close to a father to me, and of course, you've been the doting father to your little daddy's girl Gwen, but you've been nothing to me. And now you're tripping because I call you Rick? If that's the case, then I don't know why I'm here," she stood to grab her things.

"Mayra, stay," said Barbara, grabbing her by the shoulders and trying, despite Mayra's resistance, to seat her back in the chair. "I'll leave. You guys talk, and it's Rick for now, okay? Mayra? It's Rick?" She looked Mayra square in the eyes.

"Rick, move on, honey, and hear the girl out, PLEASE!" Barbara slowly backed out of the kitchen, making sure Mayra didn't follow.

Mayra wasted no time in expressing herself. "You know, don't you remember why I didn't want to come to your wedding? I was really angry and since it appeared that it was so important for me to be there, saying no to you seemed to finally give me the power over you, for once. I have to confess, it felt good when you told me that it was important to you and Barbara and that you would really love for me to be there. But I hated the way you always seemed to favor Gwen more than me even before you married her mother. I hated that. Where were you when I really wanted you to be there for me? For the first time since you walked out, I was the one with the power. This was it. Hallelujah! I was no longer the victim." Tears and mascara streamed down her face. "Tell me, why should I have come? Why was it so important then that I be in your life as opposed to these past few years? You should've explained that. I wanted to be fair and wasn't trying to make it hard but I really needed to understand things. Do you remember what you told me?"

"No," said her dad quietly.

"You said, 'Alright, well you think about it and let me know.' I suppose you were still hoping I would attend the wedding. But once you said that, I gave up. I figured, if it was really that important to have me there you wouldn't have had a problem telling me why. But I was left believing there was a problem, which is why I didn't attend the wedding.

"Daddy, you weren't there for me. And you don't seem to be here for me now. I still need you, but I'm learning how to make it on my own."

"Oh come on, your mother received her child support every month. This simply is not true and you know it."

"Daddy, you just don't get it, do you? This isn't about money. God, I hate it when I hear men say, 'oh, I take care of my obligations. The court takes the child support out every month.' Do you all think alike? Has it ever occurred to you that if all you do for your child is pay a few hundred dollars a month, you have NOT taken care of your obligations? Your obligation is to be there. You created me.

"There is so much I want to talk about with you, so many things you missed that I want to share with you the things you missed. I also want to hear about you and your success — and why you left me out of those successes, your life. I don't know. I want to know why? Why do you want me in your life now? I know you love me. I believe it now. It's probably because your time is short. It's your destiny to know and be a part of your children's lives. I'm grateful we have the relationship now.

"But I needed you to protect me then, teach me what to know, how to talk to boys. I needed you to tell them that you had expectations of them in how they treated your daughter. This would have showed them that you cared about what happened to me and that there was someone with authority and the power to enforce it or even punish those who hurt me or treated me disrespectfully.

"Daddy, a father protects his baby girl. He teaches her how to spot danger. But you didn't do that, and I was hurt so many times. There are things I can't even tell you. But you need to know what my life was like without you. I need to air my feelings and my experiences. When you really listen to all of it, without interrupting, without making excuses or trying to explain, blame, or justify what you've done, and when you cry with me, then I'll know you've been touched by my pain. Even when your father died … "

"What about my father!?" he interrupted, shocked by what she was implying.

"YOU LEFT ME OUT!"

"Wait a minute! I can't believe this! My own father died, so I'm sorry I wasn't thinking about where people were sitting or who came or who was called! How very selfish of me," he tossed back sarcastically.

"Dad, you just don't get it. It's not that. It's that you left me out of his life, out of the family. Gwen was there — with the family!"

"I don't believe this and I don't believe you. You're not like your mother."

Mayra suddenly stood up, grabbed her purse, and said, "You know, I gotta go. This was obviously a mistake!"

"Wait! That's right. Just run when the going gets rough. Especially when you're wrong. You don't want to hear that I didn't intentionally hurt you. No, it's easier to be angry, to hate, and to resent me. That's far easier than trying to work through where I'VE BEEN and to hear what I'VE had to face through our relationship and how hard it was for ME!"

"Dad, I don't hate you … but WHY wasn't my name on the

program? Just tell me that? Don't you see how that hurt me?" She stood in the doorway, wanting a reason to stay. "I DIDN'T EVEN WANT TO GO TO THE FUNERAL. I was afraid I would be left out and excluded and I just wanted to avoid that whole scene. I even hoped somehow through your father's death that you now would understand what it was like not having a father, which is why I decided to come, figuring you might treat me differently. I know the two situations can't be compared because you had your dad all your life, but I thought just maybe things would be different. I wondered if your own tears would remind you of MY many tears. Would you look back over your most memorable father-son moments and remember that you deprived me of the opportunity to have moments like that? I wondered whether you would wonder what I would remember or miss about him."

"What do you want me to say?"

"Do I have to tell you that too? I want you to truly be sorry. Not because I told you to say it, but because you truly understand. Daddy, why wasn't I in the funeral program?"

"That was a mistake. That was an oversight. There was so much confusion. The truth is that Bobby's wife Helen either forgot or just thought she was protecting Barbara. Don't ask me to explain it. I asked her after I got your call. She said something about not wanting it to look like I had an affair while married to Barbara. You know she's old-fashioned, and since your mother and I are no longer married …"

"Uh, Dad, you and Barbara didn't even get married until a few years ago. Gwen and I came into the world in the same way. So because over a decade later, you marry her mother, I'm still somehow illegit and she's the first princess?"

"Mayra, please forgive her. She just didn't understand. I didn't care at all about that."

"What?" asked Mayra.

"I tried to understand why you left the funeral. I tried to put it all together and then I reread the program and saw that your name was missing. Mayra, I would have left too. I'm so sorry. I'm so, so sorry, Mayra," he stretched his arms out to hug his daughter. She stood in the doorway. "Do you know what the code is to enter my apartment building?"

"What? No," answered Mayra. "Why would I know that?"

"It's the date of your birth."

For the first time since she got there, Mayra didn't have a comeback. He had conquered her rage. So every time he came home, every time his wife entered the building, they each had to think of Mayra. This was her balm.

"If you ever want to come see me or just get away from it all, here's a key to the apartment door. Your birthday will get you into the building," he said, smiling. "Mayra, I'm sorry for everything. I can't change the past. I just can't. But I love you, I really do. You're my first born and that makes you special. You will always be first. No one can ever replace you. I love all my children, but you were first. I know I have a lot to make up for, but I will, if you give me the chance."

"Dad, you don't have to make up for anything ..."

"Yes, I do and not even you can get in the way. Just let me be your father now. Please, help me."

With that, Mayra gave in. She had never loved her father more than at that moment.

"Mayra, let me ask for your forgiveness for all the times I wasn't there. But let me also ask for forgiveness NOW for all the mistakes I'll probably make in the future. It's pretty obvious that I don't have this father thing down. I want to do better. You are a part of this family. You should just call and say, 'I'm coming, where do we meet up?' We're going to drop the ball but nothing is going to change the fact that my blood, your grandma's blood runs thick in your veins. You couldn't change that even if you wanted to. You're stuck with us and you need to make it clear that we're stuck with you. You know, I rarely heard from your mom. She was too proud. I'm not trying to make excuses. No one should have to push me. Just help me along, please. Help me to do better."

Mayra stretched forward, nestled her head onto her father's shoulder, and said, "Alright, Daddy."

Journal

As this program year draws to a close, I consider our gains and losses, even our near losses. Was it worth it? Did I push Jason too far? Did I cross the line with my so-called "intrusion" into their lives? I can't help but contemplate their futures. Mine too, for that matter. Jason getting shot, my losing this job, Kalia's unearthed wounds, and Mayra — maybe some relationships aren't meant to be reconciled. I was so sure of myself and everything I believed. I have some thinking to do. — A.D.M.

CHAPTER TEN

Resolutions

Since Drew encouraged the kids to invite parents and other relatives to the awards banquet, Dion seized the chance to call his brother and father.

"Hello, can I speak to David?" Dion asked his brother's wife.

"Who's calling?"

"Um, it's me, Dion. I'm David's younger brother. He told me I can call him."

"Oh sure, I'll get him."

Dion wondered whether his brother would come to the phone. *If I was calling Ray, I wouldn't have to wonder.* With that thought, Dion realized this relationship was fragile. This knowledge didn't upset Dion, but he recognized the difference. Dion had to convince himself all over again that there was nothing standing between him and his brother's love. *He does love me, I know he does. I do believe him.*

"Hello," said David.

With that one word, Dion's heart leaped in place. "Hey, David. It's your baby brother!"

"Hey man, how are you? Well, this is a surprise."

"Yeah, I thought I'd surprise you. Is it all right that I called you? Did I call at a bad time? I can call you back later or you can…"

"Wait, slow down, dude! I'm glad you called. It's fine, really. What's going on, what's up?"

"Oh, I'm okay. Everything's cool, you know. But I wanted to invite you somewhere and maybe you can invite Dad for me."

"Oh, really, where is this?"

"I'm on a really good basketball team with the boys and girls club and I'm really good. I'm a starter. We have a tournament and we've already won two games. I'm inviting you to the championship game, and I was just thinking that if you didn't have anything to do Saturday, you and Dad might ride down together and see my game. I know you're busy and would probably have to drive right back after the game. I understand that, but after the game is a big awards banquet, we're supposed to invite all our family members. You could even bring my nephew. Do you think you can come?"

"Well, what time and where is the game and what time and where is the banquet? I'll call Dad and see if he can come too. I'll try to make it. No sweat, little guy."

Dion gave his brother all the particulars and said goodbye. Before David got around to calling his father, Dion's dad called for the first time since Christmas. As a divorce lawyer, Marshall knew a few things about broken families. He knew that people usually have some part to play in the mess they're in. But Marshall until recently hadn't realized that Dion and Ray had done nothing to cause themselves to be fatherless. It was only when Marshall began to notice the lives of his clients' children that his sons' reality hit home. The nail in the coffin for him occurred at a client meeting after Father's Day.

"What kind of man is it that won't even call or come see his own flesh and blood?" his client asked. "I don't understand that … this boy agonizes … this boy goes to basketball games with no daddy … he can't even come to the father/son day at his church because his father is just not interested in him … I thought not suing for child support would make it easy on him, but he still doesn't even call … I have no one to teach him how to be a man, no one."

Each word pierced Marshall's heart. The fact was, *his* sons played basketball without a father, and *his* sons built race cars with the scouts, but without him. Marshall wondered if his sons had been denied the joy and pride of attending father/son day at their own church. *Did they even have a father/son day? Did they invite someone else? Would they have tried to invite me? Should they have tried to invite me? Am I worthy of such a call?*

Just two days after his dad's call, Dion was hustling to help get the house ready for a visit from his brother and his dad. Ray sat idly by.

"Is your room clean yet?" called Sharon. Dion had been cleaning his room all day. He wanted things to be just right when his dad and brother came.

"Mom, should I put my shoes in the closet or leave them in front of the bed? Should I leave the pillow out from under the cover or put it under the comforter? Should Dad sleep in the top bunk? Which is better?"

"Dion, honey, I don't think your father and brother are staying here with us. I'm not sure that they should anyway, at least not your dad."

"Why not?" asked Dion. "He didn't mention any other place to stay for the night. It has to be here."

"Well, I don't think it's a good idea."

"Mom, if you tell him he can't stay here, he might not spend the night at all and he might not go to the banquet with me tomorrow and hang out with me. You're going to make him want to turn right around and go home tonight and that's not fair! I can't believe you'd do that to me!"

"Dion, don't go there! Don't even start that! He's not staying here and that's all there is to it. You better move on."

Sharon heard the slam of a bedroom door. She started to charge upstairs but stopped on the third step.

Ray heard the commotion between Dion and their mother. He knocked gently on Dion's closed door.

"What?!" yelled Dion.

"It's me," said Ray, boldly proceeding into Dion's sanctuary. "Whoa! What's up with you?"

"He's not coming is he?" said Dion. "You've been right all along."

Ray moved toward the edge of the bed. "Make some room for your big brother. Look man, I got news for you. You've been the one who's been right all along. You're the one who keeps trying and hoping and praying about dad. You keep believing and you're the one with all the faith. You're the one who actually wrote on the prayer card your hopes that dad would finally come."

"You saw me?"

"Yeah. I didn't want to say anything because I wished I had the faith to do the same thing. I was too angry and too proud to admit that I really needed Dad. In fact, I was jealous of you. I was jealous of your faith and your trust in him."

"You were jealous of *me*?"

"Oh, come on, you haven't figured that out? Dion, there's only one thing worse than feeling rejected by your dad or even your mom. It's losing hope. Drew's been trying to tell us to never give up because one day we'll lose that chance and forever regret it. You're the one who has made his words real to me. I saw what hope looked like whenever I looked at you. Now I actually believe he just might come. He might not. But, I can hope, can't I? So don't let go now. I'm countin' on you, dawg!" said Ray.

"Thanks, Ray. I've been sweatin' David and all, but you're my brother. You're here day and night. And I know that," he said, lowering his head on his big brother's shoulder.

"Good! So when you finish your room, clean mine!" He rose to his feet and pulled Dion into a headlock, his usual way of displaying brotherly affection.

When the doorbell rang, the boys ran down the steps. "Dad?" they said in unison.

"My boys! What a welcome!" he said, reaching over to grab one hand of each of his strapping sons to pull them into a loving embrace. "My boys."

"Surprise, surprise!" added Sharon, who withdrew into the kitchen, leaving the men with their reunion.

"Dion knew all along you'd be here," said Ray, still snuggled to the right side of his father.

"Dad, where's David?" Dion said.

"He couldn't come, but he'll be here next time. Hey, sorry I missed the game, but traffic was horrible."

"You didn't miss the game Dad, it's tomorrow. Then comes the banquet," said Dion. "You are going to stay for the banquet, aren't you? That part's really for the parents. Drew said he has something for the mothers and something for the fathers."

"Really, well guess what — I'm staying. I have my things in the car because I'm staying at the Day's Inn, but I thought we could go to the movies and get some pizza. If we're going, we have to leave now though. We want to go to get back in time to rest up for our big day, okay?"

"Yeah, Dad. Hey, so you're staying for the whole weekend, right?" asked Dion.

"Yes, of course, I'm staying."

The next day, after Dion's basketball game, Marshall arrived at the house thirty minutes early to pick the boys up for the banquet. He politely asked Sharon if he could help his sons dress for the banquet.

"Sure, go on up. I hope their rooms are clean."

Marshall ventured upstairs, turning first to Dion's room. "Hey, son. Nice room. Cool! It's clean — whoa!"

"Ha ha, dad. I do okay. Which tie do you think I should wear?" asked Dion as he sifted through about a dozen ties spread out on the bed.

Marshall examined the selection. "Let me see, hmmm — wait a minute, these are little boy ties — they're all clip-on. What's up with that? Don't you have any real ties?"

"I do!" offered Ray. Embarrassed, Dion reached for the full-length ties.

"Dad, I don't know how to tie them. Neither does Ray."

"Yes, I do!" Ray fired back.

"No, you don't, because no one ever taught us how to tie those ties. So Mom keeps buying these baby ties."

"Then it's time for the both of you to learn how to become men, and learning to tie a tie is a good place to start."

By 6:30 P.M., the Matador Room at the Holiday Inn was filled to capacity. Drew gathered the twenty-seven kids in an adjoining conference room.

"Okay guys, gather around and listen up. This year has been unbelievable. I don't know what to say about you guys. You have been incredible. I never imagined we'd have the year we have. It far exceeded my expectations. I thought I'd school you guys on the ways of life. I learned far more from you than I could've ever taught you. Thank you.

"I don't know what tomorrow holds, but I know that this

year has been the best year of my life. I will always look back on these days and these sessions with you and know that it was here that I became a man, that I finally grew up." Tears began to well up in his eyes.

Jason was no longer smiling. "Drew, what are you saying? Is there something we should know? You'll be here this summer and next fall, right?"

"Yeah, Drew, what's up?" asked Ray.

"Nothing. It's just that, well, you never know. I don't plan on going anywhere. But sometimes things happen that are out of our hands, and all I'm saying is that as long as I'm alive, I'll be there for you. Count me as a big brother, friend, even counselor for life, you got that?"

"Yeah, but you're not going anywhere. Did my mother get you in trouble?" asked Jason. "If she did, I'm through with her. I'll just go live with my dad. I'll find somewhere to go."

"Jason, relax. This has nothing to do with your mother. And even if it did, that's none of your business and it should-n't interfere in any way with the respect and love you must show toward her. She's the one who's there for you day in and day out. If she's done anything you don't like, it's because she loves you and she's doing what she thinks is best. End of story. You got me?"

Jason didn't respond.

Drew continued. "People, we've come too far to regress to our unsympathetic ways. We are all in this together with your mothers. You're on the same team. Jason, you and your mom Vicky are on the same team," he said, leaning his head toward Jason. "You guys are better than the best. As we prepare to go out there, keep in mind you represent Springridge. Always hold your head up. Fight the good fight of faith and remember, God loves you, your parents love you, and so do I. Now, let's go out there.

You guys head back to the banquet hall and I'll go find the speaker. I'm sure he's around here somewhere."

Drew made his way to the front desk and found that a message was waiting at the reception area to inform him that the evening's keynote speaker, a local professional athlete, had cancelled. Drew didn't know what to do, but he didn't have much choice. He made an executive decision — he would deliver the keynote address. He didn't tell anyone — not Mayra and not the board.

After the awards had been distributed and everyone had dined, Drew walked to the podium. He mumbled under his breath, "This job is toast anyway, so what the heck."

He surveyed the room, glanced in the direction of the board's table, took a deep breath, and began to speak. "WELCOME to the community center directors, to Councilman Smith and Councilwoman Solorzano, distinguished guests, church and other community leaders, Pastor Bates, whose Grove Hill Baptist Church is one of our major sponsoring organizations, to you fine parents, and to the greatest group of kids and young men and young women this world has seen. I hope you have enjoyed yourselves thus far and I hope the food was satisfying. I want all the mothers in the house to stand," he said, glancing and waving at all the mothers he had come to know during the previous ten months. "Give it up for the mothers!"

"Now, all you dads stand, and let's give it up for the dads! Whoo Whoo Whoo!" There were only a third as many fathers present, yet they received as voracious an applause as the mothers.

"Yeah, yeah — that's what I'm talking about!" said Drew, joining in the applause. "Now, we normally bring a notable in to serve as keynote speaker and dazzle you with words and wisdom. But due to a last minute scheduling conflict, our speaker cancelled. So I decided to take this opportunity to share some insight that I've gained from these amazing children. They deserve a whole lot of commendation and applause."

The board members looked on in amazement, some with disdain. All eyes turned to Vicky Phillips who had just walked in.

"When I accepted this position, I had no idea how this year and the time I've spent here would change my life. I've spent nearly a year watching, listening to, and engaging your children, so I want to share some things that I have learned.

"Just to give you a little information about who I am — I am a graduate psychology student. My master's thesis is on the emotional development of children of divorce. While it started as work, the work became my mission. The mission — to help these children reach out and try to reconcile with their fathers or mothers and bridge relationship gaps.

"Your kids shared all year during our Friday night rap sessions, and you graciously agreed to allow us the opportunity. You extended to us the distance and confidentiality we needed to penetrate hearts, minds, and even souls. So I thank you. The things we did this year and the growth we all accomplished would not have occurred but for you, the parents. As you know, these discussions often revolved around matters of school, friendships, family, and even God. We also talked about mothers and we talked about fathers. Indeed, we highlighted fathers because it's no secret that many children in our community live in single parent households.

"You know, I've seen many of your children after school every week. If you count the basketball games and practice, then I see them several days per week. I see them an additional two hours on Friday evenings. I've kept an open door. I've watched and observed your children. I've shared with them and they've shared with me. They speak with silence, omissions, apathy, and sometimes, rage. But I've also seen hope, patience, forgiveness, and unconditional love. For nearly a year, we have talked, rapped, wrote, laughed, cried, and even screamed. But most of all — simply put, we kept it real. And the message that came through loud and clear was that despite the distance, the no-shows, the hurt, and the perceived rejection — their hands are stretched out still.

"I gave your sons high fives after the touchdowns. I praised your sons and daughters after the home run or winning basket. I've tutored your youngsters. I've relearned geography. Thanks to them I can now identify Sudan and Uzbekistan on a map — blind-folded. I've been to two science fairs, baseball, football, and basketball games, Cub Scouts, and Christmas plays. I've listened every Friday night. I have heard from them, and I've heard from you. So I hope I've earned the privilege of rapping with you now. I see your issues and I understand your hurts, your frustrations, and your dreams. I have some things to say to each of you.

"To you mothers — I salute you. Your sacrifice is unceasing. You've had no one to pace the floor with as you waited out the midnight fever. There was no one to drop him off at practice while you cooked dinner. You had no one to pick her up from the day care while you were trying to navigate rush-hour traffic. Your boss refused you the time off you needed to meet with your son's teacher. You had too few chances to chaperone field trips. No Caribbean cruises for you. No one knows quite how to help you, or that yours *is* a family. You don't know quite how to ask for help. So you don't and you do without. You need child support, but the system has failed you.

"You've been hurt, labeled by society, and stereotyped. To the system, you are a statistic. You're the topic of Sunday news shows and Congressional debates. You're one of the glaring census truths and all the world wants to observe you and watch you in your cage. But they just don't know what to do with you or how to help.

"So you've fought. You fight the fathers and you fight the schools. You fight your jobs and you fight the stereotypes. You fight poverty and you fight, yes, the government, your families, and sometimes even yourself. But what you don't know is that you are not alone. There are allies and they're right around you. You just haven't noticed. These allies are your parents, the kid's grandparents, centers like this one, friends next door. They are most certainly other single mothers, but they are your brothers and uncles too. They are cub masters and den mothers and coaches. They are ministers and priests and your church sisters and brothers. They are the children themselves, and believe it or not, the fathers of your children are your allies. You only have to learn how to ask for help and how to accept it. And by all means, ask their fathers, give them a chance to meet their children's needs.

"I watched my own mother struggle and cry, fight and cry some more. But I never saw her reach out and ask for help. No one knew. When we used to go to church, we'd have a need, but she just wouldn't say a word. 'Everything is fine,' she'd say. But nothing was further from the truth.

"I suffered when she disparaged my father. When she said he was a loser, I felt like the loser. So, I salute you, particularly if you've worked to keep the relationship between your children and their fathers alive. I salute you if you speak kindly of your children's fathers. No football or baseball game or piano lesson is worth more than that visit. You know, I once heard a preacher say, 'love never fails.' So I say to you, when all else fails, love their fathers. Be kind and reach out, or help your child reach out. Be flexible and be willing to compromise. Be persistent. The 'I can do it all myself thing' doesn't cut it all the time.

"You might think to yourself, *he shouldn't see the child since he didn't pay.* Well the courts say they are unrelated, that they are a separate issue. For God's sake, keep them separate.

"To you fathers — I salute you too. I know you have been maligned. Some of you have been vilified. You've been labeled and misunderstood. The joy and closeness some of you may have once shared with your children is gone and you feel powerless to get it back. You can no longer come home to the embrace of your precious little ones. Some of you have never known the joy of family life, either because you never married the mother of your children or because you were raised without your father. Few have acknowledged your pain. Instead of trying to understand you, society and the courts bash you. The mothers say they no longer need you. They say children don't really need a father. Perhaps someone has convinced you of that lie, God forbid. I know they say there are two sides to every story. Well, I have always believed there were three. The mother's side, your side, and the truth, which is a little bit of what you say, a little bit of what she says, and something you both left out. And here's the truth — your children *do* need you. They love you. You are an indispensable part of their lives."

The crowd in the room was totally silent.

"Communication is essential for your relationships. You must communicate with them, and I know, it's not always easy. This is how it happens. You let the first month pass, perhaps you didn't make the child support payment, and guilt grips you and keeps you from making the call in month two. But when you finally get the nerve, you make sure you call when no one's at home, because often there's interference."

Applause erupted from the male contingency in the audience.

"Well, let's keep it real. You just don't want to talk to the mother for whatever reason — whether you've made the support payment or not, or if she brings up other issues you're just not ready to address. I'm not here to pass judgment on you. I'm not here to talk about whether you paid child support this week or whether something else was left undone. That job is for the courts, you guys, and the kids' mothers to work out. I'm here today to merely ask you to call your kids. Send your child a card. Call when you know someone's gonna be home, or even call when you know no one's there and leave the most caring and expressive message you can.

"You may think you're out of the picture, but you're not. You are as much a part of their lives, either by your presence or by your absence, as you were before you left … or before she left. Proverbs says you are your kid's glory. They might not admit it, but that wall they've erected is penetrable. You CAN crumble it. They want you to. They need you to. I hear someone saying, 'it's been so long.' To you, I say — reach out anyway. I once told my father to get lost while desperately hoping against hope that he'd resist me and love me anyway. So when you call, what should you say? Well, be sure to first write down the things you must say to them. Make a list of all the areas of their lives you want to talk about. Keep the list by the phone. Keep a journal. Write down everything that reminds you of your child — then tell them. Heck, use a micro-cassette recorder or anything that will get the job done.

"Develop a collection of something, anything. Stamps, model cars, mugs, tee-shirts, even postcards. Share this collection with your child. At the beginning of the month, address and stamp twenty envelopes or even postcards addressed to your child. Every other day, send one saying, 'thinking of you' or 'hope to see you soon' or 'did you see the game?' or 'guess what happened at work today' or 'what do you want to do next summer?' or 'do you have a special need I can help you with?' Attach newspaper clippings, pictures, or anything. Send a word puzzle and challenge your kid to complete it and send it back. Let your son or your daughter pick the NFL's winners for the next week. Promise a prize to the winner or dinner at the end of the season.

"Visit your child at school one day. It's so important for those school officials to see you in the flesh and know you're around and that you care. Meet the principal and their teachers. Even sit in on your child's class for twenty minutes. Then have a delightful lunch date in, yes, the school cafeteria. Let their friends see you and know that you're there. I promise you, they'll think twice before bullying your child.

"Mark your calendar, set your visitations, and let, *nothing*, and I do mean *nothing* keep you from honoring that commitment. Buy postcards, stamp them, and write messages. Tell your child you'll take him to the place on the postcard.

"You'll rediscover a source of love, unconditional love that you never could imagine. You will contribute to this world. You will reduce the nation's crime rate. You will reduce the nation's dropout rate. You will reduce the teen pregnancy rate. And you will cut learning disabilities by a sizeable margin.

"To all the parents, even parents to be — How do I say this? Some of you are still married and happily so. My earnest prayer to God is that you remain so, that nothing will ever come between you and your love for each other. If you ever think your differences are irreconcilable, reconsider. When you think you've fallen out of love, try faith. When you think you've grown apart, restitch that seam and reconnect. I think of a marriage, even a family, as a body. If it's sick, you don't throw it away. Returning this body to the factory is not an option. No, you improve your diet, you go to the doctor. In fact, you see any specialist you can find who'll help save your life and heal your body. The family's health and longevity should be treated no differently. Whatever it takes, whoever can help, whatever you must do to heal the fracture and remove the cancers that are eating up life's joys — you should be willing to do it. Returning your family to the factory shouldn't be an option.

"This society has fed my generation the lie that it's all about number one, that my happiness must come first, and that I must love me first — above anyone else. I truly hope I don't offend anyone in here but it's not all about you. When you said 'I do' or 'I will,' you promised to put someone else first. When that child came into the world, you vowed to lay down your life because you knew in your heart that it wasn't about you. Someone else's well-being and happiness came first from then on. But sometimes our selfishness takes over, which makes it easy to believe it's better for the kids if we're apart than for them to hear us screaming and yelling all the time.

"Well, my question is, why are those the only two options? How's this for a third option — stop screaming. Stop yelling. Stop fighting. Compromise. Forgive. Understand. Be patient. Get help. You see, we have a choice to scream or not to scream. That is the question. Every time we lose control, it's because we choose to do so. If I decide I can't help myself, that I must scream and yell, then it won't be my wife's fault. It's my inability to control myself. It's funny, we're willing to control that anger on the job, but we let loose when we get home.

"Again, I say, think twice. When my parents divorced, their friends all said, 'free again!' But you know, no one celebrated my freedom from the tyranny of screaming parents. No one rejoiced that I was finally liberated, and I wasn't rejoicing either. So after you've thought twice, think again.

"We can't undo what's been done, but we sure can move upward from whatever stage we find ourselves. Parents, you can't do it alone, but with God's help you can. He made the family. Since He made it, you need His operating manual.

"Religion, pure and undefiled before GOD, the Father is this, to visit the fatherless and widows in their affliction. To the men here today I ask, are there widows, including single mothers, in your family? Blood or church family? It doesn't matter.

Are your nephews and nieces orphans? You know, fatherless. If they are, I challenge you to visit them in their affliction. Visit them period. Visit them and cheer them on at their games. Even offer to go to back-to-school night. Teach the young men how to think like men, grow into manhood. Encourage the girls as they grow into womanhood and teach them how to be treated respectfully by the boys around them. Ladies and gentlemen, *that* is religion pure and undefiled.

Before we look to the government, let's look to ourselves. Grandfathers, brothers, uncles, friends, youth leaders, ministers, priests, and coaches — let's rise to the sound of the alarm. Let's mobilize and meet the challenge. Let's show the enemy of our souls that he's a defeated foe, that these children were created in the Almighty's image. He's now asking us to practice pure and undefiled religion.

"One of our mothers is from South Africa. Her boys are fatherless because their American father died of cancer shortly after they returned from Africa to live in America. She said of her sons, 'Their father's brothers won't help. I've asked and even begged them to take my sons to visit, show them love, and have some male bonding. They have never made the time. I suppose that's how it is in your country, but where I come from, it's not like that. If we were home, the husband's brothers and uncles take the boys in.' My question to you is — is that what we do in America? Is she correct? Of course not. But we must rise up and be the people God called us to be.

"I could close by giving you one of those slogans of the day, you know — each one teach one, make a difference, practice random acts of kindness, and so on. But instead, I'll say this: If you pay with a little time now, any good businessman knows there's always a return on a good investment. Invest in your own families, your own blood. You must invest in YOUR future, your

retirement. These children will lead, vote, and write laws —
either righteously or with anger in their hearts. These children
are our future and our duty. Nothing should come before them.
Mothers — not pride nor anger. Fathers — not your leisure nor
your anger. The church — neither the building fund nor deco-
rum should come before these little ones.

"Suffer the little children to come unto me, said Jesus. Look
at the opportunity before us — we can save a generation. I believe
it can be done. We must believe that together we can do it!"

Drew stepped back from the podium. The crowd rose to
their feet to in a standing ovation.

"Thank you, I now have a few words for the children, teen-
agers, and young adults."

As Drew began to speak to them, the kids began cheering and
clapping wildly. They rose to their feet and clapped and cheered
for two full minutes.

"Thank you, thank you. I really appreciate your applause, but
I appreciate you more. Please, thank you," he said, motioning with
his hands to quiet the crowd.

"Let me start by saying I'm so proud of you. I have enjoyed
this year and can't think of a better place I could have spent this
year. I believe God sent you to me. Let me tell you what I've
gleaned from our time together."

"Uh oh," yelled Jason.

"No, I won't tell that part, just the good stuff," said Drew,
drawing more laughter.

"But seriously, you guys are my heroes. You're the crew!
Here's why. You are brave. Your courage is unmatched. I've seen
faith like I've never known before. You've shown unconditional
love. You have it, my friends. All I did was help you not to lose
it. You showed me the forgiveness of God every time you reached
out to a father or a mother who had let you down. We adults have

much to learn from you," said Drew, pausing to allow the applause that followed.

"There's really not anything I need to say here tonight that I haven't said all year, but I do have a few words. They are simply this. First of all, forgive me. Forgive me for the times I've let you down. Forgive me for the times I've overstepped my boundaries. Forgive me if I didn't listen.

"I wanted to do so much and I thought I had all the answers," he said, looking in the direction of Vicky Phillips. "I knew what I had lived through when my folks broke up. I wanted to spare you all the pain and guilt that comes when the door is forever closed to reconciliation. Thanks for indulging me.

"You've got to keep on fighting the good fight of faith. Don't give up simply because the going gets rough. No, with trust, faith, hope, and love you CAN conquer your fears. Who are your enemies? I'll answer by telling you who is not your enemy. Your mother is not your enemy. Your father is not your enemy. They are on your side. We are on your side. I am on your side. God is on your side. So what if your father or your mother or your church or even I let you down? We're bound to make mistakes. This is hard for me to say, but I will let you down. Your father will probably let you down again, and so will your mother. One day, you'll be looking for the pastor or the youth leader but they won't be available. Then what do you do? Here's what you do. First, forgive us and give us another chance. Second, go to God, your heavenly Father. That's what I hope you learned from me this year — that when people fail you, the Lord will take you up. He's a Father to the fatherless. I know this from my own life.

"Other people couldn't always heal my wounds. But God could and He did. I've come to tell you today that He'll do the same for you.

"Let me leave you with this — love your mother and love

your father. YOU reach out; you make the first move every now and then. Keep forgiving and keep loving. Never give up because if you do, you just may lose the opportunity forever. Don't do what I did. My parents divorced and I only saw my father sporadically. I was angry, resentful, hurt, and lost. I didn't know which way was up. I took it out on him, and even after my dad tried to reconcile and tried to patch things up with me and tried to become a part of my life again, I let a little quarrel divide us once again. I refused to forgive him, and then, it was too late. My father suddenly passed away right after he had come to ask me to live with him. That was the one thing I had wanted for years and I blew it. So don't blow it. Instead, forgive. Because when you do so, the things you have wanted all along will be right there. It may not always come in the package that you want, but it will come. You will find love, and you will find peace. You will have hope, and you will be whole. You'll realize your dreams, but you must first dream those dreams. Be strong and be courageous and may God forever bless you. I truly do love and thank you."

Journal

With the Malden Foundation's increase in funding to Springridge, I simply cannot resist the board's offer to renew my contract. Who could've guessed that Jason's mom would put in such strong words of praise to the foundation's executive director? Who would've guessed Tony would spend the rest of the summer with his father? Who would've thought Mayra would give me another chance? One of the biggest joys of all, I must confess, was attending the father/daughter tea at the church — with Kalia. I think she's going to be okay. I pray they all will be okay. — A.D.M.

Appendix A:

Guidelines for Restoring Relationships and Assisting Fatherless Children and Their Families

The effects of divorce and fatherlessness are intricate and varied. But small, simple actions applied faithfully can go a long way toward mitigating this unfortunate legacy. Single fathers, single mothers, as well as church leaders and laypeople all have a role to play in assisting fatherless children. As you read the numerous suggestions in this appendix, prayerfully consider what your role is.

For Fathers

- **Send monthly postcards**
  At the beginning of the year, buy a set of postcards or greeting cards. Set aside one afternoon to address and stamp them all. Once a month, send the postcard or greeting card out with your monthly bills. If you're sending

greeting cards, enclose articles of current events, pictures of you and other relatives, or even money. Write a brief note to let your child know how much you care about him or her. Include some important facts about your life and don't forget to discuss interests you have in common.

• **Obtain Activity Schedules**

Contact your children's youth minister or the director of other youth organizations and centers to obtain a schedule of your chidren's activities. Also contact sports clubs and coaches to obtain practice and game schedules.

• **Create a Yearly Calendar**

Set aside important dates in your children's lives. Include birthdays, sporting events, Back to School night, school breaks and holidays, PTA meetings, and so forth. Don't forget to include locations and contact information, if necessary. Make a commitment to attend some of these events or meetings and follow through.

• **Schedule Routine Telephone Calls**

Set aside a time to speak to your children each week — for example, every Thursday at 8 P.M. Ask your children to share what they have learned that week and offer to assist with study by phone. You can even quiz your children over the telephone.

• **Create Phone/Contact List**

This list should include names, numbers, and email addresses of the school principal, guidance counselor, medical professionals, pastors, coaches, scoutmasters, neighbors, and so forth.

- **Provide Academic Help**

  Help your children study for exams, do homework, and write reports. You can challenge them to recite history or explain a scientific principle or test their knowledge of geography or geology. This can be done via the telephone or email. Via the Internet and with email, you can even help them conduct research. Thirty years from now they'll remember how you took the time to help them.

- **Share Your Spiritual Life**

  Take your children to church – yours or theirs. Pray with them. If there's some burdensome issue in their lives, take the time to pray *with* your children, even by phone. If you prayed for your son or daughter, drop them an email and let them know. "Hey, I prayed for you about _____ today. Is there anything else you want me to take to God?"

- **Plan a Vacation**

  Select at least one out of the fifty-two weeks in a year for a vacation with your children. Whether it's a trip to the beach or an entire week in your apartment, set it aside and plan it out. Include down time — movies, sports, and board or electronic games. Cook at least one dinner together. Encourage your children to talk. Share. Don't grill them, but help them warm up, particularly if it's been a long time between visits. Tell your children about you and your side of the family — their heritage.

- **Create a "Father Fact Sheet"**

  Provide your children with all necessary biographical or contact information for you, including your full name, date of birth, family history, medical history, family tree information, favorite colors, position title at work, email address, work phone number, cell phone number, and so forth.

- **Be Available and Involved**
Don't let your absence from the home prevent you from caring for your children when they're sick, attending recitals and sports events, and helping to transport them to practices.

- **Take Your Daughter Out**
At least once per month, take your daughter out to lunch or dinner, the museum, a stroll in the park, or even for a game of basketball. During this time, you can stay connected to her by asking about the things that are happening in her life and providing fatherly wisdom and advice. You should also create opportunities to express concern for and interest in her relationships with boys. The father is the one from whom she'll learn (or not learn) how to interact with, relate to, or react to boys. You can roleplay and script the types of responses your daughter should give in response to much of the seducing talk of young suitors. You should also reaffirm your support for the ground rules laid out by her mother. You should communicate your desire to meet her boyfriends — just as if you were physically in the home. This can be accomplished by taking them both out or arranging with her mother to allow you to be present in the home when the young man comes by.

For Mothers

- ### Allow Visitation Even in the Absence of Child Support Payment
  The courts have determined that, legally, one does not control the other. Moreover, the call to arrange the visit or the visit itself is not the time to raise the child support issue. That should be a separate phone call made after the visit. The intangible things your children's father brings to those children are far more valuable than the money. Let the courts resolve that matter. Also, be flexible with child support. Understand the difficulty of paying the support, while also trying to pay for birthday, Christmas gifts, and travel expenses. Be creative and make every effort to work with your children's father.

- ### Cultivate a Relationship with the Stepmother
  Custodial mothers should make every effort to establish a cordial relationship with their ex's new wife. After all, this person will be caring for your children while in that home. Open the lines of communication; offer your contact information. When you invite the father to events involving the child, if possible, invite your children's stepmother too. This effort will reduce hostilities that would otherwise affect or even strain your children's visits with their father and stepmother.

- ### Include Fathers in Major Life Events
  Be sure to invite your children's father to all of their major events and activities, including baptisms, dedications, communions, graduations, concerts, games, and weddings. Many mothers believe the father hasn't "earned" the right to attend

some of these events, but we mothers must recuse ourselves from the role of judge on that question.

- **Contact Local Organizations**
Obtain yearly calendars and schedules of games from coaches, Boys and Girls Club coordinators, and youth pastors. Give these to your children's father.

- **Contact Churches**
Investigate the effectiveness of each church's youth and family ministries and select a church that addresses the needs of twenty-first-century families. Pray and join the church where God leads.

- **Conduct a Swap Night**
Agree with other single parents or even married parents to swap kids to allow each participant a child-free evening for rest, relaxation, and so forth. Single parents need a break, perhaps far more than other parents. Be sure to factor rest into your life. Your effectiveness as a parent as well as your physical and emotional health are at stake.

- **Encourage the Father/Child Relationship**
Nudge your children to phone their father periodically; refrain from denigrating their father, particularly within earshot of the children.

- **Involve Immediate and Extended Family in Your Childrearing Efforts**
Use family gatherings or reunions to earnestly reach out to brothers, uncles, your father, or even grandfather to step

into the role of father, if possible. Ask them to phone or email your children if they're geographically separated.

- **Create a Safety Net of Helpers**
  Try to create a network of friends or other parents, who can step in to pick your children up from school, drive them to practices, or babysit on short notice. Keep these phone numbers with you at all times. Be sure to reward these friends with small gifts or tokens of your appreciation.

For Churches and Community Organizations

- **Carve Out a Place in Your Ministries**
  Make a place in your ministries for these children, as well as their mothers *and* fathers. Don't leave them out there to wander through the maze of reconstructed families and long-distance relationships on their own.

- **Conduct Counseling Sessions**
  During small group sessions, stimulate discussion on these issues; let new members know that your church is concerned about these issues and will provide assistance if needed. Find gentle ways to ask the tough questions of your new members regarding their family status and whether they need help with relationship mending. These are tough questions, but it's hard for single parents to ask for help. If they are divorced, separated, or never married and have children, they need help.

- **Reach the Non-Custodial Fathers**
  Coordinate with the mother to contact the non-custodial

father and include him in the ministries of the church where his children are involved. Provide non-custodial fathers with a church calendar and be sure to include them on the church mailing list, even the church email list. As your church phones other members to advise of youth activities, outings, and productions, the church should, likewise, reach out to these fathers and try to include them. (This assumes there are no compelling circumstances to render this suggestion not practical or legally impossible.)

- **Hold Monthly Discussion Groups**
  These sessions can be designed for fathers to gather and share issues, struggles, and successes. Fathers need to know they're not alone out there and can share what strategies and resources were most successful in their efforts to maintain relationships with and meet their responsibilities to their children. In addition, churches can facilitate these sessions for the children of divorced, separated, or never married parents. They need to be able to share their feelings and struggles with living apart from one parent, usually their father. They also need tools to help them cope, reconcile, and still function emotionally, academically, spiritually, and so forth.

- **Organize Letter/Email Writing Sessions**
  These can be used to help fathers and their children communicate with each other. Provide envelopes, stationery, or a computer for dads to email their kids. Help out. Have routine outings for *those* dads and their children. Buy tickets en masse for minor league teams, college basketball games, and so forth.

- **Establish a Visitation Bank**

  Churches and organizations dedicated to restoring broken familial relationships can establish a "visitation bank" to provide non-custodial fathers or the children themselves with funds to visit the other when regular visitation is not possible because of geographical separation. Raise funds to cover transportation and hotel costs for needy fathers to visit their kids.

- **Develop a Hospitality Exchange**

  Churches can organize members to serve as hosts for fathers who are in from out of town to visit their children. A motel is not the most ideal spot for the father/child reunion. This hospitality ministry can also provide meals, assist with transportation, and provide an itinerary for a father who may not be familiar with the new city where his children live.

- **Plan Monthly Outings**

  Get men in your church connected with fatherless children. Such a mentoring program can take place one Saturday or Sunday afternoon a month. Each man can take a child on an outing. The important thing is to spend time communicating, being real, and teaching them.

- **Provide Weekly Tutoring**

  Coordinate a weekly tutoring session on a rotating basis to minimize the likelihood of burnout. Since statistics point to lower academic performance for children who don't live with both biological parents, then this need must be addressed. The church may even wish to provide the schedule to the children's fathers and open the doors to them as well.

• **Conduct Fathering Sessions**
Identify teenage fathers in the community and invite them to fathering sessions. Collect baby items by donation, including diapers, formula, toys, and gifts. Allow young fathers to earn these items in exchange for participating in the parenting sessions. Sessions should include professional advice as well as common sense advice from the fathers in the church. You can also arrange visitation sessions so fathers can visit with their children in a safe and supervised environment.

• **Schedule a Fix-It Day**
Have men and women of the church visit single mothers to make repairs. They can work on everything from automobiles to windows, bicycles to computers.

• **Host a Quiet Achievement Dinner**
Host a dinner to recognize the academic, sports, religious, and other accomplishments of all the youth. This is an opportunity to heap praise on children who may not have the best report card, or who were not the star athlete, but who demonstrated great character, or improved one or two grades, or even quietly contributed to the family in a way that was noticed only by that child's mother.

• **Create an Activity Calendar**
Maintain a calendar of your youths' activities and have father-figure volunteers rotate attending games, concerts, and other activities. For girls' activities, the men should attend with their wives or other female relatives.

Appendix B
Resources

Focus on the Family
Colorado Springs, CO 80995
800-A-FAMILY
www.family.org

Institute for American Values
1841 Broadway, Suite 211
New York, NY 10023
Tel: 212-246-3942
www.americanvalues.org

National Fatherhood Initiative
101 Lake Forest Boulevard, Suite 360
Gaithersburg, MD 20877
Tel: 301-948-0599
Fax: 301-948-4325
www.fatherhood.org

Men and Fathers Resource Center
807 Brazos St., Suite 315
Austin, TX 78701-2508
Tel: 512-472-3237
www.fathers.org

The National Center for Fathering
P.O. Box 413888
Kansas City, MO 64141
Tel: 913-384-4661 / 800-593-DADS
Fax: 913-384-4665
www.fathers.com

The Center for Successful Fathering
13740 Research Blvd, Suite L-2
Austin, Texas 78750
Tel: 512-335-0761 / 800-537-0853
www.fathering.org

Dads and Daughters
34 East Superior Street, Suite 200
Deluth, MN 55802
Tel: 888-824-DADS
www.dadsanddaughters.com

Prison Fellowship
1856 Old Reston Avenue
Reston, VA 20190
Tel: Not available
www.pfm.org
(suggestion: search "fatherless")

Fellowship of Christian Athletes
P.O. Box 90022
Washington, D.C. 20090
Tel: 202-303-2870
www.fca.org

Endnotes

[1] Wade F. Horn, Ph.D., and Tom Sylvester, Father Facts, (Gaithersburg, MD: National Fatherhood Initiative, 2002), 118.

[2] *Fathering Magazine*, Men's Health Network Press Release, "Study Finds Teen Pregnancy and Crime Levels are Higher Among Kids from Fatherless Homes," citing Dougherty, Tim and Lillian Kurosaka, University of California, Santa Barbara Press Release, presented at the Western Economics Association Conference, July 1, 2003.

[3] Horn, *Father Facts*, 111.

[4] Allen Beck, Susan Kline, and Lawrence Greenfield, "Survey of Youth in Custody," 1987, U.S. Bureau of Justice Statistics, (Washington, DC: GPO, 1988).

[5] Horn, *Father Facts*, 47.

[6] Ibid, 111.

[7] Ibid, 129.

[8] Ibid, 111.

[9] Ibid, 139.

[10] Ibid.

[11] Ibid.

For information on distribution and bulk
orders for special organizations, please contact
Foundation House Publishing
PO Box 2526, Wheaton, MD 20915
Phone: 301-681-9137
www.lifewithoutdaddy.com
www.foundationhousepublishing.com